D0765431

WALKING THROUGH NEEDLES

WALKING THROUGH NEEDLES

Heather Levy

Copyright © 2021 by Heather Levy
Cover and jacket design by Mimi Bark

ISBN 978-1-951709-38-9
eISBN: 978-1-951709-45-7
Library of Congress Control Number: available upon request

First hardcover edition June 2021 by Polis Books, LLC
44 Brookview Lane
Aberdeen, NJ 07747
www.PolisBooks.com

POLIS BOOKS

*To Bambi for accepting every part of me,
even the sharpest pieces.*

"*Pain. I seem to have an affection, a kind of sweettooth for it.*
Bolts of lightning, little rivulets of thunder.
And I the eye of the storm."
—Toni Morrison, *Jazz*

Chapter I: Sam, 1994

Sam twisted her old yellow ducky blanket, the one her grandma said she was swathed in at birth, and wrapped it tight around her throat until she couldn't breathe.

Slowly, she counted. She thought of Arrow's lanky body stretched out in the next bedroom, the one that had been the untouched guest room for so many years. She moved her fingers between her legs, found the spot until the familiar tickle grew. She made it to seventy-three, but the May evening was too warm and muggy, the covers clammy beneath her. She couldn't concentrate enough for the tickle to explode heat throughout her body, so she removed her blanket from her neck and nuzzled it instead, trying not to cry again.

Sam wished for rain and thunder, for the windows of the decaying farmhouse to shake from it, the glass rattling in tune to her pulse. She wasn't scared of storms, but Arrow was. He'd make any excuse to come to her room if there was the tiniest burst of lightning. She'd see his little jump after each flash outside her window and smile knowing she'd always have that over him, no matter how tall he got. He might be almost sixteen, but she was a year older and taller than most guys at her school. Sometimes she'd forget his age because he was strong and hard like a grown man. Like his father, Isaac.

When she thought of Arrow and Isaac infiltrating her house, her insides boiled with the unfairness of everything. She never asked for a stepfather much less a stepbrother. She never asked for any of it—

the small courthouse marriage only three months after her mama met Isaac, Isaac and Arrow moving into the farmhouse when the tulips shot out of the ground all cheerful and bright just to quickly shrivel back to nothing—but her mama said it would be good to have a male influence, whatever the hell that was supposed to mean.

Sam looked at Isaac and saw someone too sure of himself to be trusted. He sauntered through her house like he'd built it with his own hands.

Isaac's hands. She tried not to think of them, tried not to study them when Isaac was working on the farm, but it was difficult. They were beautiful. Large, long fingers, and tan so that the pale half-moons of his fingernails appeared vulnerable, like she could take a needle and easily poke it through the soft pinkness. If he had been born during the Renaissance, Michelangelo would've used him as a model. She had sketched pages and pages attempting to capture his hands, but he was always moving, constantly on to the next task with that unnerving sureness.

The only thing Sam had ever been sure about was getting out of Blanchard. She never went as far as saying she'd leave Oklahoma; the thought was too scary to imagine beyond visiting all the famous museums up north, a region of the country as foreign to her as living with males in her house. Knowing Isaac and Arrow had lived all over Oklahoma, even outside the state, Sam couldn't help thinking they knew more about the world and would use it against her, make her feel naïve for having always lived in a tiny town. They didn't know she was smarter than them because she listened when people thought she wasn't. She knew things Isaac wouldn't want her mama to know. She had overheard the stories about why Isaac and Arrow moved from Anadarko to Blanchard, and she would use the knowledge if she had to.

Her old border terrier, Hades, barked somewhere outside, the sound muted as Sam wrapped her blanket around her neck again, twisted it tight, tighter. She thought of Isaac's hands, of Arrow's sad, big brown eyes. She wondered if Arrow felt the same as her, if he wanted to be somewhere else, far away.

She imagined him in her room, watching him touch the knickknacks on her long dresser, his hands pausing then reaching out to her, caressing her face, his fingers lowering and pressing into her throat.

Tight, tighter. She counted again, her hand working faster, Isaac's hand, Arrow's hand, moving in her, through her, the tickle spreading wider and warmer, Arrow's eyes pleading something, his mouth grazing hers, the blackness behind her eyes lighting up white, then heat blazing through her in sharp spasms.

She loosened her ducky blanket, gasped for breath. She knew she had come close to passing out this time. Somewhere in the fuzzy pleasure of the moment and losing count, she thought, *I could die.* This time was different, though. She had pictured faces, not just disembodied hands. The thought burned her cheeks so much tears came.

She'd had too many shameful thoughts since Arrow and Isaac moved in, and she often imagined God opening the ground below her, sucking her into fiery lava, her skin and muscle melting away and exposing bone like that scene with the Nazis in *Raiders of the Lost Ark*.

When Sam had these thoughts, she wanted to slip out of her body, pretend the thoughts belonged to someone else. She had a strong urge to go to the old guest bedroom, Arrow's room. When she was younger, she used to sneak out of her room to sleep on the guest bed when she missed her daddy. She'd imagine her daddy sleeping next to her. He'd call her his little Biscuit, same as Grandma Haylin, and she wouldn't even ask him why he wasn't sleeping in the downstairs bedroom with Mama. She wouldn't ask him why he left and never came back.

She rarely entered the room now since Arrow took it over. It didn't smell the same. When she used to splay her body on the guest bedroom mattress and press her face into the pillow, she'd detect the hint of Aqua

Velva and Marlboro Reds, the essence of her daddy. Two months of Arrow in the room and she could suck and suck, but all she could smell was the faint scent of laundry detergent and the same musky teenage boy smell that filled the school gym after PE.

Once, when she wouldn't leave his room, her chest aching to find her daddy's scent again, Arrow threatened to sit on her head and rip out a fart if she didn't get out. Not wanting to leave, she made like she was stealing his headphones. He had held her down on the bed, his face inches from her own, so close she could almost lick his downy facial hair.

She closed her eyes with that image of Arrow, his warm breath on her face, her body trapped under his weight, and her hand slid into her underwear again.

***

Sam stared at her cold scrambled eggs. Since she was able to talk, she had told her mama of her deep hatred for scrambled eggs, but Isaac liked his eggs beaten to death so it didn't matter what anyone else wanted anymore.

"Sammy, eat your breakfast."

Sam wished the death stare she gave her mama would somehow shoot some awareness into her brain like when Grandma Haylin did it. Since her stroke last year, her grandma's left side didn't work as well, and she typically didn't leave her room until the first soaps came on, but Sam knew she was up early as soon as the smell of fresh biscuits beckoned her from her bed.

Grandma Haylin pushed the plate of biscuits toward Sam and winked. "Go on—take another. Probably be another month before I feel like making them again."

Her mama pouredd Isaac's coffee and set the pot down, one hand on her round hip, the other running through her ash blonde hair in exasperation. "I'm serious, Missy. You only have five minutes to eat before you need to leave."

"I *am* eating," Sam said with a mouthful of biscuit and jam.

Her mama shook her head. "Your eggs."

"If I eat them, can I take the car?"

Arrow smiled a little from across the table. Probably thought Sam would drop him off in style for some girl to see. No way.

Her mama went back to pouring coffee for herself, and Sam felt a *no* coming, which would mean walking a half-mile to the high school with Arrow shadowing along.

"Not today, Sammy. I'm working an extra shift at the shop, and your daddy's working late at the Hunt farm."

"He's not my daddy." Sam hated when her mama forced *daddy* on her in front of him.

Her mama huffed out a sigh, and Sam dared a look in Isaac's direction.

He returned the look with his cocky grin before turning to Mama. "Jeri Anne, honey, I can drop you off at the shop, take a break to come getcha later."

Her mom set a mug of coffee—light cream—in front of Isaac. "Are you sure? That's awfully far."

"It's no problem. Let the girl enjoy herself while she's young."

"Well, okay then." Her mama leaned over and kissed Isaac's cheek before sitting at the table, murmuring, "Sweet man."

Sam caught Grandma Haylin's smirk.

Without missing a beat, Arrow asked, "Can I get a ride?"

Before Sam could say no, her mama pointed her fork at her. "What do you say to your daddy? Letting you drive our car today."

Sam was surprised Grandma Haylin didn't remind everyone that the car, a blue 1970 Chevrolet Chevelle, belonged to her. Just because she rarely drove it anymore didn't mean she gave it up.

"What do you say, Sammy?"

She tried the death glare on her mama again. Still nothing.

Sam stared directly into Isaac's eyes and released the most apathetic "thanks" she could manage before shoveling cold eggs into her mouth as fast as she could.

"Arrow gets to ride with you," her mama said.

Sam spit out the half-chewed eggs, shooting Arrow a death glare that worked this time.

Sam tried not to think of the night before in her bed as Arrow fiddled with the Chevelle's radio. She glanced at his hands, his fingers, and a pleasure-tremble went through her so fast she missed a stop sign.

"Holy shit," Arrow said, slapping the dashboard. "Can you please not kill us?"

"Whatever. I'm a better driver than you'll ever be."

"Try driving the Hunt's old ass tractor."

"No thanks. No desire to be a farmer."

Arrow laughed. "But you *live* on a farm."

Sam looked over at him struggling to dig something out of his backpack.

"What?" he said. "Your plans don't include marrying some redneck asshole and spitting out eight kids?"

"Hell no."

"Me either."

This time Sam laughed. She realized it was the first she'd laughed in weeks.

Arrow smiled at her as he finally found what he was looking for— one of Sam's Greek mythology books—and set it on the armrest.

"I forgot to give this back yesterday."

"You finished it already?" Sam tried to stifle the fear she always got when introducing someone to books she loved. Not even her best friend, Chrissy Baker, feigned interest in Greek mythology. "So, what'd you think?"

"I don't like that Pan guy."

The fear transformed into thrill at knowing he'd read it and formed an actual opinion.

"Why not?"

"He's just creepy."

She felt Arrow turn towards her, but she kept her eyes on the road.

"Okay, so he stalks that nymph chick who clearly doesn't want him and has to ask that river god to make her into some reeds just to get away from him, and then Pan makes her into a fucking flute so she'll never get away from him. He's creepy."

Sam grinned. When she read the same story to Chrissy, her friend thought it was romantic how obsessed Pan was with Syrinx.

"Did you know the word syringe comes from her name? Syrinx, syringe."

She caught Arrow rolling his eyes.

"Is everybody's life sad in Greek mythology?"

"No," Sam quickly said, but then she couldn't think of a happy story.

"Why were you crying last night?"

"What?" Arrow's question was so unexpected, Sam's brain felt like it had short-circuited for a second.

"Last night…I heard you when I went to the bathroom."

"I wasn't crying," she lied. She knew her face was redder than boiled beets. If he heard her crying, he might've overhead the other things she was doing in her room.

Arrow paused a long moment before saying, "Okay. But, you know…if you were and you want to—"

"I wasn't, okay? Jesus, mind your own business."

Arrow shut up after that, but she refused to feel bad for him. People didn't cry into their pillows for other people to overhear them and want to talk about it.

She had missed her daddy. That was it. Usually, she could tuck the feelings away and not think about them, but seeing Isaac doing the things her daddy used to do—leading grace before meals, feeding the goats, kissing her mama—it killed the stupid hope of her daddy coming back after ten years. She knew he'd never come back. She didn't even know where he went. The only things he left her were his chestnut hair and dark eyes.

Sam pulled into the high school's parking lot and found an empty spot.

Arrow paused before opening the passenger door. "I'm sorry you were sad."

Sam looked at him, and he seemed like a little boy with his big eyes, his face so eager.

"Get out, *Eric*."

He flinched at hearing his real name spit at him. Her mama had done the same before when Sam would get angry and call her Jeri; it was as if she had called her a bitch.

Arrow's jaw tightened, and she thought he might be angry, something she hadn't seen in him yet. She wanted to see him angry, but she didn't know why.

He didn't look angry, though. Disappointed, maybe. Like her mama.

"Meet back at the car by four," she said, softer, but he had already slammed the car door.

Chapter 2: Eric, 2009

Eric Walker spread thinset on the floor, careful that the grooves he made with his trowel were deep enough to secure the bubblegum pink ceramic tile he was about to gently press down. God bless fucking America—pink tile.

Apparently, Mrs. Burkart thought remodeling her bathroom with a new neon version of the original pink tile he tore out was "restoring" her historic home. She was a frosted cupcake of a woman, all sprinkled cheer and spray-tan—likely some administrative assistant for an oil and gas bigwig.

No one was around, so Eric had cussed loudly as he destroyed the 1940s blush-pink subway tile. It reminded him of an old farmhouse he once lived in and of a beautiful tall girl who hated the pink bathroom they had to share.

Eric set a new plus-sign spacer, laid more adhesive, pressed another tile, set another spacer—over and over until the small bathroom looked like the inside of a Pepto-Bismol bottle. When he finally stood up, his left leg buckled under him until he regained feeling. His shitty leg. If anyone ever asked about the jagged scar on the back of his upper calf, he told them it was from an old football injury although he'd never set foot on a field. Only a handful of people knew the real story and half of those people could be dead now for all he knew.

Mrs. Burkart's Persian meowed loudly, and Eric stopped buffing the last of the grout dust from the fresh tiles. Like every other day that week as he worked on the bathroom, the cat was warning him of her owner's arrival. Mrs. Burkart walked over to check out his finished work, the cat twisting to get free from her arms and doing a good job of snagging a silky blue blouse that probably cost more than his entire outfit, work boots included.

The woman gave up and released the cat. "So, you're all done, huh?"

Eric surveyed the space again to make sure every pink tile was dust-free. They were. "Yeah, looks like it." He heard his voice crack from underuse and shifted his weight to his right leg.

Mrs. Burkart held her large red Coach purse, but she didn't open it. By the way the sun filtered through the bathroom window, Eric estimated it to be damn close to five. He needed to hit the bank before it closed, but Mrs. Burkart continued to stand there, admiring the work done.

"This looks so great. I can't wait to take a bath in here." She looked at him and smiled, the creases around her eyes deeper than he remembered. Maybe she was older than he thought, but the fake tan made it hard to tell. "You ever sneak in a shower when an owner's at work? Just to clean up?"

He looked away from her and muttered, "No."

"You can sneak one now, if you want. Pretend I'm not here. Or not."

He glanced up to see her smile again, the kind that made his groin tingle and tighten.

He almost accepted her offer, but the oppressive August heat made him think the better of it. He needed the cash for a new air condenser unit a hell of a lot more than he needed this frilly woman. "Uh, thanks, but I gotta head out. Got another job early in the morning."

"On a Saturday?" The smile sagged a little in disappointment that her handyman fantasy wasn't going to happen. "Sure. Okay."

After she cut the check, Eric hopped into his black F-150 and sped over to the woman's credit union, which was way south in Midwest

City, the opposite direction of his home in historic Gatewood. He would've gone to his own bank, but he knew there'd be at least a three-day hold on the funds with the ninety-seven dollars he currently had in his account. He had more than that on hand, but he liked to keep his money close.

The thought of cool air blowing throughout his fixer-upper made him anxious, and his foot grew heavier on the gas. He peeked at his truck's clock and eased his foot some. He had time and didn't need another speeding ticket.

For a Friday afternoon, the bank wasn't as busy as he expected, but he had to go inside to cash the check since he didn't bank there. Waiting in line, he noted a dark-headed man trying to corral a toddler. The girl had long chestnut-colored hair, slightly lighter than her dad's, and bright eyes that peered at Eric from under a table displaying a huge fake plant. Beautiful girl. Eric smiled at her and she released a burst of tinkly laughter before running back to her dad. He watched her squeeze her dad's legs, almost felt her tiny arms grasping for purchase as she attempted to climb up her daddy like he was her own personal tree. The man pulled her into a hug and the girl nestled against his shoulder. Eric didn't know he was holding his breath until a teller called out to him.

Just as he made it to the window with his endorsed check, another head of chestnut hair, long and pulled back into a low ponytail, distracted him. He followed the back of the tall bank employee's head, her lithe movements somehow familiar as she assisted a teller in the drive-thru. Someone bumped into Eric's legs, nearly knocking him over, and he looked over to see the toddler running back to her father at the opposite end of the teller windows. Something in the way the man smiled at his daughter, so warm and inviting, reminded Eric of his father and his chest constricted.

He looked up to see the bank employee with chestnut hair turn around. When he saw her buttermilk complexion, the subtle rose on the high cheeks, and her eyes—God, her eyes—his stomach bottomed out.

"Sir? How may I help you?"

The blond teller in front of him looked concerned.

"I—I'm sorry. I'm not ready."

Eric turned and, going the wrong way, ran into an older man waiting in line. He half-stumbled, stopping himself from sprinting out of the bank. Inside his truck, he closed his eyes and knew he was rocking back and forth, something he hadn't done since he was fifteen. He tried to control his rapid breathing as hot acid rose and seared the back of his throat.

It couldn't be her. It couldn't, but in his gut he recognized her ramrod posture before he even caught sight of her eyes, those infinite pools of black oil, always searching, always curious and playful but never forgiving.

All those years, wondering but too scared to know, to make contact and be rejected, and she was here. Not teaching Greek mythology or art at some college but working at a goddamn credit union. Oklahoma City was large and spread out, but he still couldn't believe he hadn't run into her before now.

Eric opened his eyes and quickly shut them again, wiping the tears away with his knuckles.

He started the ignition on his truck and spent another five minutes unable to move. He knew she hadn't recognized him, or she didn't act like she did. If he went inside to talk with her she would be upset, and he couldn't do that to her at her workplace. If he waited a little longer, she would leave and likely go home, and he could follow her. He could leave her a note, maybe. Put it in her mailbox to find the next day and buy him time to think of what he would say to her.

He knew following her home was creepy as hell, but he wasn't ready to see her face-to-face. Not yet.

He turned the air conditioner on full blast, found his invoice pad

18

on his passenger seat. He ripped off a sheet reading Arrow Contracting Inc. and wrote out a note to her. He read it, reread it, balled it up and tossed it onto his floorboard. He tore off a new sheet and wrote out: *Please call me. I'd like to talk—Eric.*

Eric sucked in the cold air and felt somewhat better.

A half-hour later, he watched her exit the bank from the back and get into a silver Subaru. He followed her onto the highway and back into Oklahoma City, surprised when she got off on the 23rd Street exit, the same way he went home. She continued on near an elementary school, turning north into a nice historic neighborhood. He knew this neighborhood well, had done remodels on a few of the two-story houses in the last year. If she lived here, she was less than five miles from his house. The thought shocked him so much he almost missed seeing her turn right onto one of the streets.

Eric eased to a crawl as she continued to her house, which looked to be the smallest on the street but just as well-kept. Like the other streets in the neighborhood, hers was lined with established elm and dogwood trees, crepe myrtles, and colorful flowerbeds his mom would've envied.

He waited until she parked in the driveway and entered the house before he pulled up on the other side of the street. He saw no other car parked at her house, but then he noticed a garage tucked in the back of the property.

Maybe she wasn't alone. Maybe she was married and had a family…a kid. The thought forced memories he didn't want to think about to bloom into full color.

He pulled out his note and read it again. What explanation would she give if she had a husband who checked the mail and read this? He reached down, running his hand along his passenger floorboard until he found the original crumpled note. He smoothed it out as best as he could and read it again. Without thinking, he kissed the paper. He ran to her mailbox and dropped it in.

The sun was a finger above the horizon once he pulled up to his two-story Craftsman home. The nearby Plaza District was buzzing with food trucks, live music, and window shoppers for some art festival going on. He could walk there, maybe get a bite to eat, something to drink, but he couldn't handle being around a lot of people. He never could, even as a kid. His home, even in its chaotic state, was his sanctuary.

He had bought the house for the businesses sprouting up in the neighborhood and the promise of rising property values, although he nearly changed his mind once he saw the inside. The price was cheap and the original oak wood floors hidden by orange shag carpeting were in good condition. It was one of the many foreclosures from the market crash, and the previous owners had their large dog take a dump in each room as a present for Eric. At least he hoped it had been their dog.

He walked into the house's dense heat, his shirt already damp with sweat, but the air condenser had to wait until the next day. Seeing her drained him to nothing. The emptiness was made worse when no one greeted him. No dog, no cat. Plastic covered the parts of the house he was protecting from new drywall and paint. In the living room, there was a flat-screen TV sitting on the fireplace mantel. A brown leather couch sat against the far wall, the middle sagging where he slept on it each night. He figured he would buy bedroom furniture eventually but eventually never seemed to come—just more projects to make the place function. On a rare recent evening of drinking at the bar down the street from him, he had brought a bleach-blonde back to his place. Before giving him the most lackluster hand job ever, she told him he was too old to live like a college kid. She was right, although Eric only had a journeyman's license and never made it to college.

Sam did.

He knew that much about her. He had seen an old friend from Blanchard comment on her Facebook post two years back: *Finally have my masters!* Eric liked the public post, and Sam must have blocked him shortly afterward because her page wouldn't show up when he searched for her.

Maybe she met someone. Maybe she didn't want him to see what life she had now, that she had finally moved on.

The more he thought of it, the more his note seemed like the worst idea. She would read it and then what? Even if she did contact him, things would never be the same. Not after nearly fifteen years since he last saw her. Not after what happened.

"Fuck," he grunted before grabbing his truck keys.

Golden lamplight flushed Sam's front windows as Eric quietly edged to her mailbox. He opened it and circled his hand inside, hunting around in the dark. Then he searched the ground over and over using the illumination from his cellphone.

The note was gone.

Chapter 3: Sam, 1994

Sam couldn't stop thinking about it, however much she tried. It happened the same day a huge May storm spurring several nearby tornadoes trundled through Blanchard.

Arrow had stolen Sam's Nine Inch Nails CD again and she stomped over to his bedroom and entered, no knock, to get it back. Arrow didn't attempt to cover himself—he stood there naked with his underwear in hand, the tan skin of his chest and arms almost cartoonish against the pastiness of his legs, his bare waist. He gazed at her, face strangely serene, his hair messy from sleep, and Sam couldn't seem to make herself move to leave his room. In that moment, her body tightened and prickled and every Sunday sermon her mama dragged her to since birth slapped her good and hard in the face.

The space just below Arrow's waist was all she could think about the entire day, and she knew he knew it as she drove them home from school, avoiding eye contact.

The sky had an ominous green tint as rain lashed at the car. Then the rain turned into a solid sheet Sam couldn't see to drive through, so she pulled to the side of the road to wait it out.

She looked over at Arrow leaning away from the passenger window as if it would protect him from the storm. His mouth was tight with worry. It was strange. When she saw people worrying about things, it automatically made her calm.

"Were you in a tornado before?" she asked, trying to distract herself from thinking of that morning. "Is that why you don't like storms?"

She had been in two tornados, though the farm had suffered only minimal damage. Arrow stared at the radio, his knees bouncing and almost hitting the dashboard.

"No, not a tornado," he said.

"But you don't like storms."

"Who does?"

Sam knew plenty of crazy people who chased tornados for fun, something she would never understand.

"Some people like them. Grandma Haylin says storms clean out bad energy."

Arrow's eyes widened as if she'd said something magical. "My mom used to say the same thing."

Arrow had never mentioned his mom before, and Sam always avoided the topic. All she knew was that she died from cancer when Arrow was thirteen.

"Do you miss her?"

Arrow gave her a look like she'd asked the dumbest question in the world.

"I mean," she quickly said, "what's it like without her?"

Sam couldn't imagine not having her mama and Grandma Haylin. She never thought about them dying, not even after her grandma's stroke.

"What's it like without your dad?"

Sam looked out at the rain starting to subside.

"It's different from your mom. He's not dead. At least, I don't think he is."

"Isn't it worse, though?" he asked. "Not knowing?"

She didn't know how he had turned the question around on her. Frustration erupted before she could push it back down.

"What's worse is having strangers move into my house and no one asking me if it was okay."

Arrow chewed on his bottom lip, and Sam felt her anger fade as fast as it had come.

"No one asked me either."

Sam looked him in the eyes for the first time since walking in on him dressing that morning. He did feel the same as her. Trapped in other people's decisions and without a voice.

She reached out and took his hand, which was warm, not clammy with nerves as she expected. He started at her touch. A little smile touched the corners of his full mouth and he returned the squeeze she gave his hand.

"Let's get home before our parents freak out."

Arrow nodded, his hand seeming reluctant to let her go.

The storm continued to move over the farm that evening, the windows clattering with every gust of wind. Sam hardly heard the knock on her door. She twisted on her bed, quickly turning down her stereo and ready to get a tongue-lashing from her mama for playing The Smiths too loud. Her mom hated anything but Glen Campbell and Rich Mullins, but she didn't complain much as long she didn't have to hear it.

Arrow hovered in the doorway for a moment, the shadow of his tall form spilling in before he shut the door behind him. He latched the hook lock, and Sam instantly sat up in her bed, tense, laughter seeping out as fake and high as the freshman girls at school.

"Your daddy's going to kill you if he catches you in here again."

Isaac, for some reason, didn't like Sam and Arrow being in each other's rooms. He was always onto Arrow about something, flashing glimpses of a rage she hoped would never be directed at her.

Arrow leaned against her door, arms crossed. "He went to town. Said he needed a drink after tracking your dumbass goat through the rain today. Maddie got loose again."

Maddie was her favorite goat on the farm, and she was a total diva. Sam had raised her, had helped the mother goat give birth when Maddie was stuck. Maddie was the only animal she hadn't named after a Greek god or goddess. She had named her after her best friend from elementary school, the friend who moved to Colorado before junior high and promised to visit Sam during each summer. She never did.

The thought of Maddie giving Isaac trouble made Sam smile.

"Like your dad needs an excuse to go to the bar." Sam heard herself mimicking Isaac and Arrow's drawl and cringed. "Seriously, you should get out."

She thought of Arrow locking her door, the latch she added as soon as Isaac and Arrow moved in, and she couldn't help thinking of her conversation with Chrissy the week before.

Sam had told Chrissy about Arrow coming into her room often, how they'd talk about music and books, even her Greek mythology collection, and how she didn't mind him so much now. She didn't tell her best friend how Arrow really seemed to listen to her and care what she had to say, unlike many of her closest friends, who weren't into discussing much outside of who were the hottest guys at school. Chrissy got this worried look when Sam talked about Arrow, told Sam to be careful.

Chrissy heard Arrow spent time in juvie after raping some girl two counties over in Anadarko.

Sam had heard the same whispers about Isaac and wondered how much her mama knew. Sam used to lie in her bed, dreaming up a hundred scenarios where she'd out Isaac to her mama as a rapist, but those thoughts dried up the more she got to know him and saw how hard he worked to provide for the family. He didn't seem like someone who would rape a girl. Sam always pictured rapists as creepy, ugly men who lived in their mamas' basements. Isaac was the most attractive man she'd ever seen. He wouldn't need to rape someone when half the town's women would probably willingly have sex with him.

25

Arrow and Isaac were new to Blanchard, and people in town never trusted anything new. Sam had told Chrissy it was a dumb rumor and that people went to prison, not juvenile hall, for rape. Even as she spoke the words to Chrissy, Sam knew rumors usually contained a pinch of truth. Still, she didn't believe the stories. Not really.

Sam pushed her thoughts aside as Arrow moved closer to her bed.

"You know," he said, "you should really knock before you go into people's rooms."

Sam's face instantly burned with the memory of seeing him naked. Arrow being so close to her bed made her stomach flutter even more. She pulled her hair back at her neck, tugged the thickness hard, making it hurt until it steadied her nerves. Arrow eyed her white tank top, making her fully aware she wasn't wearing a bra. Her breasts, already tender from her period, seemed to grow more sensitive the closer he got to her.

"You better leave, *Eric Duane.*"

Arrow grinned and narrowed his eyes at her. "Make me, *Samantha Grace.*"

"Fine. Guess you'll learn the hard way."

She tossed the covers off and dove for Arrow's legs like she was about to rope a calf. Only, she forgot Arrow did, in fact, rope calves down at the Stewart farm for the hell of it, and within seconds he had her right wrist and ankle in a vice-grip, pressed against her back.

Heat stirred sudden and sharp between her legs at feeling his weight on her and not being able to move.

"You're as slow as that old ass dog of yours," he said, pushing her stomach into the hardwood floor when she tried to rear up. He sat on her back, bouncing up and down on her pinned wrist and ankle enough to make her cry out, the heat between her legs growing, pulsing.

Sam pushed up as much as she could, but Arrow wouldn't budge. "Let go, you sadistic motherfucker!"

Arrow laughed, his voice growing deep like Isaac. "You don't even

26

know what sadistic means."

"Neither do you!"

He bounced a little harder on her back as she tried to jerk out of his grip.

"I swear to Jesus, Eric Walker, I'm going to castrate your balls with a rusty nail, nice and slow!"

"I don't think Pastor Doss would like that dirty mouth of yours. Shit—actually he probably would." He pressed on her more and she thought her wrist, ankle, or both would snap. "I know your mom wouldn't."

"At least my mama's alive to care what I say, you pansy-ass scared-of-thunder baby!"

Arrow released her and stood up fast as if she'd tossed ice-cold water on him.

Sam stood up too and rubbed her wrist, afraid to look at him. She was always doing that, saying the wrong thing to the wrong person. She didn't want to see his face, didn't want to see the hurt in his eyes, but she felt his pain reaching out to her.

"Arrow, I—I didn't mean…"

She couldn't tell if it was her breath or his, but all she could hear was the loud inhale and exhale of air as Arrow stared at her, the heat at her center still pulsing, needful. Morrissey's plaintive singing of "Please, Please, Please, Let Me Get What I Want" purred from the stereo, and Sam would've laughed from the absurdity if it weren't for her heart threatening to rupture through her ribs.

"You were right…about my mom," he said so low she barely heard him. "It's different from your dad. It's different, seeing someone die."

Sam didn't know what to say, what to do. She wished the tingling in her body would go away. It was too incongruent with what Arrow was saying.

"I hate it here," he said, pausing to look at her. "I hate being a stranger all the time."

Sam remembered her words to him earlier in the car.

"You aren't a stranger to me." She wanted to say more. She wanted to tell him it was going to be okay, that he would make more friends at school and the rumors would die away like they always did.

His eyes were pink as if he would start crying. She didn't do well when people cried, so she reached for his hand, held it tight.

"I'm sorry you lost your mom," she said.

He took her other hand. "I'm sorry you lost your dad."

She didn't know if she had pulled him closer to hug or if he did, but her arms were around him, her face pressed to the side of his face, his hands tentatively touching her upper back. The hug seemed to last forever, his arms tightening around her, pulling her closer. Her heart was in her ears as he reached up and touched her hair, then her cheek. It was like her daydream. Maybe this was a dream because it didn't feel real.

He turned his face and their lips brushed, soft at first and then harder. She would never tell him it was her first real kiss and she could tell it wasn't his.

This was so wrong, she knew it. She shouldn't be kissing him, and she didn't know how to stop it.

She didn't want to stop it.

They kept kissing, Sam mirroring Arrow when he pushed his tongue against hers. She couldn't say how long they stood pressed to each other or what song was playing now. She only wanted to be closer to him, to feel the growing tickle explode throughout her body. She pictured his hands on her throat, and the pulsing in her grew faster.

Part of her was scared of what could come next, the thing her friends told her about, giggling and exchanging knowing glances, but Sam could never picture it as real for herself.

Arrow's hands lowered, slipped into the back of her pajama shorts, and all she could think about was where she wanted his fingers to touch, so close her abdomen tightened, the ache between her legs

28

almost too painful but, no, that wasn't it, her period, the string—her stupid tampon—and her face was on fire and she wanted to slap his hand away but she couldn't force herself to move.

"Eric," she breathed out, "stop."

Arrow stopped and got quiet before whispering, "Please don't tell." Then he went to her door, unlocked it, and left her room, but not before looking back at her, his eyes full of the same anxious excitement Sam felt shimmering in her chest.

Chapter 4: Sam, 2009

Sam waited until the new teller she was training balanced out her drawer before she went back to her office, shut the door and pulled the wrinkled invoice sheet from her purse. No matter how many times she read Eric's note, it kicked the breath out of her.

I'm sorry I wasn't ready to talk before, but I'd like to see you. Please call me—Eric.

When she saw him the day before, it was like watching a ghost floating her way. He was staring at a dark-headed toddler waiting in line with her father. Eric's expression was so tender and sad Sam almost jumped over the teller wall to hug him, but that was the sixteen-year-old in her. The thirty-one-year-old woman told her to stop looking his way before he would inevitably notice her. But, Jesus, he looked the same. Any boy left in him had been shaved away, making the angles of his tan face sharper. The honey waves she had once run her fingers through were cropped closer to his head, but he was the same Eric—taller and filled out with more muscle, but the same. She had forced herself to help one of the tellers, sensing when Eric's coffee-colored eyes found her. Her nerves marbled her skin with pink, sweat pearling on her skin, but she carried on working as if he really was a ghost.

Her heart slowed some when she saw Eric run out of the bank, but it raced again when she later watched him in her rearview mirror as he trailed her home. She couldn't believe he followed her, and she thought about confronting him after she parked her car, but she had no idea what to say to him. She could ask him why he disappeared fifteen years ago, why he never once tried to contact her, but she knew whatever answers he gave wouldn't be enough.

As soon as she had stepped inside of her house, her little white Bichon Frise, Zeus, yipped at her feet. He stood alert and growled, and she cracked her window blinds enough to see Eric tuck a note into her mailbox and hurry back to his truck parked across the street. She knew he was scared to talk to her.

When he left, she went and got the note. After she read it, she threw it away. A minute later, she dug it out of the trash and pressed it to her heart, unable to hold in her tears.

And here she was the next day, still rereading the note, his phone number now memorized but she couldn't bring herself to call him. It wouldn't do anything but dig up memories. Bad memories—too many for one person. Good memories stirred in her too—of sneaking out to the barn in the middle of the summer nights, fresh hay cool against their skin, talking until the sun bled orange onto the surrounding fields.

Sam traced a finger over the white scar on her right hand, her fate line severed by it. She thought of Eric's left leg, the long scar marring his calf.

She took out her cellphone and entered Eric's number. Her finger hovered over the button to call him. Her phone vibrated in her hand and she nearly threw it down from the jolt of fear it sent through her chest. She saw who was calling and suppressed a sigh. "Hey, Mama. I'm at work."

"I know. I just want to make sure you know about the storms that are gonna hit tonight."

Sam held in another sigh. "They're not coming anywhere near Oklahoma City."

"But you know how storms can shift and with you living in that tiny house with no storm shelter, I just think it'd be best for you to come on down here where you can be safe."

Sam gave up and the sigh broke free.

"Mama, I'm not driving out to Blanchard for the possibility of a storm that's already northeast of here."

She left out the fact that her mom's access to a storm shelter was through the assisted living complex where she now lived. Her mom told their extended family in Texas it was a condo, made it sound like a luxurious suite, and Sam never corrected her.

She glanced down at the note in her hand and decided to change gears with her mom. "Eric Walker's living in the city. He wants to meet up with me."

Rarely did Sam ever hear her mom cuss unless her lupus was hitting her joints hard, but she caught a whispered, "goddamn fool."

"What's that, Mama?"

"You heard me, girl. What on earth does he want?"

Sam had an idea of what he wanted—forgiveness—something she wasn't sure she could give him.

"I think he just wants to talk."

"You know darn well that's not all he wants. I say let sleeping dogs lie if you know what's best for you."

Sam knew the conversation, as usual, would go nowhere with her mom. She could never tell her mom everything that happened so many years ago.

"Maybe you're right."

"You know I am, Sammy. He has a darkness in him, just like his father. You know he does."

Sam did know, but she knew it was in her too. Maybe more so.

She ended the call and stared at the invoice sheet, at Eric's neatly printed handwriting. She always had horrible handwriting, as Eric had told her many times.

She hadn't forgotten Eric. Most days, memories of him interrupted her thoughts. She could never forget him, but he had forgotten her, had left her after the worst time in her life. That part she could never forgive.

She fed Eric's note to the shredding machine under her desk, watching the confetti come out the other side and feeling relief and regret in equal measure.

"Excuse me, Sam? There's someone here for you."

Sam looked up from the shredder under her desk. Her newest teller stood at her office door next to a stocky man with a senator's haircut, all close-cropped and plastered down with pomade. He already eased inside the office, blocking the teller's confused face.

"Are you Samantha Mayfair?"

"Yes."

"I'm Detective Chad Eastman," he said, holding up his badge in one hand while offering the other to her as she stood. His palm was warm and dry.

"How can I help you, detective?"

Detective Eastman shut Sam's door and sat in her guest chair.

"I'd like to ask you a few questions about your stepfather, Isaac Walker."

Sam sat down, too fast, her vision blackening at the edges. *Isaac.* Hearing his name after so many years made her stomach tighten, her lunch pushing up into her throat.

Detective Eastman leaned back in the chair, cool and confident as if he were inside his own home. Like Isaac. She instantly disliked him.

"I also have some questions about your stepbrother, Eric Walker."

"Eric? Why? Is he okay?"

The detective's expression changed from businesslike to acute awareness, a cat ready to pounce. "We have no reason to believe he isn't. We're trying to reach him for questioning."

Sam repressed a cry of relief that immediately turned into confusion. "Questioning over what?"

Detective Eastman leaned forward, his cold blue eyes piercing her.

"Well, you know we've had a bit of a drought, especially down south."

Sam couldn't remember a time when they weren't in a drought.

"Yes, of course."

"A couple of men were out fishing in Blanchard, a pond out near Morgan Road. They noticed a side mirror poking out of the water. Turned out to be a white Chevy pickup, so they called the local police."

Sam swallowed, the questions she had formed sandpapered into nothing from her dry throat.

"The truck's registered to your stepfather. We didn't find a body. Not yet anyway."

The detective smiled at her, and Sam couldn't decide if he was trying to be reassuring or intimidating.

"Miss Mayfair, when was the last time you saw Isaac Walker?"

Chapter 5: Sam, 1994

Almost a week had passed since the night Sam and Arrow kissed while tornadoes ripped through the next county, destroying a church and four houses. It was like the storm had destroyed Sam's concentration too, and she was glad school was almost out for the summer. All she could think about was Arrow and she hated herself for it, for how wrong she knew it was.

She didn't know if Arrow felt guilty, but she knew something had changed in him that week. After he kissed her, he barely looked at her. At first, she thought he was just scared of their parents or Grandma Haylin finding out about what they had done, but then she wasn't sure.

She had to get him alone to find out, so she waited and watched for him.

She saw Arrow walking into the barn to get feed for the chickens. No one was around, she made sure of it. She wanted him to be his usual self with her again, not be so serious and weird.

She entered the barn as quietly as she could and snuck up behind him. She playfully ruffled his hair. He swung around fast, fist aimed to land, and Sam had to jump back so as not to get hit.

"Jesus, Arrow, it's just me!"

His eyes were wide and fearful, which confused the hell out of her.

"Sorry, I thought—I thought you were—"

"What? The fucking bogeyman?" Sam's words rushed out breathless from almost getting punched in the face. "God, you're such a kid sometimes."

Arrow straightened his normal slouch, his brown eyes glaring at her, and he didn't seem like a kid anymore.

"You're the one sneaking up behind people *like a kid.*"

He turned to the feedbags and crouched down, his back to her, and she wanted to kick him right in the ass. He had to know why she followed him into the barn, and it wasn't to help him feed the animals.

She kicked dirt on his boots before she crouched down next to him. He opened his mouth to complain, but she nudged him and smiled before he could get any words out.

"I'm not a kid," he said, his mouth softening.

He leaned into her and she thought he'd kiss her, but he didn't. She pulled in closer, but he abruptly stood up.

"I've got to finish chores before my dad gets back."

Sam slowly stood and crossed her arms.

"Well, don't let me stop you."

"Don't be like that."

"Like what? I've got chores to do too."

She turned to walk out of the barn and tripped over an open feedbag. Chicken feed dumped out onto the barn floor as she landed.

"Shit." Blood dots formed on her right knee, the air burning the scrape.

"You okay?"

Sam looked at the hand Arrow offered her. She pushed his hand away as she got up, trying not to let him see her wince.

"What do you care if I'm okay? You act like nothing happened with us, but it did."

Arrow opened his mouth like he wanted to say something, and Sam waited until the air grew hot around them.

"Are you scared they'll find out? Is that why you're ignoring me?"

His face dropped as if she'd insulted him.

"I'm not ignoring you."

36

"But, you, you kissed me, and now you act like…"

She looked down at his red-dusted boots, too embarrassed to keep eye contact. The shame of kissing him, the pleasure of it—she knew it was wrong to like it, but she also knew deep down she wasn't alone in liking it, and that somehow made her feel less ashamed. Now, she wasn't so sure. Maybe Arrow decided he didn't like her like that.

"Sam," Arrow said, his gaze trailing down to her right knee. "You're bleeding."

She ignored the growing pain in her knee. The ache expanding in her chest, sucking out the air in her, was much worse. He didn't care about kissing her or what it did to her. He had probably kissed a dozen girls and she was just one. He was going to pretend like it never happened.

She could pretend too. She could pretend he didn't exist, but the thought of not talking to him made tears blur her vision. She wasn't about to let him see.

"So, that's it, huh?" she said.

Arrow looked away from her. "You should clean your knee."

Sam stood for a moment, waiting for him to offer to help her. When he went back to his chores, she left the barn, her face feeling like it'd explode from her need to cry.

She wanted to forget about the kiss with him and not think about anything. She wanted to draw, one of her few escapes. When she drew, she thought of nothing but the movement of her hand over paper.

She went back to the house to clean her knee and get her sketchpad and pencils.

Sam wasn't sure how long she had been drawing, but she knew it was getting close to dinner. Sketching in her favorite spot in the woods usually distracted her from everything she didn't want to think about, but it wasn't working.

She set her sketchpad down on the elm log she was sitting on and stretched her long legs. She'd been drawing for so long her right hand had cramped. She flexed it and stared at the fallen pine needles around her. She picked one up, touched her index finger to the pointy tip. She pushed the pine needle under her fingernail until all she could focus on was the pain blooming in her hand. She closed her eyes and sank into the familiar sensation.

"Whatcha doing out here, girlie?"

Startled, Sam threw the pine needle down and looked around until she spotted Isaac leaning against a thick tree trunk behind her. She didn't know how long he had been there or what he had seen. She was certain her face was red with embarrassment.

"Just drawing."

Isaac moved closer to her, and she noticed he was holding a cigarette in his hand, but she had never seen him smoke. When he stood in front of her, she realized it wasn't a cigarette but a joint. He took a long hit and smiled as he exhaled.

"I guess we're both doing things we shouldn't be doing," he said.

"It's not illegal to draw."

He grinned. "Why did you do that?"

"Draw?"

He sat near her on the elm log, took another hit. "What you did to yourself."

She looked at the pine needle covered ground and pressed her hands hard into the bark of the log. She didn't want to talk about this. She had never talked about it with anyone.

"I won't tell anyone," he said. "Cross my heart."

Sam glanced at him, watched his hands as he held the joint to his lips again and sucked. "Can I draw you?"

The question seemed to surprise him. He snubbed out the joint, put it in his front shirt pocket.

"Why would you want to draw some old guy like me?"

"You're not that old." Really, she wasn't sure about his exact age, but she knew he was a little older than her mama who was thirty-four. "You have good hands."

He laughed a little and held up his hands. "Really?"

She nodded, afraid of saying too much. She didn't want him to think she was a silly girl obsessing over him or anything.

"Well, I'll tell you what. I'll let you draw me if you tell me why you were doing that to yourself."

Heat flushed her face again, but she realized she didn't have to tell him the truth at all.

"Okay, but you first," she said, and she directed him to sit still on the log with his hands in full view.

"This alright?"

"Yes. Just be still."

She began sketching his hands, first tracing their outline, the curve of each fingertip.

She was almost finished when Isaac wiggled his fingers.

"Time for your end of the bargain, girlie."

She paused sketching, trying to form a lie. She couldn't think of one.

"I don't know. I guess it feels good."

He appeared to contemplate this.

"What kind of good?"

She shifted on the log, the words in her not even making sense to herself. It felt good because pain made her feel in control of her mind. It made the dark thoughts she had disappear for a while. Thoughts of her daddy, thoughts of never being able to get out of Blanchard and being stuck on the farm helping her mama and Grandma Haylin for the rest of her life.

"It just…I don't know. It helps me not think about my dad."

Isaac moved closer to her, and his knee touched hers.

"My dad left me and my brother when we were little too."

Sam looked up at him. His face was serious, not open and friendly

39

how it usually was.

"And I'm going to tell you something. It was the best damn thing he could've done for us."

Sam didn't understand how a father leaving could ever be good.

"He wasn't a happy person, and he made life hell for everyone around him." Isaac leaned forward, rested his hands on his thighs. "When he left, it was like the sun could shine again. We could breathe."

"Didn't you miss him?"

Isaac frowned a little. "Sure, I did, but the pain he left behind, it made me stronger. I had to stop being a kid and help my mom and brother. I had to be strong for them, for myself."

Isaac took her hand, gave it a quick pump before letting go. It was the first time he had ever touched her. She had never given him a hug, even when her mama urged her to.

"We can't control when people hurt us, but pain can be a good thing. It makes us resilient. Powerful." He cocked his grin at her. "It's nothing to be ashamed of for liking it."

Sam smiled at him. His words made her feel less like a freak.

"Let's finish up here and get back to the house before your mama starts to worry."

Sam took up her sketchpad again and began shading in the creases of each finger. She tried hard not to think of those fingers touching her.

***

Sam stared down at the half-read Euripides' *Medea* beside her in bed, the words distorting the more she tried to concentrate on them. The evening was so hatefully sweltering she could hardly stand wearing underwear. She did anyway in case her mama checked in on her after she got back from her evening out with Isaac, but she had taken off her shirt. Sam glanced over her bare shoulder at her door, half-expecting Arrow to be there apologizing for being such an asshole.

She didn't understand why he stopped coming to her room, why he stopped talking to her or wanting to kiss her again. The *whys* got stuck in her throat, she felt them when she took a sip of water.

She thought of what Isaac had said, about pain making you stronger. She didn't feel stronger, though. She felt confused about everything.

She set her book aside and dug out her portable CD player and headphones from her nightstand. She closed her eyes, the effort to hold back tears burning her face. Cocteau Twins surrounded her, the unearthly beauty of the music temporarily lifting the need to be touched by Arrow again. The sounds carried her deeper and deeper until she no longer heard her dog's barking or the whine of animals in the barn. She didn't know which song she fell asleep to, but she awoke to "Otterley."

She was on her back, and she felt a weight next to her on her bed. A hand reached out and found one of her hands, a thumb caressing hers. She didn't move. After the song ended, she slowly removed her headphones and turned onto her side. With her old nightlight the sole illumination, she could only see the outline of his face, not his expression.

For a brief moment, she imagined it was Isaac, not Arrow, next to her, and fear traced a fingernail down her spine. The rumors of rape flared in her mind, and she held her breath, her entire body frozen.

Arrow pulled closer to her, his hand lightly touching her shoulder, and the fear evaporated.

His lips brushed her own, so soft, but she pushed away from him.

"Why did you ignore me?" she asked.

"I wasn't trying to, but—"

"You admit it, then."

He said nothing but she sensed his silent yes.

"I don't get you. You kiss me and then you act like it was nothing. What do you want?"

But she knew. He moved his hand over her naked chest, exploring

41

like a blind person in a new room, every surface gently touched and memorized, her skin tingling with goosebumps. Yes, she knew what he wanted. It was what she wanted too, and she knew he came to her because their parents were away for the evening and Grandma Haylin was at the church bingo.

He moved his hand lower, over her stomach, and she let him. She saw how nervous and young he looked and realized he didn't know what he was doing any more than she did.

"Sam, I know I shouldn't, but I like you. I just…"

"Just what?"

Arrow stopped moving his hand and stared at her, into the dark bubble of her bedroom.

"I don't want you to get hurt."

Chapter 6: Eric, 2009

There were many building supply stores in Oklahoma City, but Eric always found himself driving the forty minutes south to Blanchard when he had a new remodeling job. The building supply there was reasonable, but that's not why he went. Today, like most days when he drove out to Blanchard, he cruised down County Line Road, Nine Inch Nails or Tool blasting. He drove down a packed dirt lane leading to a small acreage, to the place where Sam grew up.

The current owners had torn down the two-story white farmhouse, built a brown brick single-story home in its place. Eric wanted to scream and cry the first time he saw the new house, and he did allow himself some tears once he saw that they'd kept the old red barn. They painted it white, but he saw that the inside was remarkably the same. How many times had he snuck onto the property since that first time? Probably dozens. Each time Eric told himself it'd be the last, that it was wrong and dangerous to trespass, but being there helped him feel whole again.

Two years and the owners still hadn't worked the land, and Eric wondered why the hell they bought it. There were twenty or so chickens in a poorly made coop, and the owners had a thin dairy cow he usually saw inside the barn instead of out grazing the fields.

He parked at least a hundred yards from the beginning of the dirt road and walked to the property, red dust billowing in clouds behind him. He made sure no one was around and crept past the new house

43

to the barn. The mid-afternoon sun made the whitewash appear to glow, reminding him of the church Jeri had forced him to attend, how the Sunday morning sun reached its fingers out from the sides of the building. Each time he approached the barn, his heart sped up with the thought that Sam would be there waiting for him when he entered. The disappointment of knowing he was alone dragged his stomach down to his feet until he felt like he was tripping over memories of her.

He entered the barn, the cow acknowledging him with a low moo. The wooden ladder leading up to the loft was splintery but solid, and Eric slowly climbed, feeling the ache in his damaged left leg with each rung. There wasn't much space at the top, and he had to crouch over to the corner of the loft where he used to sneak away with Sam, talking and making out on the hay for hours. He had never been with anyone like he was with her, without any thought about time.

He kneeled down and crawled to the space just under the large hinged window. It was closed, trapping the summer heat inside the barn. Eric rolled his eyes. The new owners had no idea what they were doing. He was tempted to lift the window, let in some air for the cow, but instead he ran his hand down the wall until his fingers found grooves in the weathered oak. His fingertips traced the carved heart, the 'E' and 'S' inside, and he was back where he wanted to be, where he needed to be.

"How often do you come here?" a woman's voice called from below. *Shit.* He thought he had been careful, parking his truck well outside of the property. There was no good explanation for him being there but for the truth. It had been his home once, no matter how short a time. He stooped back to the ladder and looked over, expecting to see an angry homeowner. It was as if a hard wind blew him back, knocking him on his ass. He quickly recovered and looked over the ladder again.

Sam peered up at him, her face set in an expression he could study for a thousand years and never know the meaning of. She stood erect and tense like she was about to change her mind and run off.

She wore a pale gray V-neck shirt, tight blue jeans hugging her curves. Her long dark hair was down and parted in the middle, and a simple gold necklace rested above her breasts. She was more beautiful than he remembered.

"Barn cat got your tongue?" she said.

"No, I'm just—I didn't expect you here."

"Well, I am."

He felt silly trying to talk from the loft, so he climbed down the ladder, the pain in his calf increasing by the minute. He was glad he was wearing one of his nicer plaid button-up shirts with good clean boots, but he didn't shave that morning and now regretted his laziness.

When he reached the ground, he wasn't sure what to do. It had been a week since he saw her at the bank, and he figured ever speaking with her again was a lost cause. He had so many questions he wanted to ask her, namely why she decided to see him now. He tried to act casual by leaning against the ladder. Really, he wanted to sit somewhere to get pressure off his left leg before it gave out on him.

"Still bothers you, huh?" Sam said, eyeing his calf.

"Yeah, but it's okay most of the time." He was a good three inches taller than she was, but Sam seemed to tower over him, her eyes pressing him closer to the ladder. "Did you follow me here?"

"You're not the only one who can stalk people."

"I didn't stalk you. I just had to cash a check and there you were." He saw she looked doubtful. "How did you find me?"

"It wasn't hard. Public records."

So, she followed him from his house, and he hadn't even noticed her vehicle behind him.

He took a tentative step forward, and Sam stepped back, crossing her arms.

"I can't believe these assholes tore down the house," she said. "Had another hundred years in it, at least."

"I know. Field's gone to dust too."

45

"It's depressing as hell. Why did you come here?"

He didn't know how to explain it to her, how coming to the property felt like coming home. "I miss it. It was good land, still is."

"You miss the land." There was so much bitterness and hurt in Sam's face, Eric almost broke down in front of her. "Then why the hell did you leave?"

"I didn't want to leave. Your mom—I don't know why but she didn't want me around. She called services, and I went into foster care."

Sam closed her eyes and exhaled slowly. She looked like Jeri when she had been stressed and about to lose her shit. "My mom wouldn't have done that. I would've known."

"Ask Grandma Haylin. She knows all about it."

Sam released a sound as if Eric had punched her chest.

"Grandma…she died a couple of years after you left. Another stroke." Her voice broke, and he could see she was fighting tears.

Eric closed the gap between them and held Sam. He felt her stiffen in his arms.

"I'm so sorry," he said, and Sam relaxed a little.

He had loved Grandma Haylin. She'd been kind to him, treated him like family. He owed her so much.

"I needed you, Eric, and you disappeared. I didn't even know if you were alive until…until a few years ago."

So, he was right and she had blocked him after he liked her Facebook status. He couldn't be angry about it now that he knew why she shut him out. She thought he had abandoned her.

He looked down at her sandaled feet. Her toes were painted shiny red, and he wanted to touch them. He imagined someone, a boyfriend or husband, holding those perfectly painted feet, kissing them. "The first year in foster care, I wrote letters to you. All the time."

Sam pulled back from him. "I never got any letters from you."

He shook his head. "I promise I did. None got returned."

He imagined Jeri ripping up every letter. Of course she would protect her daughter from him whatever way she could. At the time, he thought Sam wanted nothing more to do with him. He had never felt so alone in his life, not even after his mom died.

"What did you write to me?"

Eric forced himself to look into her eyes, and he thought he saw the old Sam, the young, strong-willed Sam who was too smart for the town where she was born and raised.

"Stuff about the families I was staying with and my new school. Things like that."

"That's it?" she said, disappointment in her voice.

"No. I wrote about how much I missed you. That I…that I would find a way back to see you."

Sam shook her head as if she didn't believe him. He needed her to believe.

"Well, you didn't come back," she said. "And I was okay."

His heart sank to the dirt. "Why did you follow me here?"

Sam stepped back from him, her eyes red and lips hardened.

"A detective came to my work."

Eric stared back at her, confused.

"Police found a white Chevy in the pond, the one off Morgan."

Then Eric understood. His father's truck.

"The detective asked a lot of questions. Questions about you and Isaac. Questions that made me think…"

It took all his power to ask, "What?"

"That something bad happened to him."

He saw worry in Sam's eyes, worry for his father. It made his stomach turn.

"Police already talked to my mom. She hasn't even mentioned it to me. Probably doesn't want to worry me." She shrugged. "I told the detective I don't know where you are."

"Why'd you say that? I have nothing to hide."

Sam shot him a fierce look and he knew what she was thinking.

47

That December day fifteen years ago.

Eric didn't want to relive that day, the sound of Bing Crosby's singing and the smell of Grandma Haylin's freshly baked gingerbread cookies following him to the woods lining the farmhouse. Deep into those woods, he walked, his pocketknife ready.

Whenever he thought of that day, it was in bursts, in white flashes of fear and the sound of Sam crying over his leg gushing blood, her own right hand cut deep, the gray sky dotted black with scattering birds.

"Eric, we need to find Isaac."

He knew what Sam was getting at. His father would never part with his truck. Change the license plate to avoid the police, sure, but not leave it at the bottom of a pond. If the police thought something happened to his father and didn't find him, there'd be questions Eric didn't want to answer.

He looked Sam in the eyes, and he knew she didn't want to answer those questions either.

He took her hand. "Okay."

Chapter 7: Sam, 1994

I don't want you to get hurt.

Sam asked Arrow what he meant, but he kissed her instead of giving her an answer, his hands sliding off her underwear, his fingers pushing between her legs until she forgot his words and only wanted more from him. When he finally gave her what she wanted, she cried.

She cried because it felt good. She cried because she could never get the girl she had been back, and she wasn't sure who the new girl was yet. She was a bubble floating free, afraid of the approaching treetops.

Arrow stopped moving in her. "Am I hurting you?"

The bubble popped. "No," she lied, her temples wet with tears. It felt like being torn in half with all the blood in her body pooling to that single area throbbing with the pain, a pain so wrapped in pleasure she wasn't sure which she liked more.

When she didn't move with him, he continued until he sharply inhaled like he was the one hurting, and warmth filled her. She had seen enough animals mate to know what the warmth was, and she felt soiled like she had in church four years ago when her period first came. She had bled on her favorite blue dress, soaked right through it onto the wooden pew and she had no idea. Her mama scolded her as if she'd done it on purpose. She didn't want to think about the sticky blood between her thighs after Arrow pulled out of her, her old self exiting with him, but she was glad she was on top of her bedding. Can't wash a mattress.

49

"What are you thinking about?" Arrow whispered, his head nestled in the nook of her neck.

"Zeus and Hera."

"Why?"

She wiggled her shoulder until Arrow traded places with her, allowing her to rest her head on him.

"Zeus and Hera were brother and sister. They got married and had kids. Hera was always crazy because Zeus was a cheating asshole." Like her daddy.

"But we're not related." He lightly rubbed her head in an even, circular motion that was exactly how her mama stroked her head when she was little. It made goosebumps rise on her skin. "What? Are you scared of going to hell?"

Sam swallowed hard. She thought of her mama's face when she listened to Pastor Doss preach, the way her eyes closed and her hand lifted high toward the ceiling, the Spirit overcoming her. "Yeah. Maybe."

"Well, I'm not scared of hell."

"How can you not be scared of hell?"

Arrow withdrew his hand buried in her hair. "Because I've seen it."

The way he sounded as he said it, the sudden flatness to his voice, made her shiver. He pulled the covers over them although it was still burning up in her room.

She was about to ask him what kind of hell he had seen, the rape rumors itching on her tongue, but he cuddled close to her again, holding her like she'd disappear.

"If we ever go there," he said, "I'd protect you."

"Like Prometheus? Remember I told you about him tricking Zeus and giving mankind fire? He protects humans."

Arrow lightly yanked on her hair and gave a low laugh. "Yeah, I'll protect you like Prometheus, but I'm not gonna get tied to a rock with some dumb eagle eating my liver."

Sam tried but she couldn't laugh with him.

50

***

I don't want you to get hurt.

Sam tried to forget Arrow's words as she trudged through her chores the next day, but they kept coming back, tainting the night before until her stomach clenched painfully and she could barely breathe.

Hades followed her to the barn, his short tail wagging as fast as his stride. Sam ran fresh water for Maddie. Hades loudly barked at Maddie until the goat decided she'd had enough and plopped down in the corner of her stall. Sam smiled, remembering what Arrow had told her about Maddie's last escape attempt. Maddie had made it all the way to the edge of their property, worked her fat belly through a break in the wood fencing, and then promptly fell asleep before getting to the other side. Isaac had to carry the lazy animal all the way back to the barn, got one of his favorite shirts torn in the process.

That morning, Arrow had passed Sam on her way to the hideous pink tiled bathroom her mama loved. He grabbed her hand and pulled her into his room, kissing her fast and hard against the wall before whispering, "Meet me in Maddie's stall after lunch." He smiled, his nerves releasing a quiver into her that spread between her legs.

Isaac wouldn't be back from his Sunday fishing until after supper, so Sam had hurried through her afternoon chores as well as some of Isaac's before heading to the barn. Every time she started a task, though, she'd lose track of what she was doing when she thought of the previous night.

She touched her lips, enjoying how sensitive and raw they were from kissing. A weird sensation loosened the joints of her hips, the same sensation she experienced when she visited the Bank of America building in Dallas with her Aunt Shelley last summer. They had taken the elevator as high as they could go, and when Sam looked out to the skyline her legs turned wobbly and her hips felt like they were going to break apart. The feeling frightened her then, but now it only made her aware of the emptiness that had been filled with Arrow.

"What's got you so deep in thought, girlie?"

Sam jumped about a foot and turned in Maddie's stall to see Isaac standing by the doorframe a few feet from her, his arms crossed over his naked broad chest, his T-shirt hanging from his belt loop and his honey hair darkened to molasses with sweat. He smelled of rich earth and some warm spice she couldn't quite name, but it made her want to keep inhaling forever.

"Just how school's almost out." She forced a smile. "I'll be the only one without a car of my own."

"Now, I know that's not true." Isaac moved inside the stall closer to her. "Your friend—what's her name—Chrissy? She doesn't have a car."

"She's getting one for her birthday. She's not sixteen until October." Right before her own seventeenth birthday in November, and she thought of Arrow's birthday in late September.

Sam shifted closer to Maddie. The goat kicked at the ground, and Sam pet her to calm her.

"Wow. I really thought she was older." He rubbed his shoulder, and Sam tried not to stare at his muscles flexing. "Girls develop so early now. Must be all those hormones they put in everything."

Sam hugged her arms across her braless chest.

"You have nothing to be embarrassed about," he said.

She knew how some of the men around town saw her, not as a girl, but like an object they wanted to capture. She couldn't even get a soda at the drug store without the owner, Mr. Woodcock, leering at her chest.

She uncrossed her arms, feeling oddly powerful letting Isaac see her curves. "I'm not embarrassed."

Isaac grinned like he knew exactly what she was doing, and she no longer felt powerful. She wanted to shrink into the ground.

"I bet the boys are scared to even look at you. They don't know what to do with that kind of beauty."

Sam looked down at Hades lapping Maddie's water, the blush rushing to her cheeks. She thought of what he'd said, about pain. He had seen her do something no one knew about, not even Arrow, and it didn't freak him out.

"Could I draw you again sometime?" she asked. Maybe he would tell her more about when he was younger, how pain helped him.

"Why not ask one of your friends?"

"I have. My friends think it's boring to sit still for so long."

She remembered when she asked her mama about taking a nude drawing class at a local art studio, and her mama flat-out said no. She tried not to look at Isaac's chest again. The thought of seeing him nude was too bizarre of a thought for her to wrap her mind around. Seeing Arrow naked was overwhelming enough.

"I'll probably get to draw people all the time in college," she said.

"I'm sure you will."

"My art teacher won't even let us model for each other." She grinned. "Everyone's figure drawings look like a toddler scribbled them."

"Except for yours?"

Sam thought about when she'd sit nude in front of her full-length mirror for hours, studying every curve and shadow, sketchpad on her lap.

"I try."

"Okay," he said. "You sold me. I'll model for you."

"That's great. Thanks."

She didn't know what else to say. Arrow should've come to the barn by now, but she didn't want him to get in trouble with Isaac.

"I better get back to the house and start the beans or Mama will kill me."

Isaac slowly nodded. "We wouldn't want that."

Sam moved to leave the stall, but Isaac darted in front of the exit, blocking her. He smirked like it was a fun game to him. Flustered, she quickly skirted past him and tripped over her own tennis shoes. He caught her at her waist, and she fell against his naked chest for a moment, his spicy scent invading her senses.

He was quite a few inches taller, and she felt like a child. He held her chin and forced her face up to look him in the eyes, eyes the color of coffee with a splash of cream, same as Arrow's.

"Don't be afraid of being different, Sam. You're talented. More talented than most people around here. Nothing wrong with it."

Her throat pushed out, "Okay."

His fingers pressed hard into her chin, and she felt ill as familiar excitement filled her.

"Do you like that?"

She did but she didn't want to say it.

"You're not scared to look at me. Isn't that right?"

Right then, Sam wanted to take back every time she had watched Isaac working with his shirt off when she thought he wasn't looking. She wondered if he had caught her staring at his chest now. She felt a tremor travel up her body.

"It's okay to look." His voice rolled out as a low rumble. "There's no law against looking. I like it when you look at me."

She couldn't breathe. She was sure she was going to choke on her heart beating in her throat.

There was a loud clang outside of the barn followed by cussing.

"You will not believe what that goddamn rooster just did to me."

Arrow stopped short of Maddie's stall and his face fell when he saw Sam, her lips inches away from his father's. She saw a fear in Arrow's eyes she'd never seen, a fear that made her want to run, run, run from the farm until her legs gave out.

Isaac released her and walked past his son without so much as a nod that he existed. Arrow stood there frozen in front of Sam, his mouth parted but silent, one hand holding the other she now saw was deeply scratched and bleeding from the rooster. His mouth opening

54

and closing without a word made Sam want to rush up to him and punch him as hard as she could in his dying fish face. He knew something bad, something he was keeping from her. The town rumors flashed in her head as Arrow continued to stand there saying nothing. She roughly shoved him on her way out of the barn.

She ran to the two-story house, the whitewash worn to nothing, climbed the narrow stairs to her small bedroom, and slammed her door before collapsing onto her bed. She couldn't prevent the tears from soaking her pillow, and she couldn't erase the words scratching at her gut.

I don't want you to get hurt.

Arrow wasn't her Prometheus. He wasn't her protector at all.

Chapter 8: Sam, 2009

Sam had never been to Sapulpa, the small town nestled outside of Tulsa, and she never would've guessed her first visit would be driving with Eric to track down Isaac Walker. She didn't know what she'd do, how she'd react if she saw him again. She wondered if he would look the same, and how she would look to him, now older.

Her mom had been quiet for a long time when Sam called her about the detective's visit. She imagined her mama was thinking about what happened fifteen years ago, of rushing Eric to the hospital in Grandma Haylin's car, no time or money for an ambulance. She could never talk to her mom about that day or the months leading up to it, although she knew her mom knew most of what had happened.

"Let the police find Isaac, Sammy. Why would you want to find him anyway?"

Sam could've tracked him down anytime in the last fifteen years and asked him why her, what did she do, but she didn't because she told herself she had moved on. Now, with him missing, the feeling of being unsafe nagged at her.

"I don't know, Mama. It's just weird that they found his truck so close to the old farm." She tried not to think about Eric contacting her around the same time, of how he didn't seem to have any interest in finding his father.

"With what Isaac did." Her mom sharply inhaled as if she was trying to calm herself. "If he had any ounce of remorse, he would've driven himself into that pond."

Sam knew he wouldn't have done that.

"Where would he have gone, Mama? When he ran off?"

Her mom paused. "I'm not sure. He didn't have any family, but he had an army friend he talked to quite a bit. Les Compton—I think that's his name. Lived in Sapulpa."

Sam watched Eric shift gears, increasing speed as he reentered the highway from their pit stop. He had insisted they take his truck for the hour and half drive after she told him she couldn't handle a standard as well as she used to. The last time she saw him he was a sixteen-year-old boy, barely old enough to drive. Not old enough for many things he did then. Now, here he was, a grown man talking about how he started his own contracting business several years ago. He told her about buying a big foreclosed house in Gatewood to fix up and flip for big profits, and she thought about all her bank customers who had lost their homes within the last year from the recession, how some of them would likely never recover.

He was talking about the families he lived with after her mom placed him in foster care and about one nice family who wanted to adopt him before he turned eighteen when he turned quiet.

"Did you do it?" she asked. "Did you let them adopt you?"

"No."

"Why not?"

He looked over at Sam. "I told them I already had a family."

She sensed the expectation in his voice, but she had never looked at him as family. He was more than family, but she didn't know what category to place him.

She could tell he was nervous with how much he was talking. She was nervous being around him too, but she was much better at hiding it.

"Sorry," he said. "I didn't mean to talk your ear off."

"It's good to hear what you've been doing." She almost added that she was proud of him for surviving foster care and doing something positive with his life, but it would've sounded condescending. She knew his damage was there, under the surface. Just like her.

"What about you?" he asked.

She told him she owned her house, but she didn't say she had a decent nest egg saved in case she needed to leave in a hurry. She had a master's degree in Greek Classics she didn't use but no student debt thanks to her work's tuition reimbursement program. She had traveled a bit and got lost telling him about visiting Florence and seeing Michelangelo's David.

She didn't want him to think she was some sort of psychopath, so she lied, said she went out with friends as often as she could. The truth was she had visited Italy on her own and she went home every night to her dog and her two-thousand dollar queen-sized mattress, a splurge she didn't regret. Getting close to people meant showing them the ugly parts of her too. Relationships didn't usually last too long after that.

"So, you don't draw anymore?" Eric asked.

"No."

She had stopped drawing a long time ago. It made her think of hands grasping flesh, tearing pieces away.

"You were so good, though. I always thought you'd be an artist."

The way he said it, it was like he was suggesting she had settled. Maybe she did, but she was good at being a bank manager. She liked the predictability, the order of it, and it paid well.

"Maybe I'll draw you sometime, but I warn you—I'm rusty. You might end up looking like a fucked up potato."

Eric smiled a little, one of his deep dimples flashing.

"I was never a good model for you."

"Because you couldn't stay still."

"I had other things on my mind."

"Homework?"

58

"You."

Sam shook her head, blushing.

The old electric current was still there between them, binding them with memories, with their secrets. He knew more about her than most people ever would, yet she found she couldn't trust him the same way she had as a teen. Too much had happened in those fifteen years, too many failed relationships and shameful sexual encounters that could've killed her, literally. She pushed aside the memory of an alcohol-fueled one-night stand were a guy had slammed her so hard against a wall she got a concussion. She didn't press charges because she had asked him to do it.

It took her a long time and a lot of therapy to determine no one could help her untangle her past much less her sexuality. Most therapists she had visited seemed more interested in her masochism, which they saw as a sexual disorder even after she informed them she had no distress from it. It was quite the opposite; it calmed her mind and gave her peace.

She wondered what Eric would say about her sexuality, whether he would react the same way her last boyfriend did when she finally opened up to him about it. *You're disturbed. You need help*, he had told her before moving out. Men were usually okay with spanking, but few were okay with her other, darker requests. The ones who were okay with it usually hadn't asked her consent first.

All the talk about their adult lives, she knew, was a distraction for what they couldn't talk about—the thing that had shaped them. The stupid shit logic of teenagers to lie no matter what.

Eric looked so serious. She always thought he'd grow out of his pensiveness but, if anything, he'd grown more somber as an adult. She wondered what he was thinking about. Maybe thinking about how detectives had found him, asked him similar questions about Isaac, what happened before and after the attack.

No matter what Eric was thinking, Sam knew driving to Sapulpa to see Isaac's old army buddy was probably a waste of her Saturday, but she wanted to believe they'd learn something useful.

"Maybe my mom was wrong," she said, and Eric glanced at her. "Maybe this Les guy doesn't know anything."

The man didn't have a listed phone number, but from what Eric could find he apparently lived in the same Sapulpa trailer park.

It was almost four, the August afternoon swallowing them in its heat, when they pulled up to the trailer park. It was nice, for what it was, with tiny well-maintained patches of lawn.

They circled around and Eric parked in front of a powder-blue manufactured home. In the front, there was an inviting rock garden with a small, bubbling water fountain and several ceramic Buddhas peeking out of the greenery.

For several minutes, they sat in the heat, their eyes on the house. Eric broke the stillness by taking Sam's hand.

"You should stay here. I can turn on the air for you."

"No. I'm coming with you."

It took forever for Les Compton to open the door, and Sam quickly saw why: Les, his long graying hair pulled back into a ponytail, was an amputee. His right leg was missing below his thigh, the metal of his prosthesis glinting in the sun. He dressed in a loose, white cotton tunic, no shoes, and he didn't appear to have on shorts. She hoped he had on underwear.

"Arrow? Holy hell, I thought I was staring at your father for a second."

"It's been a long time."

Les embraced Eric hard, something Sam had never seen Isaac do. Eric didn't look too comfortable with it. Les gave Eric a final slap on the back and looked over at Sam, smiling.

"You'll have to tell me who this pretty lady is. Come on in."

The tidiness of Les's home surprised Sam, and she felt guilty for thinking it. Isaac had been neat too, every sock and shirt organized by color in his drawers. Must have been a military thing.

Eric introduced Sam, and Les asked if they wanted some hot tea after they found a spot on his gray loveseat. She didn't want to be rude, so she accepted but she would've preferred anything with ice.

Eric nudged her with his knee and gave her a look reflecting what she was thinking; this man had no idea Isaac was missing.

After a few minutes in his small, sparse kitchen, Les came back with a tray of green tea and shortbread cookies. Sam smiled and took a cookie.

"You still live in this backwards state?" Les asked.

"Yeah. In Oklahoma City now."

"So, what brings you two out here? Surely you didn't drive all that way to amuse an old guy like me."

"Did my dad ever contact you in '94, sometime in late December?" Eric said.

Les scrunched up his face in thought for a moment.

"No. I didn't hear much from him after he moved to Blanchard, and I haven't seen him since you both stayed here after your mama passed."

Eric's leg bobbed up and down, shaking the loveseat until Sam touched his thigh.

"When I heard about what happened, I couldn't believe it," Les said. "I knew he had a temper, but he loved you and always wanted to do right by you."

"He had a funny way of showing it," Sam said.

Les set his teacup down and rubbed the metal ball that was his kneecap. "I guess we never really know people, not behind closed doors."

Eric was quiet in thought next to her, rubbing his left leg.

"Is there anyone else he might've contacted?" she said.

"I don't think he had many people to turn to, not after his brother Jobe died. I really don't know, he never talked much about family, but

I expect he called Vickie."

"Who's Vickie?"

Eric stood up, his entire body rigid. "We should go."

What the hell? Sam looked over at Les who shared her confusion. She had never seen Eric react like that, and it lodged a splinter of fear in her chest.

Faster than Sam expected, Les stood and gripped Eric's shoulder. "Arrow, what's this all about? Did something happen to your dad?"

"I don't know. Maybe." Eric looked at Sam, his eyes urging her to get up. "Thank you for the tea, but we need to get going."

"You're welcome to stay for dinner," Les said. "I'd love to know what you've been up to."

Sam touched Eric's arm. "Yeah, why don't we stay? We came all this way to leave already."

Eric's mouth grew tight. "Another time. I have some work I've got to do at my place."

She didn't know why Eric was lying, but she knew it had something to do with the woman Les mentioned.

"So," Sam said after a few minutes of watching Eric drive in silence, "you going to tell me what that was about?"

Eric kept his eyes on the road ahead.

"Who's Vickie? And why didn't you tell Les that Isaac's truck was at the bottom of a pond?"

"We should stop to eat."

"Jesus Christ, Eric, I went on this wild goose chase with you. Be honest with me."

Eric exited the highway and pulled into a McDonald's parking lot. He kept his hands on the steering wheel and stared out at the golden arches.

"Your mom suggested we talk to Les, not me."

"Okay, but at least we have some kind of direction with this Vickie person."

"We're not going to see her."

"Why? Who the hell is she?"

He didn't look at her, but Sam could tell he was weighing something in his mind, maybe how much to tell her. The thought that he didn't trust her felt like swallowing a bucket of ice.

He let out a long sigh.

"Vickie was married to my dad's brother."

"So, why have you never told me about her?"

"Jobe was army like my dad, but he got killed in the Gulf War. He was a good man. Vickie was one of the people we stayed with after my mom died, and she messed around on my uncle a lot."

Eric finally looked at her, his jaw tight.

"But she was loyal to my father. Always."

Sam ignored the strange mix of anger and shame seeping into her body and searing her face.

"We need to contact her, Eric. She could know where Isaac is."

"She's probably dead from an overdose by now. God willing."

"She screwed around with your dad. So what? That's why you don't want to see her?"

Eric rubbed his eyes, the line between his brows deepening.

"No."

"Then why?"

"Listen, you don't know what kind of person she is. She's not—she's not right. She's like my father."

Sam doubted that. She couldn't imagine any woman doing the things Isaac did. She took Eric's hand, laced her fingers with his.

"You mean she hurts people?" she asked.

"Vickie liked it. She liked hurting people. But not the same as him, you know?"

"Did she hurt you?"

He looked away from her and she knew the answer.

"She let him hurt her daughter, her only kid. She had her with some

63

random guy she messed with, but my uncle raised her like she was his own. He wouldn't have let anyone touch her, not when he was alive."

She knew if she asked Eric more questions about Vickie and her daughter that it would only make her relive her own hurt. She imagined a box inside herself, inside Eric too, tucked deep into some dark corner, a place where the hurt could safely live within her. She squeezed Eric's hand. She had no interest in forcing his box open. Not yet.

Eric returned the squeeze and gazed at her, his face leaning toward her, and she thought he might try to kiss her. She knew it was a horrible idea, but she wanted to feel his lips on hers. It had been too long since she'd been with someone.

Then Eric looked away from her, out at the cars lining up in the drive-thru.

"Let the police find him, Sam. It's not our job."

Her mom's words. Sam would've been lying if she agreed with them. She did want to find Isaac. All these years, she thought she was safe in her new life, but she wasn't. Her job, her quiet, hermit-like existence, it gave her the illusion of normalcy. But the lies she told fifteen years before, they would haunt her, Eric too, if they didn't find Isaac alive.

Chapter 9: Arrow, 1994

Since that day in the barn almost two weeks before, Sam hadn't spoken to Arrow at all, not even when they entered their upstairs bathroom at the same time. He understood her angry silence, though. He had left her alone in the barn with his father. He failed to protect her, to warn her, and now she hated him.

Making sure she was okay was all that mattered now, and he vowed to be better at watching over her. His father was a circling hawk, always around the corner waiting for Sam, offering her rides to the library or the coffee shop when Jeri was working at the feed shop.

The June afternoon was so hot his Hypercolor T-shirt changed from its normal blue to a pale green. He followed Sam from the town library down Tenth Street to the First United Methodist Church where she settled cross-legged with her pile of books at the top of the covered playset. He had stayed as far behind her as possible so she wouldn't see him.

Sam was a quarter of the way through one of the books when she looked up from her page. "Are you going to follow me every damn day like a puppy dog?"

Arrow pressed himself closer to the brick exterior of the church, holding his breath as if it'd make him invisible.

"I swear to Jesus, you walk louder than an elephant wearing sleigh bells. Just come on out of hiding and stop being stupid."

Arrow slowly walked over to the bottom of the playset's slide, willing himself to look at Sam. Her black eyes went through him and he couldn't speak.

"Let me ask you something, *little brother*," she sneered. "Do you know a Meredith Lang from Anadarko? She's about your age?"

He swallowed over the sudden lump in his throat. How did she know that name?

"No."

"But you lived in Anadarko before moving here?" She leaned forward, her tank top lowering enough to reveal the tops of her breasts.

"Yeah, for a while. So what?"

"And you didn't know that girl, in that tiny ass town?"

Arrow shifted his weight and shrugged. "It's no smaller than here."

"Your daddy know her?"

"Maybe. I don't know." He hated the sudden whine in his voice.

Sam stood up and walked down the long slide to him in less than five steps. "The whole town knows you know her."

"That's not true."

"Stop lying. I looked everything up at the library and read the articles. The papers didn't print her name, but everyone whispers it and I know you know her."

"I don't."

"You know what happened to Meredith?"

Arrow backed up from her, shaking his head.

"She was raped—a lot. She had to get stitches."

Her eyes flashed anger he'd never seen in her.

"She had a baby inside her. Did you know that? It was messed up real bad and it died. People talk about it. People talk about you and your dad and that girl, and it can't all be rumors."

Arrow's stomach rose until he tasted pure acid. He pictured Meredith's rosy cheeks, her soft strawberry blond hair fanned out over her pillow, the wideness of her blue eyes.

"Is it true?"

"No," he said too slowly and she pushed his chest hard.

"Did you do it? Did you rape her?"

He hated seeing so much anger at him in her eyes.

"No, Sam, I promise. I would never do something like that."

"Did your dad?"

He wanted to tell her, but he couldn't. It was like a metal trap closed tight over his mouth whenever he tried. He shook his head to free them, but the words stayed trapped.

She was quiet for a long time, her hands twisting the bottom of her shirt. She looked at him as if she was trying to work out a tricky math problem. "Would you ever hurt me?"

Sam was the first person in a long time to be nice to him, even when she was playfully mean. He could talk to her. He could tell her things he couldn't tell anyone else. She was the only person he'd ever fully trusted outside of his mom.

An image of his mom's skeletal body flashed in his mind. He didn't want to think about her, of when she lay dying in the hospital. It was the only time he ever saw his dad cry. If he thought about it too much—of his mom's funeral after the cancer ate her up, of when he and his dad moved in with his uncle's widow, Vickie's cigarette smoke choking him, seeing his dad's hand tight around her throat as he lifted up her jean skirt from behind…and Meredith—Meredith and her nails always bitten down to bloody stumps—he'd break down in front of Sam. He had to be strong for her. He had to be strong this time.

"I'd never hurt you. Never." He paused, afraid to say the words he imagined telling her many times, but not like this. "I—I love you."

Sam's eyes got teary. She looked like she was fighting the desire to run from him.

"Promise me you won't lie to me," she said.

"I promise." But he knew as he said it he'd lie again if it meant keeping her safe.

Sam leaned forward, lay her head on his shoulder, and he wrapped his arms around her.

When she lifted her head, he found her lips on his, and he closed his eyes from the sheer pleasure of her wanting him again. He needed her to know he wanted her too, so he ran his hands down the front of her shirt to the button of her cutoff shorts. She didn't stop him, so he undid the button and lowered the zipper. The more they kissed, the more uncomfortable he felt with his jeans still on.

He led her under the playset, glancing around to make sure no one was watching them. Then he pulled her cutoff shorts and underwear down her long legs to her ankles, spread her thighs, and buried his head between her legs. At first, she laughed a little from above, but then she got quiet, her hips lifting. He thought of her mouth on him too, but he didn't ask her. He liked hearing the soft sounds she made.

As they lay together under the playset, the woodchips poking their backs, Sam placed her hand on his chest. It reminded him of his mom, her hand resting over his father's heart as he lay next to her on the hospital bed, Arrow not realizing she had already died.

A shiver ran through him. It seemed too perfect to be holding Sam, the shade of the slide hiding them from others. He wanted to stay hidden with her forever.

Sam's face turned red and she smiled at him. "Where'd you learn how to do that?"

He imagined his dad's head lost between pale legs, dyed red hair covering half of a face, lips parted in pleasure like Sam's had been moments before. And he saw a girl's face and strawberry blond hair and fear…so much fear he tasted the copper blood of it. The metal trap closed over his mouth, his jaw aching from clenching it shut, but he opened his mouth and freed the words he needed to tell Sam.

"I used to watch them."

Chapter 10: Eric, 2009

Four days since the drive to Sapulpa and seeing Les, and Eric still couldn't shake the knee-drop sensation he'd experienced when Les said Vickie's name. His mom would've called the sinking sensation "a knowing," something she swore his grandmother had too.

His mom was always having *knowings* when he was young. There was the time she dreamed a giant crow plucked Eric from the playground and tore him in half. The next day, he fell from the monkey bars at school and split his ulna in two. The doctor said it was the cleanest break he'd ever seen. His mom had other *knowings*, ones that kept Eric awake at night, like her vision of her swallowing a black storm cloud. No matter how much she coughed and coughed, nothing came out until a tornado of blood ripped from her lungs and swept her away.

Eric didn't have *knowings*, he knew that much. He shook the sensation off again and focused on the small drywall repair for an elderly woman who lived down the street from him. She vaguely reminded him of Grandma Haylin, straight gunmetal gray hair cropped close, a once solid body turning weak on her. She could hardly afford to pay him for the job, so he didn't tell her the reason why her ceiling had warped and sagged in her living room, how the bathroom above had a severe plumbing leak. He had some extra pex pipe for the broken water supply line, so he fixed it. It wouldn't have done any good to fix the drywall otherwise.

69

He finished the job and declined the stale-looking cookies the lady offered. He had completed the job early and the late afternoon sun was well above the trees on his way home. He pulled onto his street, saw an unmarked black Dodge Charger parked in front of his house, and forced himself to park in his driveway instead of driving on.

He was barely out of his truck with his drywall tools when a short, solid man wearing a dark suit ambled up to him like he was taking a pleasure walk through the shittier part of the neighborhood.

"Eric Walker," the older man said, removing his sunglasses and extending his right hand. "Detective Chad Eastman. Mind if I come inside, ask you a few questions?"

Sam was right; Detective Eastman looked like an ex-politician with the clothing and hair to match.

He took the detective's hand, not caring to wipe the work grime from his own. It unnerved Eric that the man didn't ask his name but stated it like he had a long-awaited appointment with him.

"No, sir, don't mind at all, although I'm not sure what else I can tell you. I already spoke with the other detectives."

"Sometimes it helps to talk again. You'd be surprised what people remember when you jog their memory a bit."

"Well, I just got off work, so you'll have to pardon me—gotta clean my tools in the garage first or I'll never get the plaster off."

"No problem. We can talk while you clean."

"Sure."

He led the detective around to the back of the house, unlocking the side door to the old one-car garage. He tossed his keys and tool bag onto his workbench and flipped on the overhead light. Detective Eastman, without being directed, went straight for the only chair in the garage, an ancient orange La-Z-Boy recliner left by the previous owners. Eric looked forward to sitting on it while cleaning his tools each day.

"You mind if I sit?" The detective said, pointing to the recliner.

"Not at all."

The detective sank back into the chair, letting out a groan of comfort. Eric sucked in a deep breath and silently cussed out the detective as he walked over to his mini-fridge. He pulled out a bottle of water and looked over to the detective.

"You like a drink, sir? Afraid I only have water."

Detective Eastman smiled at nothing and said, "No, thanks."

Eric wasn't much for the heavy stuff, had no head for it, but he wouldn't have refused a few shots of whiskey at that moment. He took his time, drinking down the water while trying to get his nerves under control. After he finished the entire bottle, he locked eyes with the detective in a way that, he hoped, would appear to be both curious and ready to help. His heart jackhammered, the water in his stomach sickeningly cool.

"Let me just get this bucket set up, sir."

Eric lifted the five-gallon bucket, filled it with warm water at the utility sink, and placed it on the concrete floor. Normally, he would've placed it in front of the La-Z-Boy, sitting down to rest his left leg. He grabbed another five-gallon bucket nearby, flipped it over, and sat with his plaster-covered tools.

"I'm ready to answer any questions, sir."

"Sir, huh?" Detective Eastman said, smiling again. "You military like your father?"

"No, sir. Just how I was raised." Eric crouched over the bucket and dunked his drywall putty knives into the water, scrubbing them with a nylon brush.

"Don't care for authority figures?"

Eric paused cleaning and looked up. "I wouldn't say that. Just prefer to be my own boss."

"Your father was his own boss too, wasn't he?"

Eric dunked the knives again, brushing them harder than necessary. "Yes, sir, he worked for himself quite a bit when I was younger. Mostly

71

labor work. He taught me a lot about how things work, how to fix them."

It was the only time Eric felt close to his father, working side-by-side, sweating together under the sun while planting seeds or crawling under a house to fix a leaky pipe.

The detective leaned forward in the chair, his hands on his knees and his face serious. "And your father taught you other things too. Bad things, right?"

Eric stared into the muddy water, the putty knives sunk to the bottom of the bucket. He inhaled, held it for a few seconds, and slowly released it when he looked back up at the man. Detective Eastman sank back into the chair again, ready for whatever story he thought he was about to hear. The detective's self-assured expression was too much like his father. He imagined balling his fists and punching the smirk off the detective's face.

Eric stood and lifted the bucket, dumped the dirty water into the utility sink. He turned around to see the detective rocking a little in the chair. Eric leaned against the sink, arms crossed, putting his weight on his right leg.

"Did some of the things he taught you involve your stepsister, Samantha Mayfair?" the detective said.

Eric said nothing.

He had been waiting for it, and Detective Eastman finally pulled out a small steno pad from his inner jacket pocket, the stubby pencil resting inside the metal coils. The detective jotted a few notes down before looking at Eric again.

"Why do you think your father attacked you and your stepsister in December of 1994?"

Eric turned to the sink and took another deep breath. He had answered this question from police too many times before. "He thought I was going to report him to the police—that we'd both report him for the things he tried to do."

The recliner resumed creaking back and forth. "The things involving Samantha Mayfair or Meredith Lang?"

Eric's heart sped up more at hearing Meredith's name.

"Sam, sir."

"But you reported about Meredith Lang's rape to police, back in '93. That correct?"

Eric ran fresh water into the bucket and faced the detective. "Yes, sir."

Detective Eastman smiled and Eric realized who the man reminded him of: the Cheshire Cat. That asshole, know-it-all cat.

"Surely, you're aware Miss Lang denied the accusations of rape against your father. Said she went to a high school party against her mother's wishes, drank too much and was assaulted by some boys. But you have a different opinion?"

That Meredith had lied to the police didn't surprise Eric.

He kept the bucket in the sink this time and ran the stiff brush over the putty knives again. "Meredith—she was scared to tell the truth."

"You sure she wasn't scared of you? I read the report."

"No, sir." Eric gave up on cleaning the tools and moved to the workbench, his left leg aching to rest on the La-Z-Boy. He saw the detective studying his limp. "I tried to protect her."

The detective leaned forward and fiddled with his short pencil, twirling it between his index finger and thumb like a tiny baton. "Like you tried to protect your stepsister?"

"I already told the other detectives all of this."

"I'd like to hear it myself. Tell me about when your father attacked you and Miss Mayfair."

Eric's leg was killing him now, pulsing pain as fast as his heart. He sat on the bucket, straightening his left leg as much as he could.

"My father—he tried to hurt Sam, but she fought him off."

The lie was easier every time he said it.

"My father heard us talk about turning him in and he went nuts.

73

He came at us with a knife, cut Sam and sliced my leg up when I tried to get him off her."

"What kind of knife did he use?"

"A pocketknife."

"What did it look like?"

"I don't recall. Just a regular pocketknife."

The more Eric told the story, the more it seemed real. Funny how memories distorted, became whatever he wanted them to be.

Detective Eastman's blue eyes lost all good humor. "So, when he left y'all in the woods, he was uninjured?"

The Cheshire Cat grinned, willing Eric to slip up.

"I reckon so."

"But you fired a gun at him in Anadarko, to protect Miss Lang? That correct?"

"Yes, but it was to stop him from hurting her."

"But he wasn't the one who hurt Miss Lang, is that correct?"

Eric swallowed, the large bottle of water doing nothing for his parched throat. The sounds of that night, the screaming turned into choked crying…Meredith's pink mouth fixed into a silent O. "They did hurt her."

"They as in those high school boys?"

"No," Eric said. "My father. He was hurting her." He paused, pinched the bridge of his nose. "I'm sorry, it's been a long day." The detective stood up from the chair and moved close enough to Eric that he could smell the man's Stetson cologne. "Are you saying Miss Lang lied about what happened to her?"

Eric understood why Meredith told a different story, how she turned on him as quickly as a storm cloud into a tornado. She had been terrified. Eric had spent six months in juvenile hall for her lie, but he didn't hate her for it. She had hated him, though. Probably still did.

He rubbed his face with both hands. "Yes. She lied, but she was afraid."

The exhale Detective Eastman released sounded halfway between a grunt and a resolution. "We found your father, Mr. Walker."

Eric was sure the other man heard the air punched out of him.

"Well…I should say we found most of him."

Chapter II: Sam, 1994

Sam waited for Arrow outside of the high school. She watched the kids scurrying to waiting cars and the school's one bus. After what Arrow told her about Isaac the week before, she couldn't look at other kids the same way. They all seemed too young, too ignorant of danger that could be right around the corner, down the street from where they lived, next door, in their own bedrooms, under the tent of their sheets.

Everything Arrow had told Sam about his father raised the hair on her arms, his words eliciting a low, horrifying thrill throughout her body. He told her about living with his father's friend and Meredith in Anadarko after his mom died, of Isaac trying to find farm labor work there. He told her about seeing his father doing sick things, sexual things where he hurt Meredith, and the next thing he knew his father moved them to Blanchard.

As much as she wanted to believe he was telling her the truth she couldn't. It didn't help that his story for why he had spent time in juvenile hall—truancy—was an obvious lie. Arrow never missed a day of school, was never late, not once. He hated being even a minute late.

Besides, Isaac had never tried to hurt her when they were alone, and they had been alone several times before when he let her draw him. He had never removed his clothes or tried to touch her, even though she fantasized about him doing both. They only talked while she sketched. Even now, after she stopped asking Isaac to model for her, she didn't feel afraid of him.

76

Then she thought about the time in the barn, his hand on her chin, squeezing hard and asking if she liked it. In the moment, she had wanted him to hurt her, and she tried to think of what signal she had given him to make him do it. She didn't want to think about Arrow's face watching his father with her, the fear shooting from him straight into her chest. Maybe Arrow was jealous of Isaac. Or maybe he was confused by what he saw between Isaac and her and with what happened with Meredith. Maybe Isaac had accidentally hurt Meredith when he was trying to help her like he was helping Sam understand how she was different.

Sam watched Arrow wave goodbye to a classmate, some pretty blond girl, before he sauntered over to her. They walked side-by-side, not touching until they were deep into the wooded area near their house.

Arrow entwined his fingers with hers, forcing her to slow down to his easier pace.

"You look pretty."

Sam laughed, thinking about how Arrow looked at the blond girl's chest, her small breasts showing through her tank top. She looked down at her baggy black No Fear T-shirt, the one Arrow had given to her to hide her curves from his dad. She didn't know why she went along with his dumb suggestion.

"I look like a boy."

"You could never look like a boy."

She let go of his hand and motioned to her clothes. "Dressing stupid isn't going to do anything."

"You don't look stupid," he said. "You just look…"

"Ugly? That's what you want, right?" She removed her T-shirt, exposing her white bra, and ran until she was several yards ahead of him. "At least I have tits, unlike your little girlfriend."

"What are you talking about?"

"I'm not an idiot."

"What girl?"

She kept walking straight ahead, the stupid, stupid thoughts spinning in her mind, thoughts of wanting to hurt Arrow but she didn't know why. She didn't really care about that blond girl. It was something with how Arrow looked at the girl, so normal, so unlike how he looked at Sam when others were around, like he couldn't look at her for too long or others would notice.

"What girl?" Arrow yelled this time.

"You know what girl."

"You're nuts."

"You're right, it is nuts, all this lying and sneaking around and your dad gets to have a normal life. Hell no, not anymore. I'm telling my mama everything you told me."

"What?"

"If it's true, people should know, especially my mama."

She sprinted now, but she heard Arrow running behind her. He quickly caught up to her, wrapped his arms around her chest and swung her around to face him.

"Listen—you can't tell your mom anything." He shook her hard. "You can't."

"Let go of me!" She shoved him away from her. "I can do whatever the hell I want. If he really did those things to that girl—he needs to pay for it, and you should want him to pay for it."

Arrow mumbled something, looking at the fallen dead limbs of an old elm tree next to them.

"What?"

He looked up. "If you tell, I won't ever see you again. They'll take me away."

Sam hadn't thought of that, and the desperation on Arrow's face pierced her heart. He was right. Isaac would go to jail and Arrow would be sent away, probably foster care if he didn't have family to take him.

She once had a good friend, Nicole, who was in foster care after police arrested her mom for drugs. Nicole had told their group of friends horror stories of her foster father touching her in the middle of the night. Now, no one talked to Nicole, not even Sam, like what happened to her would rub off onto them. She heard Nicole smoked and drank whatever she could find now, even tried to give her thirteen-year-old foster brother a blowjob.

She swallowed the sudden sickness from thinking about Nicole, how she had followed her friends in shunning her, as she watched Arrow stare at her, tears about to flow from his eyes.

"Please, Sam. I don't have anyone else."

"Okay. I won't tell." She knew in her gut it was the wrong decision, but the relief on Arrow's face was what she wanted to see.

They continued on to the house, skipping their usual messing around in the woods. Arrow appeared disappointed, but Sam wasn't in the mood. He tried to follow her into the house, but she told him to go check on the chickens. She put on her T-shirt, went to the kitchen where Grandma Haylin was peeling potatoes, and sat at the mint-green Formica table. For a minute, she sat watching her grandma's sturdy body gently sway with the peeling, wishing she could peel away the bad things Arrow said about Isaac.

"What's the matter, Biscuit?" Her grandma moved next to her, peeler in hand.

"Nothing."

"Is it about Eric?"

Sam looked up at her. Grandma Haylin rarely called Arrow by his name.

Grandma Haylin turned back to the potatoes. "You know, if your mama expects me to continue living here, she best move me downstairs. Too many stairs to climb…and you kids are louder than cats in heat."

Oh, sweet Mother of Jesus. Sam never thought about her grandma's room being next to her own since Grandma Haylin usually fell asleep in her recliner downstairs, and she could only imagine the things her grandma had heard with Arrow sneaking in every other night.

"Grandma? Does Mama—"

"No. She doesn't know a thing. Neither of them do, and I suggest you two keep it that way."

If her mama or Isaac found out, Sam didn't know what would happen but she knew it wouldn't be good.

Grandma Haylin finished the potatoes and sat next to her. "Biscuit, you sure like walking through needles, dontcha?"

Her grandma often said things like this to her. She usually laughed off her grandma's sayings, but she wasn't laughing now.

"Well, I hope you're at least using rubbers," Grandma Haylin said in a lowered voice.

Rubbers? She had to mean condoms, something Sam didn't know the first thing about using and Arrow never mentioned them. She didn't want to have this conversation with her grandma, so she told her, "Yeah, we are."

"Good girl."

Grandma Haylin patted her arm, but the air was too thick with embarrassment to breathe right. She watched Grandma Haylin get up and fill a large pot with water for the potatoes, her eyes not looking back at the table.

"Your mama will be home soon. Go and do your chores."

Sam couldn't wait to get out of the kitchen. She was strangely glad her grandma knew about her having sex, that she didn't seem as mad or disappointed as Sam expected, but she thought her face would burst from mortification.

Sam walked to the barn to change out the hay for the goats, Hades barking at her heels until she reached down to pet him. When she entered Maddie's stall, Hades stopped short and ran off. Isaac was in the stall, his shirt off and wrapped around the back of Maddie's head, cradling her. Her goat's eyes bulged, white foam leaked out of her gaping mouth. Isaac looked up at Sam.

"What's wrong with her?" she asked, afraid of the answer.

"Damn animal probably got into some hemlock when she snuck out again."

Sam gasped—hemlock was poisonous to most livestock. She crouched down next to him and touched Maddie's side, felt how hard it was for her to breathe. "Will she be okay?"

"I don't think so. I tried to get her to throw up, but I think she's too far gone."

Sam's cry caught in her throat, a sudden lump thick and hard.

Isaac frowned, stroking Maddie between her ears where she liked it. "If my goddamn son would've fixed the fence like I told him, this wouldn't have happened."

Arrow was supposed to fix the fence? First, he lied about why he spent time in juvenile hall, and now he let Maddie escape and eat something poisonous. Anger erupted into tears she couldn't stop.

Isaac touched her cheek, brushed away her tears with his thumb. "I'm real sorry, honey."

Sam remembered how small Maddie was when she wrapped her in a blanket and rocked her as a newborn. "I don't want her to die."

"Can't be helped," Isaac said, looking down at Maddie. "We can't stop death once it's started. All we can do is try to make her comfortable."

Sam looked into Isaac's eyes and she didn't see a monster who molested some poor girl. She saw a man trying to help her Maddie, a Maddie sick and dying because Arrow didn't do what he was supposed to do.

She and Isaac sat side-by-side for a long time, petting the goat and saying calming words to her, words that calmed Sam some too. She avoided staring at Isaac's bare chest, the golden smattering of hair on the tan skin. She watched how gentle he was with Maddie, and she couldn't imagine him raping that Meredith girl. She wanted to ask him, watch his face to see if he was lying.

"I wish I could trade places with her so she wouldn't feel any pain," she said instead. "Did you want to trade places with Arrow's mom?"

Isaac looked away from her. "Of course, I did. But what good does it do to think of it? Doesn't change anything."

Sam wished she'd kept her mouth shut.

They pet Maddie more, Sam too aware of their hands overlapping at times. Her heart jumped a little every time their fingers touched.

"I've seen you with Arrow," he said, breaking the silence.

Fear struck her hard in the chest, but she kept her face calm.

"I know he likes you. I've seen how he looks at you."

Sam continued to stroke Maddie, keeping her eyes on that brown fur until Isaac took her hand and held it.

"I want you to be careful around him. After he lost his mom, he hasn't been right in his head. He lashes out a lot. He could hurt someone without meaning to try. That's why I gotta be hard on him sometimes."

She glanced at Isaac to see if he was serious. She'd never seen Arrow so much as raise his voice to an adult.

"Just be a good sister to him. That's what he needs."

She could never be his sister, but she nodded.

"I know he wants to do things with you, and maybe you want him to do things too, but he won't understand how you are." Isaac placed his hand on her leg, his fingers curling around the inner part of her thigh. "He'll think something's wrong with you. Other people will think that too. But I don't."

Her breath came out rushed and ragged like Maddie's. Isaac pulled closer to her and gently kissed her on the lips.

Cloves. That was the scent. He smelled like cloves, like her grandma's gingerbread cookies.

She kissed him back, just to see what it felt like to kiss a grown man. The coarse hairs on his chin scratched her face, but the way he kissed her made her want to liquefy and bond with that earthy scent coming from his skin. She kept kissing him, and he pressed his thumb against the zipper of her jeans. She couldn't focus on anything else but

82

the growing ache between her legs.

He moved his hand and pinched her inner thigh. He seemed to like the sound she made when he pinched her, and he did it again, harder.

"You like that?" he said.

She didn't know what to say. Her mind was too full of confusion mixed with need.

He rubbed between her legs, over her jeans.

"You want more?"

No. Yes. Neither word would come out.

Then he clasped his hand around her neck and squeezed hard, shocking her and cutting off any scream she might have attempted. She couldn't breathe and he kissed her harder, leaning against her until she was flat on her back next to Maddie. He loosened his grip on her throat and she gasped for a breath before he tightened his grip again. She dug her fingernails deep into his hand and kicked her legs, but he held onto her. Every time she thought she would pass out, he let go enough for her to breathe. She closed her eyes, expecting him to take off her clothes or his own, but he didn't. She kept her eyes closed, listening to the sound of her blood pounding, Isaac's hand pressing and pressing, his heavy breath in her ear as he rubbed between her legs.

Everything blurred to black, her body the most intense blank sheet of paper white before color burst through the center of her.

He finally removed his hand from her throat, and she turned to her side, sucking in air and dirt from the ground and coughing.

Isaac stood up. She followed his eyes over to Maddie next to her.

"She's gone."

Chapter 12: Arrow, 1994

Arrow sat across from Sam at the dinner table, willing her to smile at him or at least look at him. The setting sun outside the kitchen window cast an otherworldly glow over her face that made it hard for him to catch his breath. Her back was straight and stiff, her chin lifted slightly as her eyes drilled into the uneaten food on her plate.

Jeri looked over at Sam, who continued to eat nothing, and then over to Arrow's father, who was nearly done with his meatloaf and mashed potatoes.

"Sammy, you feeling okay?"

Sam glanced up from her plate, but she didn't look at her mom. She looked dead on at Arrow for a second before lowering her eyes again, and he knew. Something happened. Something bad.

"Maddie died," his father said from the head of the table. "We watched the poor thing pass."

"Oh, no," Jeri said. "My poor baby girl."

Jeri got up from the table, her blue eyes wide as she circled over to Sam. Both Jeri and Grandma Haylin tried to comfort Sam, hugging her, but she failed to respond in any way. She sat there, hands in her lap.

She loved that stupid goat like it was a Golden Retriever, but Arrow knew that wasn't why she sat like a statue.

He examined his dad's hands shoveling more mashed potatoes—up and down like a machine—to his mouth. Then Arrow saw them—red half-moons perfectly spaced between his father's thumb and index finger with one long, angry pink line on his forearm. He swallowed back the sudden hot spit in his mouth, his dinner threatening to come up.

Grandma Haylin joined Arrow in looking at his dad, a deep V forming on her forehead. "Why didn't you tell us before dinner?"

Jeri, huddled next to Sam, grew the same deep V. "That goat's not even five-years-old, honey. How'd she die?"

"Laziness killed her," his father said.

Grandma Haylin and Jeri stared at his father, their blue eyes narrowing.

"What do you mean, laziness killed her?" Grandma Haylin said.

Fear and anger shivered down Arrow's spine, but he risked a look at his father, who was staring him down.

"Maddie escaped again and musta got into some hemlock."

"How'd she get through the fence?" Jeri asked, stroking Sam's arm.

"Broken." His father set his fork down and turned to Arrow. "If the fence would've been fixed like I told you a week ago, we wouldn't be having this conversation."

As much as he wanted to, Arrow didn't turn from his dad's glare.

His father's breathing got heavy, his eyes unblinking. "Nothing to say for yourself?"

"It wasn't my fault. You were supposed to fix the—"

The backhand shot stars through Arrow's vision, the metallic taste of blood filling his mouth.

"Isaac, please!" Jeri yelled as his father lifted Arrow from his chair and slammed him against the wall.

Arrow heard "I'm sorry sir" come out of his mouth. He knew better than to hit back.

Jeri, frantic, begged his father to stop as Grandma Haylin hollered something about getting her shotgun. It all turned into a chorus of loud pleas blending with his own.

A huge crash rang above the noise and quiet fell.

Sam stood on the other side the kitchen table, a white Corningware dish smashed in front of her feet, leftover meatloaf scattered like body parts. His father's fist hovered above him, frozen. Grandma Haylin and Jeri stood frozen too. Sam had stopped time. That was Arrow's first thought until his father pushed himself up from the linoleum.

His dad's gaze burrowed long and deep into Sam before he rushed to the other side of the kitchen. "You deal with him," he spat out as the screen door slammed behind him.

Arrow knew his dad was going out to the barn to smoke the weed he hid from Jeri. "It calms me," he used to tell Arrow. He had said the same words about so many things—alcohol, pain pills, the Xanax the VA loved to give out to vets—and none seemed to work.

"Eric, honey, are you okay?"

Grandma Haylin's heavyset body crowded next to him. He was more stunned by her use of his name than his father whaling on him. She tried to help him up from the floor, clutching at her back with her other hand, and Jeri took over for her.

"You shouldn't have talked back, honey," Jeri said, pushing hair away from his eyes. "He didn't mean it, you know that, but you just shouldn't have talked back."

He gave a little nod so Jeri would shut up. Yes, he knew not to talk back, but it wasn't fair. His dad was supposed to fix the fence, not him, and he couldn't let Sam believe he had something to do with Maddie dying.

He couldn't even look at Sam. She did what he couldn't. She had stopped his dad. He hoped she had stopped him before dinner when Eric wasn't around to watch out for her, but he knew the answer the moment she had glanced at him.

His father always got what he wanted.

Arrow made himself look at Sam, who was watching Jeri, disbelief on her face. He wasn't sure if she expected her mom to help him, but it didn't surprise Arrow when Jeri did nothing.

He shook off Jeri and Grandma Haylin trying to examine his face and climbed the stairs to his bedroom. He wished he could smoke weed and try to calm himself like his dad, but he already knew he didn't like it, how it made everything seem unreal and blurred.

He sat on the edge of his bed, wanting so much to go to Sam's room, crawl under her covers, and wait for her. He wanted to cry, but the anger at his father dried his eyes before any tears released. He tried to keep his eyes wide open, let the dry air burn them so the tears would form. He wanted to cry for Sam. He wanted to cry for himself. He wanted to be small again and for his mom to hold him.

"He got you good."

Sam entered his room and closed the door behind her. She held a wet washcloth and sat next to him on the bed. Without asking, she pressed the cold cloth to the swollen side of his mouth, and he cringed from the pain.

"He got you too," he said.

She kept her eyes on his mouth as she patted the blood. "Does it look like he got me?"

No. She seemed normal now. Whenever she was upset about something, he could sense this force field around her, like the heavy ozone in the air before a storm. He didn't feel it now, but he thought about the half-moon marks on his father's hand.

"You can tell me."

"What does it matter?" she said, removing the washcloth from his face. "You can't even protect yourself."

Her words kicked him harder than his father ever had, and he could feel the tears breaking loose.

"Are you mad at me?"

Sam stared at him for a long time, her expression blank. "I'm mad at myself."

"Why?"

He reached for her hand, but she jerked it away.

87

When he looked at her face again, she closed her eyes and tears streamed down her cheeks. She twisted the washcloth in her hands, over and over.

"Why, Sam?"

She looked at him, her eyes dead, and smiled.

Chapter 13: Sam, 2009

Sam wasn't going to think about Isaac Walker, that Vickie person, or anyone else. It had been four days since she and Eric drove to Sapulpa to see Les, and she needed a break to feel normal again. She was going to sit on the couch with her dog Zeus, drinking oolong tea and eating a red velvet cupcake she picked up from Cuppies and Joe. She was going to watch the Real Housewives of Orange County on TiVo and laugh at all the dumb crap those women worried about—botched Botox injections, who talked trash about whom, what tropical island they were going to vacay on. Whatever was going to happen with the police and finding Isaac had nothing to do with her. And Eric…she wouldn't think about him either.

She successfully maintained that sentiment about fifteen minutes through the show before she admitted she was a bigger liar than the rich bitches on the TV screen. The truth was she couldn't stop thinking about the drive back from Sapulpa and seeing the look on Eric's face when he talked about Vickie. There was a pain there she recognized, and she wanted to take it from him to see how he'd look without it. As if it were so easy, like Windexing a smudged mirror.

She switched the TV over to a music station and grabbed a thin book from her bookcase. *Electra*, the Euripides version—her favorite. It seemed somehow appropriate to read. Only, Sam didn't want to avenge a father. She wanted to avenge the missing piece of her.

She wouldn't let herself think about it.

89

She took a few deep breaths and she was calm again, the tears never leaving her eyes.

Zeus shot up from the couch, dashing to the door and yapping his head off before the doorbell rang. Who the hell? It was after nine on a Wednesday. Sam got up, tugging on her blue cardigan. She peered out the window blinds. *Jesus fucking Christ.*

When she cracked the door, Eric pushed his way past her to rush inside.

"Uh, hello. What are you doing here?"

"I didn't know where else to go."

Zeus yelped and growled at his feet, but Eric ignored the white dog and went to the front window. He lifted one of the blinds, stared out into the dark for a few seconds. He looked relieved. This didn't make Sam feel any more comfortable about him being inside her home with her wearing nothing but a camisole top, underwear, and a cardigan barely covering her ass.

"What's going on, Eric?"

"Detective Eastman came to my house."

Eric remained standing by her window, and she noticed he was carrying himself the same way he did as a teenager, slightly stooped and wary, but his eyes stared blankly. It scared her.

"They found him."

Sam's legs went boneless. She sat on her green couch, Zeus hopping up next to her and keeping his eyes on the tall intruder.

Eric moved over to the couch, but he remained standing, his eyes unfocused until he turned to the TV and looked back at Sam.

He finally seemed to notice her undressed state because he kept averting his eyes back to the TV screen. Then Sam realized the Cocteau Twins' "Cherry Coloured Funk" was playing on the music station. It had been his favorite song from an album they'd played too many times when they messed around. "Play it again," he would say before kissing her stomach. From the look on Eric's face, he remembered all too well,

90

and she pulled her cardigan tighter over her chest, crossing her arms.

"Are you scared about seeing him?" she said, and Eric looked away from her.

Sam tried but she couldn't imagine actually seeing Isaac again, of saying what she'd wanted to say to him for so many years: *You didn't break me.*

"Do you have anything to drink?" Eric asked.

"Drink?" The sudden change in subject caught her off guard. "I have some Jameson and a little vodka."

"Jameson's good."

She went to her kitchen and came back with the two-thirds full bottle of whiskey and two glasses. Eric left the glass on her coffee table and took the bottle, drinking down a few pulls and coughing afterward. She took the bottle from him before he could drink more. The nervous energy rolling off him made every muscle in her tense.

"So, where did they find him?"

A brief look of illness flitted across Eric's face.

"The woods…by the old farm."

"The farm? In Blanchard?"

"Yeah."

Sam was confused as hell. Why would Isaac be by the old farm? There was nothing but the woods in the area, the closest neighbor a half-mile away.

"How long has he been out there?"

"They're not sure exactly but at least ten years." Eric swallowed and cleared his throat before he said, "The bones. They can tell by his bones he was stabbed. The gouges on his ribs. And his skull was fractured. Police dogs found the grave."

She felt her head go light, her face numb.

She looked at the bottle of Jameson in her hands and chugged. It blazed down her throat, but she didn't cough.

Isaac dead. Stabbed. She watched Eric, that blank, empty expression

91

on his face. He was paranoid and afraid, before when he came in. Afraid of the police following him, most likely. He was going to confess to her, bring her into his mess and ruin the normalcy she'd fought to create. Seeing him at her work that day, and Isaac's truck found at the same time. No. It wasn't coincidence. It couldn't be.

She stood up and moved away from him. "What did you do, Eric?"

He straightened to his full height, his jaw tightened. Those toffee eyes stared through her until she imagined Isaac standing there, his large hands flexing, ready. She pictured those hands around her throat, squeezing until every part of her body yielded to him. And now Isaac was gone.

"Say it, Sam. Tell me you think I killed him."

"You need to leave. I can't get involved in this. I have a good job, a house, a fucking normal life now."

"And I don't?"

He grabbed her hand, turning it palm up as Zeus barked at their feet. Eric jabbed his finger into the center of her hand right above her lifeline and the silvery scar marring it.

"You carved those initials in the barn. You did, with this hand. We both did, and now you say you can't get involved? You were always involved."

The muscles in her right wrist twitched as if in memory of using Eric's pocketknife to engrave their initials inside the heart he'd carved. He ran his thumb over her palm, sending a chill throughout her body.

"Did you do it?" she asked.

Eric released her hand and seemed to age ten years in the time it took him to sit on her couch, his face drawn and drained of color.

She saw the trouble in his eyes, but she thought she saw grief there too.

"No, I didn't do it," he said. "But I'm not stupid. I know the police are looking at me."

She didn't know what to think. He sounded broken, like he could cry at any second, not like a person who killed his father.

She sat on the other end of the small couch. Zeus squeezed into the space between them. Eric absently pet him, which Zeus allowed to Sam's surprise. She ran her hand over Zeus's fur and Eric grazed her hand with his own.

"Then who?" she asked. "Who would kill him?"

And why bury Isaac near the Blanchard farm? For a second, she imagined Grandma Haylin, her limping figure digging a grave, but it was too ridiculous to consider. Then she thought of the woman who had experienced the worst of Isaac.

"Meredith Lang," she guessed.

Eric's eyes widened.

"She had a reason to kill him."

"No," he said, so resolute. "She didn't do it."

"How can you be so sure? Didn't she hate him? Everything you said he did to her?"

"Even if she wanted to, she wouldn't have been strong enough to hurt him. She was tiny."

Sam had always wondered how much Eric cared about Meredith, and she heard regret in his voice.

Eric pet the same spot on Zeus's back, over and over, until the dog got irritated and jumped off the couch.

"She trusted him," he said, barely audible. "And..."

She took his hand and felt the tremor in him.

"That was the biggest mistake she ever made." He gave her hand a half-squeeze.

Like you. She knew that's what he was thinking.

He took the bottle of Jameson from the coffee table and downed what was probably three generous shots before passing it to Sam. The whiskey wasn't settling well with her tea and cupcake from earlier, but she lifted the bottle to her mouth anyway. She wasn't sure if she wanted to drink herself into oblivion or cry until she couldn't breathe.

Drowsiness tugged at her, but she forced herself back into alertness. She had too many questions.

"Tell me," she said.

"Tell you what?"

"Tell me about Meredith."

Eric closed his eyes and she thought he might be drifting off until he opened them, slowly. He hit the bottle again.

"What do you want to know?"

Everything.

Chapter 14: Sam, 1994

Sam had too many emotions battling inside her chest as she watched Arrow staring at her, his mouth bleeding from where Isaac had struck him during dinner. She knew seeing Isaac's rage should've scared her, but it didn't. She had wanted to do the same thing to Arrow for allowing Maddie to eat whatever poisonous thing that killed her. She could still feel it simmering, that rage, alongside worry and confusion, but she didn't want to cry again in front of Arrow.

Arrow touched her hand. "What did he do to you?"

He kept asking that same question, but she knew he really didn't want to know the answer. He wanted to blame her.

She held the wet washcloth up to his mouth, but he stood up.

"I wasn't supposed to fix the fence, Sam." His eyes implored her. "I promise I would've fixed it if I was supposed to, but he said he was going to do it."

"Fine. Whatever." It didn't matter now if he was telling the truth. It wouldn't bring Maddie back.

Arrow huffed out a sigh. "Please. What happened?"

She knew he would keep bugging her forever until she told him something. She finally blurted out, "Whatever you think happened."

Arrow walked around his room, back and forth, like he was going to go crazy from not knowing. He looked so eager to know as if he was waiting for her to say the right words to be mad at her.

She couldn't explain to him how calmness eventually washed over her as Isaac held her in place by her throat. Arrow made her feel good, but what Isaac did was different. She had been used to giving herself pain for so long, but Isaac doing it was so much better. It was as if she had been down with a fever for a long time and it broke, releasing her from hurt she didn't know was trapped inside of her.

Arrow stopped pacing his room. "Just tell me. Please."

Sam looked down at the wet washcloth in her hand, Arrow's blood blooming in the center.

"He's different. Like me," she said.

"Different? How?"

"Just different, okay?"

"You're sick," Arrow yelled. "He got into your brain like he does with everyone."

Isaac was right; Arrow wouldn't understand how she was. She tried to hug him, to reassure him it didn't change her feelings for him, but he moved to the other side of his bedroom and stared at his *Evil Dead II* poster.

"Go be sick with him. Do whatever you want. I don't care."

Sam shot up from his bed and threw the washcloth at his wall, barely missing his poster. She rushed to her room and locked her door.

Maybe she was sick. The week prior, she had made the mistake of telling her best friend she dreamed of kissing Isaac. She left out the part about him choking her in the dream. Chrissy looked like she was going to throw up. She then proceeded to tell Sam that her mom, a licensed professional counselor, would say it was daddy abandonment issues, that she was seeking positive male attention. Sam finished her ham and cheese sandwich and stopped listening. Chrissy had a new boyfriend every other week.

Sam looked out her bedroom window, at the departing sun streaking purples and pinks against the sky. Soon, it would be dark. Until then, she would wait.

Sam knew it was the worst idea she'd ever had, but she couldn't make herself leave the barn. She knew he would come here eventually, as he always did late at night, and she knew what would probably happen when he did.

She leaned against Maddie's old stall, the wound of losing her that day raw and tender. After Isaac had moved Maddie from the barn to bury her, Sam cleaned the empty stall, laying fresh hay as if her goat would pounce back into the barn and give her a playful headbutt.

She thought of her mama, how she cowered in the background as Isaac repeatedly hit Arrow. She wondered what her mama would do if she knew what Isaac had done with Sam in the barn before dinner.

The Bible said the wife was supposed to listen to the husband, do everything he says no matter what, which Sam thought was dumb as hell. Her mama believed every word, though. Grandma Haylin said man wrote the Bible and man is weak and stupid.

Sam heard someone walk into the dimly lit barn and she pressed herself into the stall's gate to steady her nerves. At first, she worried it might be Arrow, but she knew he was hiding up in his room.

Isaac walked to the back of the barn and stopped at the wooden ladder leading up to the loft. He rolled up the sleeves of his plaid work shirt, and Sam could barely make out the scarab beetle tattoo on his forearm, a remnant from his time in the army.

"Come on out," he said without turning to look at her.

There was only one good light in the barn, and she stepped out from the shadows of Maddie's stall to the middle where Isaac could see her under its yellow glow. He slowly turned around and took in her outfit, a strappy blue summer dress she had dug out from her closet because Isaac once said he liked it.

"Come here."

She did, her stomach reaching up to her throat with every step.

He stared at her and shook his head. "What are you doing out here? You should be in bed."

97

He sounded so much like a parent she wanted to cry.

"I—I thought…what happened…" She wasn't sure what to say, that she wanted him to make her feel the same way again—like she didn't have to think about anything and could just sink into what was happening.

Isaac sucked in a breath and scanned her from head to toe. "I care about your mama."

She didn't know what that had to do with anything.

"She's a good Christian woman—not like me. Or you."

No, Sam wasn't like her mama—thank Jesus. She wasn't sure what she believed anymore, but she knew she didn't believe the same as her mama.

Isaac hesitated, but then he reached up to caress Sam's cheek with his thumb. "It was a mistake. Do you understand?"

"No." She shook her head, her face burning. "I don't understand at all."

"Sam, it can't happen again," he said, slower. "You know that. You're a smart girl."

She had to feel the same way again. She had to feel whatever it was, the thing she couldn't easily define. It was like the time she went to Branson with Chrissy and did the zip line eighty feet in the air, the exhilaration of being out of control and frightened but knowing she was safe too.

She reached for Isaac's hand and before she could open her mouth to speak, he had her against the ladder, his hand over her throat. She closed her eyes, savoring the feel of his fingers tightening.

He let go of her neck and his hand trailed down the front of her dress before he backed away from her. "Goddamnit, you're killing me."

She didn't move. She knew he expected her to run off, but she stood there tall, a tower of stone.

"So brave," he said, "and you don't even know what you're doing, do you?"

She didn't know what he meant, but his arrogant tone gnawed at her.

"Like you're brave," she said, "beating up on your own son? Like some redneck asshole."

The grim lines of Isaac's tan face softened into a grin. Then he laughed at her, so boisterous that some of the goats stirred in the stalls. Normally, Sam would've kicked a guy in the balls for laughing at her, but she couldn't imagine anyone hurting Isaac and surviving.

"Have you ever smoked?" He held up his hand like he was pinching a joint.

Her lips curled to match his smirk. "A little," she lied.

He started up the ladder and looked down at her. "You coming or what?"

She thought of Arrow alone in his room, of her mama at her stupid church bingo night, the only church event Grandma Haylin seemed to enjoy, and followed him up.

Once they climbed the ladder, Sam's eyes darted over to the loft window. Under it was a heart and initials she and Arrow had spent an hour carving into the wood. Isaac went to the opposite side of the loft. He dug around and came back carrying a small metal tin. A nervous tickle fluttered in her stomach. She had never even tried cigarettes.

Isaac fiddled around with rolling the weed, licking the thin paper, his eyes locked on her as he did it until she had to look away.

As she had waited in her bedroom for dark to come, she imagined confronting Isaac about hitting Arrow. Whether or not he was supposed to fix the fence, Arrow didn't deserve to be hit. But when she saw Isaac, it was like her brain would only focus on what happened in the barn and if it would happen again. Guilt twisted in her stomach. She had a sudden urge to go back to the house, to bring Arrow some ice for his busted lip.

"Has Eric ever told you about the Center of the Universe?" Isaac said.

"No."

He sat on a bale of hay and motioned for her to sit next to him. He lit the joint, inhaled deeply, and handed it to her before releasing the smoke. She took it and attempted to inhale as deeply as Isaac, but the burn in her chest exploded into a coughing fit. Isaac laughed and took the joint back from her.

"It's this weird place in downtown Tulsa," he said. "We lived there for a while when his mom was working at the college. She was pregnant and about ready to bust. Eric must've been around eight then, and he kept hearing about this strange, magical place from the kids at school, so we finally set out to find it."

Arrow once told her about his mom losing a baby, how she went to the hospital with her huge belly and returned home with nothing. His face had gone solemn when he described how sad his mom and Isaac had been.

Isaac took another hit from the joint and held it back from Sam, teasing her. She grabbed it from him and took a long drag, longer than she should have but she held it in more than before. She still coughed a ton.

"Did you find it?" she asked.

Isaac grinned to himself. "Yeah, but it wasn't what we expected." He looked up at Sam, his brown eyes looking black under the florescent light. "You stand on this spot and you can yell, sing—whatever—and you hear your voice echoed back to you, out in the open air. No one outside of the spot can hear the echo."

She pictured a young Arrow hollering his head off, jumping up and down in delight.

Isaac handed her the joint, and she inhaled as much as her lungs would let her this time. She felt lightheaded and disconnected from her body. She liked the feeling, although it scared her.

"That place sounds cool," she said.

"It was until Eric freaked out. He was in the spot shouting and laughing with his mom, and then his face dropped like someone had stepped on his foot." He held up the joint he took back from Sam and shook his head. "Took us forever to calm him down."

"Why was he upset?"

Isaac tapped the joint on the metal tin until it went out. "He said he couldn't hear his brother's echo."

Sam touched his hand, worked her fingers until she force-held it. He didn't look over twice her age with his ash-blond hair curling around his ears and the weed haze surrounding them. He looked young and weightless, even talking about losing a baby. She wanted to be weightless too.

"I'm sorry," she said.

Isaac slowly nodded. "I don't even know if he remembers. Probably better if he doesn't."

She rested her head on his lap. After a minute, Isaac rubbed her head. She imagined her daddy stroking her hair, something she remembered him doing when she was young. She wouldn't think about him. He didn't want her. She didn't want him either, and she wouldn't waste more tears on him.

She looked up at Isaac's face, and he stared down at her, his eyes thoughtful. She was nervous to ask him the questions stirring in her for so long, but she made herself speak.

"Do you like pain too?"

He paused in rubbing her head. "In a different way."

She thought she knew the answer, but she asked it anyway. "You like to give pain?"

He nodded.

"Have you done it to other people?"

"Yes."

"How many?"

"I don't know. Several."

"Did they like it?"

He paused. "Yes."

"Have you done it to my mama?"

"Sam—"

"Sorry." She covered her face with her hands, the sudden shame hitting her, and she couldn't keep her tears in. "I'm sorry, I shouldn't have asked. I'm such a freak."

He held her hands away from her face. "You're not a freak, okay. You're young and curious, but you don't understand what you want. You think you do, but you don't."

She reached up and touched Isaac's chest over his heart, felt the muscle contract under his shirt. Hardness rose from his lap and pressed against her ear, and she looked up at him. His eyes were closed, mouth slightly parted, and he had stopped rubbing her head.

"I want," she said, but the rest of the words didn't want to come out: *I want to understand. I want to learn.*

He shifted his body so she would sit up.

"Go back to the house."

"But—"

"Go."

Sam didn't know what she had done to cause his mood to change. She made her way down the ladder, pausing on each rung, hoping he'd change his mind. She ran back to the house, the unusually cool August night raising goosebumps on her body. The house was quiet and dark, and she knew her mama and grandma were still out.

She climbed the stairs, her eyes on the golden beam of light under Arrow's bedroom door. She went to his door, opened it, and saw him lying on his side on top of his covers, his headphones on, eyes closed. She shut the door behind her and turned off his lamp, which made him turn over to see her next to him. He removed his headphones, and she could hear Tool playing.

"Did you do something with him?" he asked, anger cracking his voice.

"No. Don't be an idiot."

Arrow sat up in bed, scooting over. She stretched out next to him, resting her head on his chest. His heart was beating so fast.

"I'm sorry," she said, but she wasn't sure why she said it. Sorry for forgetting about him? Sorry she had sometimes thought about Isaac when they were having sex?

Arrow caressed her hair. "I'll kill him if he touches you again."

Sam pulled herself up and kissed him. He was too gentle in kissing her back, and she felt like she was kissing herself, which annoyed her. She pinched his nipple hard and he pushed back from her.

"What the hell was that for?"

She pinched him again, harder, and he wrestled her flat on the bed.

"Are you crazy? That fucking hurt."

"Do it to me."

"No."

She giggled so much the entire bed shook.

"You're high. Aren't you?"

She laughed and pinched him again. He pinned her down.

"Did you get high with him?"

"What are you gonna do if I did?" She tried to kiss him, but his face was too far away.

He released her arms, and she pulled him to her. He touched her face as they kissed again, and she moved his hand to her neck, pressed his fingers into her skin.

He stopped kissing her and sat up.

"Please," she said. "I want you to."

He reached up and held her throat for a limp second before his arm went slack at his side.

"No."

"Fine." She rolled onto her side. "Forget it."

After a few moments, Arrow finally draped his arm over her waist.

"Don't ask me to be like that," he whispered

Chapter 15: Eric, 2009

Thunder crashed, and Eric woke up with his heart somewhere outside of his body. Sam's tiny white dog jumped up on the couch beside him and licked his nose, startling him. He pushed Zeus off the couch, but the dog jumped back up and licked him again.

Lightning lit up Sam's living room, rain hammering the windows. No matter how much Eric tried to ignore it, storms bothered him. His mom used to say storms cleaned out the bad energy in the world, but he didn't believe it. Storms carried the bad shit and blew it all over the place.

He recalled the night before and cringed at how much he drank. He and Sam had finished off the bottle of whiskey, and he vaguely remembered talking about Meredith. Sam kept asking him questions about her—what was she like, was she smart, was she pretty—and the alcohol flowed through him and words fell from his lips. Yes, she was pretty but not like Sam, and yes she was smart but not in the same way. What was Meredith's mother like? Here, Eric broke through the alcohol enough to shut up. He didn't remember much after that.

He dragged himself up from the couch, noting he was missing his shoes and jeans and he didn't recall taking them off. He stumbled his way through the dark until he found a bathroom. His piss sounded so loud, louder than the storm outside, he was sure it'd wake Sam. He walked passed a bedroom, realized it was the master. He entered Sam's room and stood by her bed. He watched her chest rise and fall, the

104

streetlamp outside creating spidery shadows on her face and the walls.

Her room was large for a historic home, and she had a small sitting area by the window. He went to sit on one of the chairs and tripped over something. He looked down and saw a dog toy. He tossed it aside so Sam wouldn't trip on it. He thought about staying in her room, but he decided it was probably better to leave and sleep a little at his own place, so he headed for the bedroom door.

"You can stay."

He turned around and Sam sat up in her bed.

"It's really coming down outside," she said, her voice groggy. "Come here."

She scooted over to let him lie next to her, and it was like they were teenagers again, sneaking through the old farmhouse into each other's beds each night.

He faced her and watched the rain shadows stream down her cheeks.

He couldn't see the details of her face well in the darkness, but he heard her steady breathing, steadier than the metronome Grandma Haylin used to start up whenever she taught Sam piano. She had tried to teach him too, but he never caught on.

"Sam?"

"Yeah."

"Do you ever regret knowing me?"

Another thunder rolled over the house before Sam finally said, "No."

It was a lie, but he took it and cherished it as truth.

"I won't ever love anyone else. I tried."

"Eric…"

He thought he caught the gleam of real tears mixing with the rain shadows on her face, and he touched her bare shoulder, felt the strap of her top, and pulled her close to him until her face was against his chest.

"I know you don't want to hear it, but it's true."

From the first time he saw Sam at the feed shop while Jeri was working behind the counter flirting with his father, he knew. He knew he needed to know her.

"I've always loved you. Nothing's changed."

Sam's body relaxed until she molded with his own, just like when they were younger and it seemed they could never get close enough. He inhaled the scent of her fruity shampoo, the freshness of her mixed with the heat of their bodies.

"I can't believe he's dead."

"I know," he said into her hair, hugging her closer.

"I guess that makes you an orphan now."

He hadn't thought of that, but Sam saying it made the truth punch through his chest. He had no parents. He had no one. Tears came from nowhere and he couldn't prevent them. The shame of crying in front of her made it harder to stop.

"It's okay."

"Is this real?" he choked out. "Is this really happening?"

He felt Sam hesitate before rubbing the back of his head. "Yeah."

He couldn't get a handle on himself. He didn't know what it was he was feeling. Maybe regret. He could never look his father in the eyes and try to understand him, to somehow release the apprehension tunneled inside him, eating his insides.

"Hey." Sam pressed her hands to his cheeks, wiping away his tears with her thumbs. "It's okay. I'm here. It's going to be okay."

"How?"

"I don't know, but it will."

She touched his cheek as if to confirm it, but it wasn't enough for him. She didn't feel real. Nothing felt real.

He held her face in his hands, felt her stiffen in his arms when he sought her lips. Her body eased against him, and she kissed him back with a fierceness that surprised him. The taste of her mouth made him want to taste every part of her. He kissed along her neck, pushed up her top and kissed the breasts he had dreamed about for the last fifteen years. Every part of her was new and terrifying, surreal. She took his hand, pulled it back up and kissed his palm before forming his fingers around her throat.

He froze.

"It's okay," she said, her breath fast and urgent against his face. "I want you to."

He knew what she wanted from him. The thing he couldn't give her those years ago. She pressed his fingers tighter on her neck, and he felt every cord of muscle twitch under his hand.

Everything in him fought against his hand squeezing her long neck, against pressing her into her bed with his weight until he trapped her under him. The sound of pleasure that escaped her lips stabbed through his hand, up his arm, and into his chest and he thought about stopping, getting dressed, and leaving her there on the bed, half-naked.

He wanted this to be real, for her to be real for him again and make him feel real too. Not like this, though.

He let go of her neck. "I don't want to hurt you."

"You won't. I'll help you."

He held in the words he wanted to say: *Please, don't ask me to be like him.*

"I can't."

He tried to kiss her again, but she turned her face and removed his hand from her breast.

"It's okay," she said, but he knew it wasn't.

For those short, beautiful moments, though, he found himself in her touch, in hearing her shallow breath against his ear, and there was no time, no past. It was just them in the bed with the storm raging overhead. Now, there was nothing, and he was so tired.

He turned on his side, away from Sam. She stroked his arm, but he couldn't find sleep.

"I should get back to my place," he said.

Sam was quiet for a long moment. "Okay."

He couldn't leave fast enough.

Chapter 16: Sam, 2009

Sam sat at a table near the front door at a kitschy diner, a place off the highway feeding into Guthrie. She ordered a cheeseburger and fries from the server who was too old to be doing that sort of job and waited.

She didn't immediately recognize Meredith Lang from her Facebook profile pic. For one, Meredith had dyed her long strawberry blond hair a gaudy burgundy color and cut it into a jagged bob. She also had the stringy, wired look typical of a meth user. She was almost Sam's age, but she looked a hell of a lot older.

Sam waited for her food, playing a game on her iPhone and trying not to think about how Eric couldn't wait to leave her place last night. She knew why he left. He was disgusted with himself, with her too, for what she asked him to do to her. She touched her throat, remembered the feel of Eric's hands on her, how her pulse raced when he said he still loved her.

She called him again. She didn't leave another message when it went straight to voicemail.

She told herself she wouldn't let it bother her. She'd experienced much worse than a man rejecting her call, but this was different. It felt like he had rejected a core part of her, a part Isaac had accepted as natural, a part she had taken years to accept herself.

Sam wondered if Meredith was like her, craving pain.

One thing she did know was that Meredith had a good reason to

109

kill Isaac. A cup of coffee and a quick Internet search later, and she was on her way to Guthrie where Meredith now lived.

She called in sick to work and planned to stake out Meredith's apartment complex, but she wanted to see what Meredith was like while she worked. Unlike Sam, Meredith had her workplace listed on her Facebook page. Grandma Haylin always said a person could tell a lot by how someone works. Sam hated the satisfaction derived from knowing her life was better than Meredith's. "Get off your high horse," her mom was fond of telling her. Her mom had nearly guilted her out of attending college, as if Sam was going to forget where she came from by earning a degree. She could never forget their farmhouse, what happened there, even now with it torn down.

She watched Meredith, who appeared to be a decent waitress. She was quick to refill glasses, unlike Sam's server, and her smile, while never quite reaching her eyes, contained all obligatory friendliness needed for food service work. The more she watched Meredith, the less she could picture her as an innocent fifteen-year-old girl raped by Isaac Walker. She saw a capable woman. She saw herself.

Service at the diner was so slow, a couple cursed their way out the door without getting their food. An hour later, Sam's greasy burger arrived, lukewarm and nearly inedible. She ate a few bites, paid, and left, waiting in her car until Meredith exited the restaurant shortly after two-thirty.

The distance to Meredith's apartment complex wasn't far, and Sam stayed well behind the woman's dinged-up red Ford Focus. She thought of what Eric had told her the night before, Meredith the straight-A student before Isaac got to her. Plied with liquor, Eric went into a sort of trance when she asked him about what happened in Anadarko with Meredith and Isaac, some terrible memory paralyzing him. So many times, her own memories had done the same to her, but she pretended that those bad things happened to someone else, like she had watched a horror movie and simply had a hard time shaking it from her mind.

110

She had to think that way or she'd probably be like Meredith—scraping by to support some addiction.

Meredith parked and headed up a flight of rust-stained stairs to the second story of apartment units. Sam followed her, stepping over puddles left by the storms. She forgot everything she wanted to ask the woman, her hand glued to the stair railing. Meredith paused in front of a badly dented door and turned around. She looked directly at Sam, a half-cocked smile on her face.

"Can I help you?"

"Uh, yeah," Sam called up to her. "Could you tell me where the front office is?"

Meredith shifted a messenger bag nearly half her size to her other arm. "You looking for a place?"

"I might be."

Meredith slowly made her way down the narrow metal stairs. Up closer, the woman's blue eyes lined with too much black liner were so piercing they looked as fake as her tan. She scanned Sam's outfit, her expensive jeans and nice red blouse. "*You* want to live here?"

"This place is as good as any."

"Sure." Meredith smirked. "You know, it's not working."

"I don't know what you mean."

"This little act of yours. You think I'm slow? You think I don't know?"

Sam couldn't disguise the surprise on her face. She stepped forward and her leather sandals sunk into some mud. The other woman laughed with pure venom. Sam looked up sharply at her as she pulled her feet out and found solid ground.

She had an eerie feeling Meredith could read her mind and knew who she was and why she was there.

"Isaac Walker's dead. Did you know that?"

Meredith's lips tensed into a thin line. "I don't know who you're talking about."

Sam held the woman's gaze. "Oh, I think you do."

"I don't even know you, but you're about to know me if you don't leave me alone." Meredith crossed her arms, her mouth tight, everything about her exuding clear hostility.

"Isaac was my stepfather. Some…things happened with him," Sam said, unsure of how to say it. "Bad things. And I know he hurt you too."

Meredith's sudden laughter cut through Sam's stomach with its viciousness. "You must be off your meds, lady, so I'm going to kindly ask you to leave before I call someone."

Meredith turned and started back up the stairs with her large bag.

"Did you love Isaac? Is that why you didn't turn him in?"

Meredith turned around.

She ran down the stairs so fast Sam feared she'd keep going until they collided. Meredith stopped right in front of Sam and slammed her messenger bag down.

"I see you following me again, I'll fucking rip every inch of that hair from your head. You understand?"

Meredith looked ready to tackle her, and Sam stepped back. Eric was right. The woman was tiny, but she seemed plenty capable of murder.

"I just want to talk," Sam said.

"Bitch, what part did you not understand? Get the hell out of here."

"Mom?"

Sam turned to see a gangly teen boy walking up to Meredith, his backpack slung over his shoulder. He stopped and stared at Sam and then back at Meredith, worry in his sable-brown eyes.

"Go upstairs, baby. I'm almost done here," Meredith said to him, keeping her eyes on Sam. The boy didn't move, anxiety plain on his face. "*Now*, Caleb."

"Jesus," Sam heard herself whisper. She no longer listened the stream of threats running from Meredith's mouth.

Sam couldn't stop staring at the boy, at his straight, determined nose and round sad eyes.

The boy inching up the stairs could have been Eric.

Chapter 17: Arrow, 1994

Arrow leaned against the chicken coop, watching the birds peck away at the feed he sprinkled until the ground was bare and he scattered more. He looked up at the late September sky, the blue so bright it hurt his eyes. If nothing else, he would have good weather for his sixteenth birthday.

Sam told him she had a surprise for him later, but he couldn't get excited about it when he knew her mind wasn't on him. When they were together now, she wasn't herself. For one, she was too nice to him, never challenging what he said as she normally did. She never told him exactly what had happened with his father, but Arrow knew whatever his dad had done changed her.

Sam wasn't the only one acting weird. His dad would come around to his room each evening, asking him about school, attempting to rouse him to the idea of trying out for football the following year. He couldn't figure out why his dad suddenly cared how he was doing, and he started to think maybe he was being paranoid. Maybe his dad had changed and nothing happened with Sam.

"Boy, you keep overfeeding them chickens they're gonna pop like ticks and I'm not cleaning up the mess."

He smiled at Grandma Haylin and glanced back down at his feet. She had been a lot nicer to him since witnessing his dad beat him, sitting down to talk with him about school every day, letting him lick cake batter off the spoon when she baked, and sneaking extra cookies into his lunch bag. He liked her looking out for him, especially since Jeri didn't seem to know how to act around him. Grandma Haylin felt like a real grandparent, something he always wanted. His dad's parents were dead, or at least that's what his father told him. His mom's mother was in some nursing home in Idabel, drooling on herself, and his mom never knew her dad.

"You as shy at school as you are around here?"

Arrow looked Grandma Haylin in the eyes. "No, ma'am."

She lumbered closer to him and took the feedbag from his hands. "I expect not. Probably a little lady killer with those dimples and puppy dog eyes."

"Not really, ma'am."

She raised her eyebrows at him. "Only eyes for one girl, huh?"

He looked down at his feet again. "Maybe."

"You know how old Jeri Anne was when she had Sam?"

Arrow peered at Grandma Haylin and shook his head.

"Seventeen," she said, tightening the string on the feedbag. "Too damn young, if you ask me, which nobody does. And that no-good sonofabitch who got her that way was no better than a baby himself. Wouldn't even marry her."

Normally, he enjoyed it when Grandma Haylin tried to chat with him, but he felt the conversation going somewhere that made him want to disappear.

Grandma Haylin came up next to Arrow and took his hand. She placed something in his palm, curled his fingers around it. "I don't mean to raise great-grandbabies, you get me? Jeri Anne and Sam were more than enough for me."

Arrow opened his hand and saw a green ribbon of folded foil packets. Condoms. Some of the boys at school kept them in their back pockets like they were good luck charms, the small squares reshaping the denim of their jeans, badges of honor the girls blushed over. His dad had used them with Vickie when they lived with her, the tiny

115

bits of torn metallic wrapper dotting the bedroom carpet like leftover confetti from a birthday party.

He realized Grandma Haylin knew about him being with Sam, yet she hadn't told their parents. "Ma'am…I, uh…"

"Happy birthday, lady killer."

She tousled his hair and limped back toward the house.

He stared down at the condoms in his hand, shocked and embarrassed, before shoving them into his back pocket.

He grabbed the feedbag and headed back to the barn to store it away. The goats were out grazing, so the barn was quiet when he entered. He went to the back, put away the feed, and looked over at Maddie's old stall. He expected it would remain empty for some time.

A crazy image entered his head, and it made him sick. He imagined Sam in the stall, naked and tied up by her wrists, her eyes glazed over like a Jesus freak at Jeri's church. Then he imagined himself pushing into Sam from behind, her bound and helpless, and his groin stirred.

"Dreaming of that cake Grandma Haylin made, son?"

His dad came up next to him and Arrow's heart sped up.

"Or, are you dreaming of something else?" His dad's face was dead serious for a moment before he broke out laughing and slapped Arrow hard on the back. "I have something for you."

His dad placed his arm around his shoulder as if it were the most natural thing in the world. Arrow tried to relax his body, but his dad's arm felt like a boa constrictor coiling around him tight, tighter.

His dad pulled a slender box from his back pocket and handed it to him. Arrow opened it and saw it was a pocketknife, a nice one with an ornate mother of pearl handle. He thought he recognized it but didn't know from where. He couldn't guess how much it cost, but he knew it was too expensive for him.

"Belonged to your Uncle Jobe," his dad said, taking the knife from the box and switching the blade open. It was a three-inch blade and his dad pressed it lightly against his own palm. "He left it to me after he got killed protecting this country. He was a true hero." He turned it over to show Arrow the light glimmering from the iridescent handle. "Now it's yours. Won't be long before you can serve too."

Arrow would never join the military, but not because he didn't want to serve his country or even to die for it. It was the possibility of not dying that scared him, knowing how his father came back from tours of duty a different person each time until Arrow wished he would never come back at all.

Arrow carefully took the knife from his dad and ran his fingertips over it. He smiled. "Thank you, sir."

He looked at the silver blade again, at the beauty and detail of the handle. A strong hand came from behind him, wrapping around his hand and forcing the blade to his throat.

"This is a real weapon, son," his father growled into his ear, his breath hot on Arrow's neck. "This isn't that stubby dick knife you're used to." His father pressed the cold blade harder against his throat, just under his left ear, before releasing him. "Learn how to use it. Maybe someday you can serve your country too. Be useful."

He backed away from his father fast. He touched his neck and didn't see blood on his fingers. He held up the knife and thought about using it right then on his father. Feeling it sink into his dad's stomach.

His dad laughed, shaking his head. "Oh, Lord. You should see your face." He grabbed the back of Arrow's neck and squeezed hard, pushing his head down a little. "I'm just messing with ya, son. Happy birthday."

Arrow slowly closed the blade, swallowing the fear and rage quaking up and down his body.

His father strolled to the barn exit.

"Next time you wanna mark up the loft with little hearts and such, I suggest you skip the stubby dick and use that one instead."

Chapter 18: Sam, 1994

Sam didn't know what bug had crawled up Arrow's butt and had babies, but he barely touched the chocolate cake she helped Grandma Haylin make for his birthday. She kicked him under the kitchen table and smiled, and he barely glanced at her before going back to smashing his cake into tiny bits with his fork.

Her mama was going to stay overnight at the Woodland farm to help care for Betty, the wife of Harold Woodland, who lived a few miles away from their farm. Betty was even older than Grandma Haylin, and she had suffered a stroke that left her right side all droopy and useless. Several of the women from church were taking turns feeding and bathing Betty for Harold, which her mom constantly told them was her Christian duty and they should do the same.

Before she took off after Arrow's birthday dinner, her mama caught her elbow as she washed the dishes. "Leave the front gate open tonight, Sammy."

"Why?"

They always locked the gate to the property after someone stole some of their livestock.

"Your daddy's going out with some of the boys."

Sam stopped herself from saying Isaac wasn't her daddy. She wasn't sure what to call him now. She continued drying off a plate. "So, you think he'll get drunk tonight?"

"If Lloyd Fletcher's with him, I'd say it'd be a miracle if he didn't."

118

Her mama laughed. "Don't need him crashing into the gate in the middle of the night."

"Who's gonna crash into gates?"

Isaac came up behind her mama and hugged her, his arms wrapped tight under her full breasts. He pushed her blond hair to the side and kissed her neck, his eyes on Sam as he did it. Her mama giggled when he pulled her around and kissed her on the mouth, longer and deeper than he usually did in front of others. Sam couldn't help but think he was doing it to mess with her.

A few days before, she had been sketching some of the goats playing in the field behind the barn as Isaac cut back the wild brush lining the property. He had taken off his sweat-soaked T-shirt, and she teased him, suggested he take off everything so she could try nude drawing and be a proper artist. He looked around first, then told her to come to him. The tone he used, like a teacher scolding a student, sent wild sparks in her head that spread down to her hips. She slowly walked over to him, and he took her ponytail in his hand, pulled it so hard she cried out and tears immediately sprang to her eyes. It was the first time he had hurt her since the time in the barn. Afterward, he told her she couldn't handle him. It felt like a dismissal, like she failed a test.

She watched as Isaac drew her mama into another embrace.

"Mama says you're going to get drunk and crash the truck tonight."

"I did not," her mama said, her face flushed from Isaac's attention.

Isaac smiled at Sam. "I promise I'll be good as sin."

"Oh, I just bet you will." Her mama laughed more and poked Isaac's side; he poked her back.

Sam looked at the remaining dishes soaking in the sink, a rush of angry heat reddening her face and making her dizzy and confused. What did she care who Isaac kissed? She'd leave the gate closed and maybe his drunk ass would smash right into it, and then he'd stop grinning all the time.

Her mama gave her a side hug, which she shrugged off. She gently tugged on Sam's long braid, but Sam ignored her. When her mama left the kitchen, Isaac pressed up behind her, pulled on her braid too, much harder than her mama had. He kept pulling, but she refused to cry this time. "Don't wait up, girlie."

Sam finished the dishes alone in the kitchen, Grandma Haylin settled in front of the living room TV to watch *Dr. Quinn, Medicine Woman* and *Touched by an Angel* back-to-back until she would inevitably fall asleep in the recliner. Arrow had disappeared to his bedroom right after dinner.

Sam had waited to give Arrow his birthday gift because she didn't want anyone else to see it, especially Isaac. She stopped by her bedroom, then entered Arrow's room.

"Hey, don't you ever knock?" He sat up in his bed.

She quickly erased the hurt from her face. She almost turned around, but she had spent too long on his gift not to give it to him. She wanted him to see it and feel like an asshole for being rude to her.

He saw what she was holding and stood up, his face brightening. "That my surprise?"

"Maybe." She moved it behind her back and he came up to her.

"What is it?"

He tried to look behind her back, but she swung around to dodge him.

"Let me see it."

Sam thought of the fancy pocketknife Isaac had given to Arrow, the one Isaac made Arrow get from his bedroom to show everyone during dinner. It was like he was trying to prove he was a good father for giving his son a present. It was a beautiful knife. She thought of her own gift and it suddenly didn't seem so great.

"You're going to hate it."

"No, I won't."

She was too slow, and Arrow snatched it from her hands. She watched him remove the newspaper wrapping and hold up the wooden frame. He looked up at her, wonder on his face.

"It's me."

"Yeah," she said, knowing her face was reddening.

"I'm Prometheus, right?" He pointed to the drawing, to the palmed fire a young man held high to the stormy sky, an angry Zeus in the background.

She nodded.

His smile was as bright as the fire she took two hours painstakingly drawing with her colored pencils.

"This is the best present I've ever had."

If that was true, it was the saddest thing Sam had ever heard. She did try her best to make it look good, though.

He set the frame down by his dresser and hugged her. His door was closed, so she kissed him. It was always different kissing him when she knew they were safe from their parents catching them. She hated those times they had to be careful, their eyes never closed too long, their ears always listening for footsteps.

Arrow grinned at her and he almost looked like Isaac, that devilish expression he had given her as he kissed her mama. "Wanna see what Grandma Haylin gave me?"

"She gave you something?"

She couldn't imagine Grandma Haylin going out of her way to do anything for Arrow.

He went to his sock drawer, dug around, and brought back a green foil packet, which he placed in her hand.

Sam kneaded the packet, the snot-sliding material inside it, and threw it at Arrow.

"Gross! She gave you condoms?"

She had seen them floating around at school, some of the girls passing around flavored ones in the locker room as if they were pieces of gum. Grandma Haylin giving Arrow condoms was as believable as her giving him a million dollars.

Arrow pulled her onto his bed with him, his hands floating down, pressing her closer. "Let's try it."

"Go ahead. You and your pillow have at it and I'll watch."

"I'm serious." He glanced at his door, which didn't have a lock like her own. "We'll be quiet."

Sam pictured Grandma Haylin asleep in the living room, the TV glowing on her lined face.

"Okay."

The condom, Sam decided, was disgusting. It was slimy, it smelled weird, and Arrow took forever putting it on. Sex didn't feel any different to her, although she didn't realize Arrow was done until he pulled out. When he suggested they start using them every time, she agreed it was a good idea, although she didn't know how they could buy some without people in town talking. Arrow wasn't always good about pulling out in time, and neither of them could afford the chance of pregnancy. She didn't want to end up like Nancy Wallace, pregnant at seventeen, her full ride to Oklahoma State University a fading dream now.

Sam left Arrow sleeping in his room. She saw the door to her grandma's room was open and knew she was fast asleep in the living room, so she didn't have to be super quiet sneaking back into her bedroom. She crawled under her covers and hugged her hands between her legs to warm them.

It was late, but she couldn't relax her body to fall asleep. Sometimes Arrow did things during sex that gave her relief, but not this time, and she felt like a rubber band stretched taut.

She pulled her underwear off, found her ducky blanket at the bottom of her bed and wound it around her neck. She tried, but none of the images she thought of helped her find the tickle.

When she tightened the blanket around her neck more, she heard the stairs softly creaking. *Grandma Haylin.*

Sam's bedroom door opened, and she quickly yanked her covers up. It wasn't her grandma standing in the doorway.

"Arrow?" she whispered.

No one answered.

Her voice dribbled out a much quieter, "Isaac?"

He shut the door, locked it. Sam couldn't control the electric excitement coursing through her. He was really in her room and she was wide awake.

He sat on her bed, and she smelled alcohol and earthy sweat coming from him, somewhere buried deep was the strange comfort of cloves.

"Are you drunk?" she asked.

"You didn't leave the gate open."

She had forgotten all about the gate. "Sorry."

He reached out and touched the blanket still wrapped around her throat, and she wanted to disappear. "What's this? Is this what you do?"

She swallowed hard, too aware of her underwear on the floor. "Sometimes."

"It's not the same, is it?" he said, his voice low.

"No."

He tugged the blanket away from her neck. Every part of her body began to tingle.

He pressed his mouth against her ear, his hand resting on her neck. "This is what you've wanted. Tell me."

She wanted so much for his hand to squeeze her throat she thought her body would ignite.

She nodded.

His fingers pressed hard into her neck and he kissed her. She moved her hand back under the covers to stir the growing tickle, but he squeezed her throat so hard her vision blackened. Then his hand was under the covers too, on her, and a pleasure spasm felt about to rip through her, but he stopped just before it did.

It happened so fast, him pulling the covers back, exposing her

123

naked waist to the cool air, and suddenly his head was between her legs, his stubble scratching her inner thighs before his teeth found flesh and bit down. She suppressed a scream. Then his mouth was there where he bit her, on the center of her, and she disappeared into a tickle that grew and exploded into wave after wave and she wanted it to go on forever it felt so good.

She heard the clink of him undoing his belt buckle, and her body went cold. She tried to push up, but he leaned against her with his full weight, his legs pressing hers wider.

"Isaac—"

His hand squeezed her throat, cutting off her words.

This was too much. She couldn't do this. She clawed at his hand, and he pressed her neck harder until she saw stars.

He put his mouth to her ear again. "Be still."

She pushed against him as hard as she could, her voice trapped under his fingers.

"I don't want to hurt you, but I will if you make me. Be good."

She froze. His words were a knife wrapped in silk.

"Better." He caressed her face and kissed the tears on her cheek. "We'll see how strong you are."

Chapter 19: Eric, 2009

Eric pulled up to the 7-Eleven down the street from his next job, a kitchen backsplash replacement in Edmond that would take him most of the day. His stomach churned from how he had left Sam's place, and it tightened with even more knots when he ignored her calls. He couldn't eat, but he needed to at least get coffee into his system or he wouldn't be able to function.

He poured coffee from the pot he hoped was the freshest and placed a lid on the large foam cup. He was two people behind in line to pay when he saw the dark suit and stocky build of Detective Eastman sidle up beside him.

"Mr. Walker," he said, laying a heavy hand on Eric's shoulder. "I'm going to need you to come with me."

Eric stared at him, unable to conceal the shock on his face. "But I—I'm on my way to work."

"Tell them you'll be late." He motioned to the foam cup. "Leave the coffee. There's some at the station and it's a damn sight better."

Eric went back to the coffee area and set his cup down. He looked over at the side exit where his truck sat outside. He thought about running for it, but what would be the point? He followed Detective Eastman out the front where he saw the black Dodge Charger waiting for him.

"Are you arresting me, sir?"

The detective smiled at him. "Would you like me to?"

Eric glanced over at his truck. "If you're not arresting me, why should I go with you?"

"Well, I figured you'd want to do whatever possible to help the investigation. Help us find who killed your father."

Eric reluctantly agreed to accompany the detective to the downtown Oklahoma City police station. He had asked if he could follow in his truck, but Detective Eastman said it'd better for them both if they took the Charger.

"Why are we going to the Oklahoma City station?" Eric asked from the back seat on the drive down. He was sure the detective had to be in Blanchard's jurisdiction where police found his father's remains.

"Other stations try to be accommodating." Detective Eastman sped up more on the highway. "Why? You want to drive all the way out to Blanchard? I try to avoid the place myself."

"You don't live there?"

Eric saw the man grip the steering wheel tighter. "Not anymore."

"Why not?"

"All the small-town talk, everybody knowing everyone else's business. I had my fill of it." The detective watched Eric in his rearview mirror, the wrinkles around his eyes deepening in his examination. "Or maybe it had its fill of me. Sound familiar?"

It did, and Eric stayed quiet the rest of the way. He tried to focus on what questions the detective might ask him, but he gave up. Besides finding his father's bones, he had no clue what evidence the police had collected. He figured they wouldn't bring him in again unless he was a suspect. He took a few long inhalations to steady himself.

They parked, and Detective Eastman checked them in at a front desk before taking Eric back to a small room. He felt like he'd just entered some shitty crime show on TV, something Grandma Haylin would've watched if she were alive. If Grandma Haylin saw him now, she'd probably tell him to keep his mouth shut and be polite. That's what she always told him whenever Jeri dragged him to church services, and it worked for him then.

Detective Eastman brought Eric a cup of coffee and sat across from him, a box marked with numbers between them. The detective stated both of their names and explained that the conversation was being videotaped for accuracy, and all Eric could think was that he probably looked like crap, unshaven, wearing yesterday's clothes, maybe even smelling a little like Sam's perfume after almost having sex with her.

Eric stared into the cup of black coffee and thought of Sam's eyes, how he was glad he couldn't see them when he broke down crying next to her in her bed.

"So, I'm not one for wasting time, Mr. Walker." Detective Eastman wasn't smiling, which Eric found much more unsettling than the man's usual grin. "How your father died—it wasn't pretty. His clothes found at the burial site and markings on his ribs show he was stabbed multiple times in the back, and he sustained a nasty blow to the back of his skull."

He tried to picture his father injured and dying and he couldn't.

"You have any ideas who might've done that to him?"

Eric sat up in the metal seat and stared at the older man who looked so confident across from him. Confident Eric was his man.

"No, sir. I don't."

The detective leaned back in his chair, crossing his arms.

"We searched the surrounding area for possible murder weapons."

Eric followed Detective Eastman's eyes to the box.

"Our search dogs led us to an interesting find. Found it in the barn loft on your stepmother's old property."

Eric kept his eyes on the box. He knew what was in it, and his empty stomach clenched.

The detective took the box, opened the lid, and pulled out something sealed in a plastic bag. He set it in front of Eric within reach of his hands. He had to stop himself from touching the mother of pearl handle, from rushing to find a sink to scrub the blade clean.

His old pocketknife, age-worn and a little rusted.

"It was in a metal tin, hidden away. Has your father's prints. Yours too." Detective Eastman's Cheshire smile was back. He stared at the knife in front of Eric like he could somehow summon the truth from it, but Eric knew all too well there was always more than one truth. "My daddy gave me a knife just like it. Your daddy gave you this, didn't he?"

For a moment, Eric saw the man's smile wither. Then it was back again, even bigger.

Eric pushed the knife back across the table. "No, this was my uncle's and he left it to my dad. He let me use it sometimes."

The detective leaned forward with his hands spread on the table, his smile gone again. "Fifteen years—that's how long it'd been since you'd seen your father. Is that right, Mr. Walker?"

"Yes, sir."

"That's a long time, but we have the best forensics team in the state testing for blood. I'm sure we'll know more about this knife soon."

Eric closed his eyes and swallowed hard. He knew exactly what they'd find on that knife, and it wouldn't be good. When he opened his eyes again, the detective looked much older under the dull florescent lights.

"I think it's time you start talking, Mr. Walker. I think it's time you tell me about Meredith Lang."

Fear crawled up Eric's spine and he shifted in his seat, straightening his left leg until the pain stopped throbbing down his calf muscle.

"What does she have to do with my father's murder?"

The man reached across the table and took Eric's untouched cup of coffee. He took a good, long drink. "They sure do know how to brew a cup here. Not the usual horse piss you find at most stations."

"I thought you don't like wasting time, or did you just mean your own?" Eric said, cringing with his words. *Just keep your mouth shut and be polite.* Too late.

Detective Eastman set the foam cup down a little too hard and

128

some coffee sloshed out onto the table. "I had a visit to Anadarko, saw Meredith's mom, Vickie. Very helpful lady. Needs to get herself cleaned up, though."

Eric's heart picked up when he thought of Vickie, of that dyed red hair in a halo of cigarette smoke. His mom never smoked yet she died of lung cancer, something he had wished on Vickie too many times to count.

"Once she learned about your father's murder, she was very eager to tell us about what happened the night Meredith was raped," the detective continued, pinching the edge of the foam cup.

That night, lightning and thunder cracking, Eric waking and searching next to him, but Meredith was gone.

"She says your father had to fight to get you off Meredith and then you got his gun."

Eric's chest constricted until he couldn't breathe.

"She says your father convinced her to protect you, you being young and all. He didn't want to see you go to jail, not after they found out Meredith's baby was fine despite your apparent efforts."

The lights overhead seemed to dim, narrowing Eric's vision, and he closed his eyes. He saw blood on Vickie's hands, up her forearms, and he quickly opened his eyes again.

"That's not—that's not what happened."

The baby was dead. Sam said so all those years ago. Everyone said it. The raped girl in Anadarko lost a baby.

"Your Aunt Vickie showed me pictures of the kid. Good-looking boy. Has your dimples. Your father had dimples too, huh?"

Eric couldn't get a breath. He couldn't speak. He watched an unnatural look of delight cross Detective Eastman's face, the huge grin never matching the dead blue of his eyes.

"So, let me ask you something, Mr. Walker. Who's the proud father?"

Chapter 20: Arrow, 1994

Arrow jolted awake, Trent Reznor's repeated screams of "kill me" ripping through his ears. He had fallen asleep to the Nine Inch Nails CD he stole from Sam's room. As he'd done for the last few nights, he'd gasp awake when the end of "Eraser" came on.

He removed his headphones and heard a strange sound coming from Sam's room. It was a high, hiccupping cry, and it scared him. He didn't want to leave his room to see if the cry was Sam's—he knew it was and he didn't want to know what was causing it. He had to, though.

He quietly opened his door and padded over to her room. He didn't hear anything else besides the cry, and he cracked her door open. Sam was under the covers, lying on her side away from him. Arrow closed the door behind him and she stopped crying, her sudden silence and the rigidness of her body making him pause.

He moved over by her window so she could see it was only him, but he was afraid to sit on her bed. He recognized that thick force field-like energy around her and it told him to go away, you're not welcome.

"What's the matter?"

Sam pulled the covers up to her neck. "I had a bad dream," she said, sniffling. "Go back to bed."

"What was it about?"

"I don't remember. Just go back to bed."

He ignored her and his sinking feeling and sat on the edge of the bed. He tried to rub her back, and her body shuddered like she was cold. That's when he smelled it—the bleachy-scent of semen cut with soil, sweat, and alcohol. It was all over her.

His dad.

His hands balled into fists. He wanted to punch himself, slam his head against her wall, anything for letting it happen. He should have watched over her better and it was too late.

"Sam."

"Please, just go." Her voice sounded like it belonged to someone else, someone frail and about to die. "It was just a dream. I'm okay now."

Arrow left her room. He couldn't feel his legs, but they moved him back to his room, to his dresser and to the drawer where he kept his new pocketknife. He opened the blade and crept past the soft snores coming from Grandma Haylin's room, down the stairs, and to Jeri and his dad's bedroom. His father lay on his back on top of the covers, his large hands braided together and resting on his naked chest.

He held the knife high, his arms shaking, over his father's rising and falling chest.

He had to do this, he had to stop him, for Sam, but his hands trembled when he thought about sinking the knife into his dad's heart. His only parent left, but he knew his dad would do it again. Meredith flashed in his mind. Everything would happen again.

He held the knife higher.

He heard movement coming from the front of the house, the clinking of keys being set down on a table.

Jeri. She was back from the Woodland house.

Arrow lowered the knife, went out to the hallway, and let out the breath he'd been holding. His ears were ringing, the feel of an icy hand gripping the back of his neck hard as he made himself move, quietly, back up the stairs to his bedroom.

He stood by his dresser, shuddering so hard he almost dropped the knife.

The right time would come. Saying it in his head calmed him a little. It would come, he knew it in his heart. He made the promise to protect Sam and he would keep it.

Chapter 21: Sam, 2009

Sam sat in her car outside of Eric's two-story Gatewood home, eating a Sonic burger she picked up along the way. The surrounding Plaza District had been "up-and-coming" since she had moved to Oklahoma City twelve years prior. Knowing how much Eric used to love fixing things, she knew the house would eventually end up the nicest on the block. In its current state, it would've fit nicely in a horror film, the streetlamps doing little more than illuminating the rotted wood exterior and sagging covered porch.

She wondered if Eric knew about the boy. Caleb. That's what Meredith yelled to him when he remained standing on the stairs, staring down at his mother with those soulful eyes that drove Sam stuttering like a damn fool. Eric had to know about him, and he didn't want her to find out for some reason.

It was almost ten, the moon high, when Eric pulled his truck into his driveway, nearly hitting Sam's car parked on the side street. He got out, steadied himself against the driver's side door before moving to his porch, and Sam knew he was drunk.

She got out of her car, looked around at his neighborhood again, and hit the lock button on her key fob several times. Eric turned around at hearing her car alarm chirp.

"Your drunk ass could've killed someone."

Eric squinted under the dark covered porch. "Sam?"

"We need to talk."

He turned back around to his front door, struggling to put his house key into the lock.

"I've had enough talking today."

Sam took his keys from him and opened his door. "Trust me—you'll want to hear this."

She wasn't sure what to expect on the inside of his house, but she didn't expect the sparseness. A remodeling zone, sure, but his house had zero furniture. They moved past a large, empty room to the back of the house, which seemed to be the only space in use, with a thin blanket and pillow shoved to the side of a brown leather couch.

"I don't have a lotta time to work on it," he slurred out like an apology, sinking into the couch.

"It has good bones." Bones that would take a shit-ton of muscle and skin to make it livable.

Sam sank into the couch next to Eric and held her breath. The smell of alcohol, cigarette smoke, and sweat wafted off of him. Bar smells. He looked exhausted, the circles under his eyes and stubble on his face making him seem much older.

She was tired too, but she tried to focus on the questions she wanted to ask Eric, which now seemed impossible for him to answer given his drunken state.

One thing Sam knew for sure now was that Meredith didn't lose the baby. It wouldn't be the first time town rumors had the truth wrong, and the local papers only stated general information about an Anadarko girl's rape, no names mentioned. She thought of her old best friend Chrissy, how she fed Sam all the gossip about Isaac and Eric as soon as they moved to Blanchard. Everyone had talked about them—the old veterans hanging out at the diner, the church ladies getting their hair done, even Grandma Haylin, who was never a fan of Isaac long before she knew what he was capable of.

After Isaac disappeared, Sam's mom had asked the local paper to leave out the gory details of the attack, as if people would judge her for what her husband did. She would've been right. Sam knew the police questioned her mom about Isaac's murder, but her mom said nothing about it for some reason. Sam knew she'd have the conversation about it with her mom soon and she didn't look forward to it.

On her drive over to Eric's house, anger at him had hummed low and constant but it didn't feel justified. For all she knew, he didn't know about Caleb. There was another emotion trying to surface—resentment—but she wouldn't allow herself to fixate on it for too long.

Sam's eyes caught a framed picture on the wood floor leaning against the wall. Prometheus, benefactor of mankind—it was the drawing she had made for Eric on his sixteenth birthday. There was a line down the middle of the stormy scene as if someone had torn it in half and carefully taped it back. She couldn't believe he still had it after all these years.

She looked at Eric. He was staring at the drawing, his chin resting on his chest and his eyes glazed.

He was probably too drunk to understand anything, but she didn't care.

"I saw Meredith Lang today."

Eric's head shot up so fast, Sam jerked back from him.

"Why?"

"Because I needed to. I needed to see her reaction about Isaac."

"Fucking great. You know the cops are going to follow you. Probably followed you there."

"They didn't."

Eric stood up, wobbled some, and went to his kitchen. Sam followed him. He took a plastic cup next to the sink and filled it with water, drinking it down like his life depended upon it.

"You didn't tell me how delightful Meredith is."

"I don't know her."

"But you did."

"I don't want to talk about it."

"Fine. Let's talk about Caleb then."

Eric's face was blank. Maybe he was too intoxicated.

"I saw Meredith's son. He's your goddamn twin."

He looked at the empty cup in his hand.

"He's a sophomore. Almost sixteen. I looked him up on social media."

Sam could see everything about the kid. Where he went to school, what his room looked like, his favorite music and video games, his friends and hangouts. Everything.

Eric stared past her, his face pale.

He leaned over the sink, violently throwing up on a stack of unwashed dishes. Sam looked away, the smell of whatever he had to drink hitting her nostrils. That anger at him fizzed up again, but she forced it down, rubbed Eric's back until he got it all out.

She poured him more water from the tap, and he took a large gulp, swished it around and spit it out.

"Where's your bedroom?"

"There," he said, pointing to the leather couch.

She assisted him back over to the couch and removed his work boots when he struggled to get them off. He was wearing the same clothes from the night before, his hair a greasy mess. His eyes were unfocused, a dreamy smile playing on his lips that stirred a memory awake.

It had been two months after the attack and Eric's leg had mostly healed. She remembered Eric being out late, well past dinner. It was the end of February, the air frigid with a recent snow, and he came back covered in dirt, no coat. As cold as it was outside, he was sweaty, a strange grin on his face, said he had helped the eldest Stewart boy kill one of the wild hogs eating up their winter crop, lost his coat in the process. Shortly after that night, he was gone.

She watched Eric reach for his blanket on the couch.

"Actually," she said, "let's get you into a shower before you pass out."

Eric tried to protest, but she successfully dragged him up and found his bathroom. She helped him undress as the shower water warmed up. She couldn't get over how different his body was from when he was a teenager. It was like he had slipped from his gangly boy frame and stepped into Isaac's labor-hard body. Her eyes lingered too long. Eric noticed and took it as an invitation. Drunk as he was, he pressed her against the bathroom vanity, his mouth on her neck, hands working to remove her blouse. He kissed her, and she shoved him away.

"Hey—let's get the bar funk off you."

He grabbed a fistful of her hair and pulled hard as he held her by her neck. Shivery pain danced up her back to the spot he held firm.

"This is what you've wanted, right?"

Sam closed her eyes, heard the words Isaac told her that first time he was on her, pressing her body down on her bed: *This is what you've wanted.* No questions with him, everything an absolute.

At sixteen, rape was something she read about in books, saw vague depictions of in movies. It didn't seem to fit what Isaac had done to her. Rape was so much more than the physical act. He had removed any choice from her and twisted her desires to be his own, had broken her ability to sense bad intentions in men until she went through years of therapy.

Eric squeezed her neck tighter, his lips forceful on her mouth, his erection wedged hard against her pelvis. Memories seared between her legs, as if Isaac were inside her, whispering in her ear how proud he was of her, of how much she took from him without breaking, and she'd beam with his words like a student getting praise from a favorite teacher.

Eric could be Isaac, with her eyes closed, but she didn't want that. She had a choice now.

"No."

She shoved him off. He looked confused, but he didn't try to kiss her again.

"You need a shower. You fucking stink."

She left him in the bathroom and wandered through the remodeling mess, every wall staring back blank and cold. She found a large toolbox on the living room floor and searched through it until she found what she was looking for. She positioned a nail and hit it a good three times with a hammer to drive it into the plaster wall. She stepped back after she hung her old drawing. It wasn't the best or worst drawing she'd ever done, but it mollified something deep in her to see it in Eric's home.

She turned to see Eric, hair damp and boxer briefs on, watching her, the lust from minutes before gone from his eyes and replaced with a different kind of longing, the kind that reminded Sam she would never be what she knew he wanted—a wife who could give him kids, a normal life with normal desires. She had pretended with too many men before, and she wouldn't do it again. The thought alone drained her.

He glanced at the wall. "Looks good there."

"Come lie down."

He obeyed like a little boy, looking too tired to resist, and stretched out on the couch. She covered him in the thin blanket, and he tucked it around his body.

He looked peaceful and she didn't want to ruin that for him, but she had to ask.

"Did you know about him? About Caleb?"

He shook his head.

"You know what this means, Eric. You could have a half-brother."

Or a son? Her stomach tightened into a painful knot when she imagined it, so she tried not to think about it. She repeated the lie to herself: he didn't have sex with Meredith, and even if he did he would've been too young to get her pregnant.

Eric's face scrunched up, tears springing up in his eyes.

She didn't expect him to be this upset. He used to tell her when they were younger how he wanted a brother, how his mom was pregnant when he was eight but miscarried.

"This can be a good thing," she said, feeling stupid as she rubbed his arm through the blanket. "If it's true, I'm sure he'll want to meet you." She wondered if Caleb would have wanted to meet Isaac. Unlikely, if he knew anything about him.

"You don't understand. She'll never let me see him." He calmed down some as he stared at her drawing on the wall. "Maybe he's not... maybe you're wrong."

Sam had no doubt the kid was of Isaac's gene pool—that straight nose and toffee eyes were Walker all right.

"I can see Meredith again, talk her into testing Caleb or something. Prove he's related to you."

Eric grasped Sam's wrist hard. "Stay away from her. Promise me."

He looked so panicked.

"Okay," she said.

He pulled his arm back under his blanket burrito and closed his eyes.

Sam had no intention of staying away from Meredith. There was a reason why Meredith kept Caleb away from Eric for sixteen years, why she manufactured a lie Sam had believed as truth all this time. Detectives would keep digging, and they'd have more questions for Sam and Eric, questions she knew wouldn't be good for either of them. Witnessing Meredith's indifferent reaction when she heard Isaac was dead—there was something there, Sam knew it, and she would find out.

Chapter 22: Sam, 1994

Something was wrong with Sam's head, her thoughts swimming amoebas, unformed, unnamed. She pressed the bruises on her inner thighs, the purple and green fading to a soft yellow the color of freshly churned butter. She liked pressing them, over and over, deep enough to steal her breath.

Four weeks. Eleven times.

She was learning fast how to be stronger, how to take the pain Isaac gave her, but he was an unforgiving teacher. If she ever tried to speak without permission or cried too much from the pain, he'd ignore her completely, sometimes for days. It became a game to her, to see how much she could take, to show him she was made of steel. She could take anything.

But she quickly learned she wasn't anything close to steel. She was a sponge, soaking up everything he did, tiny bits of her breaking away each time.

Once, she had passed out from the pain, waking up to find him inside of her, his eyes unblinking and looking past her as if she wasn't under him. It was the first time he had given her pain without offering pleasure too, and she hated him for it.

After that time, she almost told Arrow everything. She wanted to tell him, especially when he was lying next to her on her bed like he was now, her flinching at his slightest touch until she forced herself to relax. She wanted to explain to him why, but he had to know. He had to, his

140

eyes always skipping over the marks she tried to conceal. She wanted to scream to him how much she hated Isaac, but it would be a lie. The truth was she looked forward to Isaac coming to her, of him giving her more pleasure than she knew how to give herself, than Arrow could give her, because he gave her pain alongside it, pain making her feel more solid and real than anything.

She couldn't tell Arrow because it was her fault. Isaac had warned her. He said she didn't understand what she wanted, and she now knew she didn't, but she didn't know how to make him stop. What she had done to herself for years—poking herself with needles, burning her inner thighs with melted wax, choking herself with her blanket—it was nothing compared to what Isaac enjoyed.

She didn't want to think about the barn, of what happened there the week before, but the memory kept picking at her brain, removing the scab. She thought of the sound of Isaac's breathing behind her, the goats bleating in the stalls around her, her mind numb when she realized he could kill her.

The wound pulsed between her legs. She wouldn't think about that night, of any of those things, when she was with Arrow. She had to be normal for him. She had to play pretend with him. Everything was fine.

She stared at a freckle near his earlobe, holding her breath, pain from the wound making her nauseous every time she breathed in too hard.

"Are you okay?" Arrow asked.

She nodded and closed her eyes as he ran his hand up and down her arm. His touch was so different from Isaac, so gentle.

"You smell different. What is it?"

Sam showered under the hottest water she could stand every time Isaac was done with her, the trickle of blood down her thighs no longer frightening. Even Isaac seemed shocked by what he had done. He cradled her since she couldn't stand, saying, "It'll be okay, honey." He later snuck some pills to her that made her drowsy and eased the pain but did nothing to make her walk right. She ended up faking the flu for three days.

She shifted onto her back, which didn't help the pressure between her legs.

"My mama gave me her old perfume."

She actually stole her mama's Vanilla Fields, but her mama hadn't used it since Isaac bought her Poison for her birthday. Even with the hot showers, Sam was paranoid others could smell Isaac on her, so she doused herself with so much Vanilla Fields she smelled like a bakery.

"It smells good," Arrow said.

She realized her shirt had pushed up when she turned onto her back, and she pulled it back down since her lamp was on. She didn't like Arrow seeing the marks Isaac left. Bruises, teeth marks, scratches—her body was his blank canvas.

Arrow abruptly stopped tickling her arm, his full lips sucked into a straight line. "Tell me what's wrong."

"Nothing's wrong."

She knew he wanted to have sex, but she couldn't, not with the wound.

"I just don't want to tonight," she said.

"You act like you hate it now."

She slowly turned back onto her side, facing him. His eyes searched hers, and she wondered what he would say if she asked him to bite her neck, thought about what Isaac would do if he saw marks not made by him.

"I don't hate it. I'm just tired."

She watched the worry crease his forehead and she thought again about telling him.

"Fine." He pulled back the covers and left her bed. "I'm tired too, and I still haven't studied for my Spanish test."

She watched him put on his T-shirt and his face paled when he looked at her.

"Sam."

"What?"

His eyes scanned her bedsheets. "Fuck."

She looked down and there was blood on her bedding. She jumped out of her bed and saw blood smeared on her inner thighs all the way down to her knees. "Oh, shit!"

Arrow looked like he was going to throw up. "Is that your period?"

She couldn't let Arrow see the wound.

"Would you get one of the old towels from the hallway? Please? Quick."

Arrow didn't look like he wanted to move, but he left the room and came back with a wet cloth and an old towel for her. Then he pulled the bloody sheets from her bed and helped her put on fresh ones.

She left her bedroom and went straight for the pink-tiled bathroom that made her feel like she was trapped in a giant Barbie house. She locked the door and found her grandma's old, silver hand mirror. She held it between her legs, her bloody underwear at her ankles.

It definitely wasn't her period. It was the tear Isaac had made, which seemed to have grown longer. The blood, which had stopped, didn't scare her as much as the swollen redness and yellow puss oozing out of the area. She pressed down on it, thinking she could squeeze it out and it'd feel better, and nearly passed out from the pain.

She sat on the toilet and cried because it was the only thing she had energy to do. Arrow knocked on the bathroom door, whisper-asking if she was okay. She didn't answer and a few moments later Grandma Haylin was at the door.

"Let me in, Biscuit."

Sam pulled up her underwear and cracked the door. She caught Arrow's worried face before her grandma pushed in, closing the door behind her. She looked at the blood staining Sam's underwear and almost looked relieved.

"Lady time wake you, honey? You need help cleaning up?"

Grandma Haylin looked like she hoped Sam didn't need assistance.

Sam felt dizzy, as if a strong fever were coming over her. She shivered until her entire body shook and wouldn't stop, and her grandma's face grayed with alarm. She held Sam by her shoulders, examining her face as though she could diagnose her with her eyes.

"Honey? Do you think you have the flu again?" She touched Sam's forehead and her mouth dropped. "I'm gonna get your mama."

"Grandma, I—I don't feel well."

And that's the last thing she remembered before there was nothing.

Chapter 23: Eric, 2009

It was two in the afternoon and Eric was still hung over. He had hit happy hour after Detective Eastman was done questioning him, but drinking did nothing but narrow all his thoughts to a kid he thought died almost sixteen years before. Then Sam showing up at his place, seeing him in that state, the strain in her eyes when she said the boy's name—Caleb—it made him want to go back to the bar and drown some more.

The pounding in his head subsided some as he sat in his truck across from a small, beige apartment complex off a narrow, poorly paved road. Of course, Vickie lived here, the shittiest low-income housing Anadarko likely had to offer. He willed himself to cut the engine and go to the second-story unit, to see the woman face-to-face for the first time in over fifteen years.

The only positive thing about living with Vickie, after losing his mom, after moving and losing his friends and the home he knew, was Meredith, her strong welcoming hug, her strawberry-blond hair smelling like fresh-cut apples, like something good could finally happen to him.

Her tiny room was a clean sanctuary in the house, some Section 8 rental property on the verge of crumbling into a pile of termite-infested wood. She had made space for him, shoving her dresser into a corner so a twin mattress could rest on the floor next to her own. She was a talker, but he didn't mind. He liked listening to her dreams about becoming an actor, leaving Oklahoma and moving to Los Angeles, her description of the city all glitter and magic. Even then, he knew she'd never get to LA, not after seeing how his father watched her dance around the house, Mariah Carey's "Emotions" blaring on the stereo. It took Eric that first week of living there to realize his dad already knew where to find the toilet paper rolls and coffee filters and that he never slept on the couch.

He couldn't think about Meredith or his father, of everything that happened then and all the things he could've but didn't do.

He found himself standing at the front door of Vickie's apartment unit, the peeling brown paint revealing lighter beige underneath. He shouldn't be here. He should be anywhere else but here, but he needed to know why she was talking to police about him. And Caleb. He needed to know about him, but he couldn't face Meredith. Not yet.

He steadied his breath and knocked. Vickie's crazy red hair poked out of the door before her sleepy face. Her eyes—fake green contacts—instantly widened when she recognized him.

"Holy shit."

He swallowed, his mouth drier than the late August afternoon. "Vickie."

She smiled and he noticed she had maybe seven good teeth left. She had clearly moved from cocaine to meth. She opened the door wide, revealing her short, kimono-style red robe. "Come on in."

He followed her inside the combined living and dining space, the kitchen an open U less than ten feet from the entrance. Dirty clothes scattered about on the stained carpet, a half-dozen or so Big Gulps crowded the small coffee table. The smell of sour milk and unwashed female parts wafted toward him when Vickie plopped down on the couch covered in cat fur, although Eric didn't see a cat around. He smelled one for sure.

"Sit down." She patted the cushion next to her.

"I'll stand."

146

Vickie sneered and lit a cigarette, leaning forward as she took a drag. Her sagging breasts were halfway hanging out of her robe, and Eric was sure she was aware of this.

"What brings you all the way out here, honey? Been a long time."

A cat materialized and rubbed against Eric's leg.

"You lied to detectives about me, about what happened with Meredith."

The cat jumped onto the couch at Vickie's prompting and she pet its skinny black body.

"I didn't lie about anything. Maybe you just have a bad memory."

"My memory's just fine."

Vickie pushed back into the couch and gave Eric a long appraisal before smiling. "Good Lord, you haven't changed a bit. Look just like your daddy." She patted next to her again. "Sit down—you're making me nervous. I promise I won't bite."

His heart jumped at her words. Stupid. She'd never touched him, not physically. She didn't need to. Her words had been saccharine when she was high, but when she was itching for something she turned her hate on him so fast. On Meredith too.

"Why did you lie to them?" he asked.

Vickie hacked up something and took another quick drag of her cigarette. He always hated that about her—her chain-smoking but never taking more than four small drags per cigarette, letting them burn to the filter and forcing Meredith and him to breathe all the smoke.

"They needed to know about you, know the truth."

Eric's left leg ached but he remained standing.

"What truth is that? The one where my father's a saint?"

Vickie's face twisted in anger. "Your father was a good, hard-working man. You're lucky I don't call the police right now, have them lock your ass up for killing him."

"Do it."

147

He knew Vickie wouldn't call the police, not with all the drug paraphernalia he saw in her apartment. He always knew she was obsessed with his father, but he didn't expect her to carry such a bright torch for him after so many years.

She coughed again, deep from within her chest and he thought she might keel over on the couch. "I know you did it."

"Believe what you want." The cat rubbed against Eric's leg again, purring. "My father came back, didn't he? Fifteen years ago, he crawled back to you and you took him in, hid him from police."

"I never saw him. He probably drove out to Les's place to get far away from you."

Lies. He expected nothing less of Vickie.

"You tell the detectives that?"

"Told them all I could remember."

"You tell them what you let him do to your daughter?"

Vickie grinned and it was an ugly sight.

"You mean what you did? Trying to kill your own daddy."

He never wanted to punch a woman as much as he did right then, but then he knew that was exactly what she wanted so she could have something to show the cops.

She took a tiny drag of her cigarette and laughed. "Mr. Fucking Innocent."

Vickie knew nothing about innocence. She only knew about his father getting tired of her drug binges and moving on to someone he could control and slowly destroy while she watched and did nothing.

"I wish I had better aim that night," he said.

"Well, you didn't."

Vickie stubbed out her cigarette and lifted a huge purse from the carpet.

"Got something to show you. Maybe it'll make you feel better."

She dug for her wallet and pulled out a photo Eric didn't want to see because he knew it'd cut him deep and he might not recover. He

148

couldn't even make himself search the internet like Sam had done. Vickie handed the photo to him and he forced himself to look at it, at the boy on the verge of becoming a man. His hair was longer than Eric had imagined but his smile was like Eric's had been most of his life: anxious and unsure.

Caleb.

"That tall whore of yours know about him?"

Eric didn't think—he took one of the half-full Big Gulps from the coffee table and threw it hard against the wall, soda splattering everywhere. Vickie smiled coyly as if she thought he was being cute.

"Don't fucking call her that again."

How did she know about Sam? From his father? From Meredith? It made him feel unprotected, like standing next to a tall tree during a thunderstorm.

"I wonder. Does she know you're a murderer?" Vickie flashed her nasty smile at him. "The detectives know now. That act of yours. Wounded little boy who lost his mommy. Bet your little girlfriend buys it. Of course she does." She grinned again. "Yeah, she likes to think she's sneaky, following people around."

So, Meredith had talked to her mother, told her about Sam's visit. He had to control himself, ignore Vickie's smirking, or he'd do something stupid like strangle her. He didn't drive to Anadarko for that.

"What about Caleb?"

Her smile dropped. "What about him?"

"People said Meredith lost the baby. You lied. She lied." His vision blurred with tears, but he held them back. "I need to see him."

Somehow, he thought if he could just see the boy face-to-face he would know; his gut would tell him if Caleb was his.

Vickie leaned back into the fur-covered cushions. "What makes you think he'd want to see you?"

Chapter 24: Sam, 1994

All Sam knew was one moment she was in the upstairs bathroom and the next she was awake in an ER room, her mama stroking her head with Grandma Haylin on the other side of the triage bed. She had looked around the room and Isaac was sitting in the visitor's chair, the expression on his face one she had never seen on him.

He looked scared.

"Where's Arrow?" she had said, feeling herself panic as she slipped away again, her skin burning, but she saw Isaac's face before she closed her eyes. His narrowed eyes and jaw locked tight made her wish she had never said Arrow's name.

The next time Sam was fully awake, a woman with a white lab coat was the only person in the room with her. A doctor, Sam guessed. She had long, dark hair pulled back into a ponytail and high cheekbones, and Sam wondered if the doctor had Indian blood in her. Her daddy had some in him, or that's what her mama once told her.

"Hi Samantha," the woman said.

"Sam."

The woman nodded. "Sam then. How are you feeling?"

She felt like shit, but she was more concerned that no one else was in the room with her.

"Where's my family?"

"They're in the waiting area, but they'll be back soon." She gave Sam a reassuring smile. "My name is Dr. Tohtsoni."

Sam sat up in the hospital bed as much as she could and decided it was a bad idea. Her entire body ached, and the stupid IV needle hit a painful nerve when she accidentally bent her arm.

"I just have a few questions to ask you, if that's okay, Sam."

"What kind of questions?"

"Just ones that will help us get you better." Dr. Tohtsoni moved closer to the bedside, her smile plastered on. "Sam, do you know what septic shock is?"

Sam nodded. She only knew what it meant from a World War II documentary she had watched in school. Young men dropping dead left and right in the trenches from simple wounds, their blood poisoned with infection.

"And do you know why you got it?"

She thought about the swollen red skin between her legs, the rip in her flesh Isaac had made. She slowly nodded at the doctor.

The doctor looked uncomfortable when she reached for Sam's hand. The woman's hand was ice-cold, even colder than her mama's, and her mama had the coldest hands of anyone she knew.

"When a woman has a baby, sometimes she can get a vaginal tear like the one you have, and sometimes she can get it other ways."

Sam turned on the empty glazed look she gave her mama when she knew she was being grilled and wanted to be anywhere else.

Dr. Tohtsoni squeezed her hand for no reason. "Do you have a boyfriend, Sam?"

She thought about Arrow, how much she wanted to see him right then.

"Sort of."

She didn't know why Arrow wasn't at the hospital, and she wondered if Isaac made him stay behind at the farm.

The doctor opened her mouth and her smile dropped some. "Sam, I'm going to ask you something, and I want you to feel safe telling me the truth." She gave Sam's hand another little squeeze. "Has your boyfriend ever done anything that made you uncomfortable? Something that you

151

didn't want to do?"

"I don't know."

Dr. Tohtsoni searched Sam's face. "Has he ever forced you to have sex with him?"

Sam turned her head and gazed out the window. The sky was gray and rain sprinkled soft and persistent against the glass. She watched the thousands of tiny diamonds hovering, quivering a moment before crying down the large pane—perfect weather for sitting with a cup of cocoa and a good book.

"Sam, it's safe to tell me."

No, it wasn't. Isaac would find out and bad things would happen. He told her so. If anyone found out, she'd be taken away from her family, Arrow too—all because of her.

The doctor touched Sam's shoulder. "Can you tell me how you got the marks on your back?"

Sam shut her eyes. She wouldn't get upset, she wouldn't. She had to be strong and say what she needed to say. She had to keep everyone safe.

She turned her head back to the doctor. "I fell off the ladder in our barn."

The doctor smiled a little, and Sam knew she didn't believe her. "Well, you're very lucky neither of you were hurt."

Neither?

"We had to remove your morphine drip once we knew," Dr. Tohtsoni said, her dark eyes mirrors of Sam's, "but your baby's going to be fine."

The world grew dark around the edges and a faint ringing started in Sam's ears.

"Baby?"

The doctor seemed to catch on to her surprise.

"You're pregnant. About eight or nine weeks along."

Fuck.

Eight or nine weeks along…several weeks before Isaac came to her. *Thank God.* Dread quickly replaced her relief when she thought of Isaac finding out.

"Does my family know?"

"No, they don't know yet."

Sam grabbed the doctor's arm and knew she probably looked insane as fear washed over her. If her family found out, Isaac would know about her being with Arrow, and he'd do something horrible. A burst of terror streaked through her chest as she pictured Isaac beating Arrow to death.

"Please don't tell them. Please."

Dr. Tohtsoni's mouth grew serious. "Minors do have certain privacy rights, Sam. However, I highly urge you to talk with your family about this so they can help you. You'll need prenatal care."

If she kept the baby, there'd be no college scholarships, no leaving Blanchard. "What if I don't want to keep it?"

The doctor let go of Sam's hand like she was suddenly contagious.

"We'll give you some information, but I hope you look at all options. There's adoption, for one. But, if not with your family, you should talk with someone you trust. Maybe someone at church, like a pastor."

Yeah right. Sam imagined Pastor Doss going straight to her mama with the news. God, her mama—what would she say? She rubbed her stomach. She thought of Isaac again and a tremor passed through her.

No one could find out. Ever.

"Sam?"

She looked up at the doctor.

Your boyfriend—if you want to press charges, we can help you."

Sam stayed silent.

"You have to start protecting yourself. Not just for you but for your child."

My child. She touched her stomach again. *Arrow's child.*

Chapter 25: Arrow, 1994

Arrow couldn't wait for Sam to come back home. Jeri told him she'd be in the hospital for at least two more days. She might as well have told him two weeks.

Maybe if anyone had told him what was wrong with Sam he could focus at school and not be so anxious that he couldn't eat his lunch. All Grandma Haylin would tell him was Sam was sick and was getting better now. Jeri wouldn't talk to him, and he didn't understand why. They wouldn't even let him visit Sam, like he was a little kid who wouldn't be able to handle it. She couldn't be worse off than his mom had been when her cancer took over. He had a sudden thought of Sam with no hair, shriveled up to nothing in a hospital bed and he shivered. He went to the barn to check on the goats' water. It wasn't cold enough for a freeze, but the animals stirred more when the temperature dropped, constantly kicking over their troughs. He smelled pot smoke as soon as he walked in and wanted to turn right back around. As far as he knew, his father never smoked weed during the day, but Arrow recognized the smell coming from the loft.

"Son," his dad called out.

"Yes, sir?"

"Get up here."

Arrow thought of his pocketknife tucked away in his dresser drawer. He wished he had it with him.

He climbed the ladder, bracing for whatever his dad might try to do. His dad was lounging by the loft window, the heart and initials Arrow had carved with Sam framed by his bent knees.

Arrow crouched over to him and found a spot to sit. The smell of alcohol almost knocked him backwards. His dad took a hit from the joint and offered it to him.

"Well, take the damn thing," his father slurred, pushing the joint into Arrow's hand.

He pinched what was left of the joint and took a light hit, holding the smoke in his mouth, not his lungs, before releasing it. His dad looked high enough for the both of them.

"Bet you're ready for Sam to come back home." He glanced at Arrow before taking another long toke that killed the joint.

"Yes, sir."

"You miss her?"

No point of lying. "Yes, sir."

His father shook his head and leered. "Yeah, I know exactly what you miss."

Arrow knew it was coming, something bad. He just knew it and he looked over to the top of the ladder, calculated how fast he could get down.

"She's not like most girls, that's for damn sure," his dad said. "She's got a good head on her, not like half the dipshits in this town. And she knows when to keep her mouth shut and listen when she's supposed to."

Arrow wanted to yell at his father that Sam hated him, feared him like Meredith had, but he pressed his lips tight until his jaw hurt.

His father huffed out a drunk sigh, his hand over his chest as if it hurt him to breathe. "You really don't know her, how she is, do you?"

"I know how you are."

Arrow flinched, expecting his dad to take a swing at him, but his dad laughed instead. The goats moved below, riled up.

"You know why she's in the hospital?"

155

Arrow shook his head.

"She's sick because of me. I took her down to Maddie's old stall," he drew out, his face dead serious. "I took her there and I tied her up like an animal."

Arrow didn't want to hear this and he scooted back from his dad. His father grabbed his ankle.

"She passed out after an hour. I couldn't believe she lasted that long." He kept his grip on Arrow as his face collapsed, his body folded over. "Oh, Jesus—Jesus Christ, I did that."

Arrow stared at his father, shocked. He couldn't erase what his father said, couldn't process it. The words sat in his stomach, churning hate and confusion.

"Why?" he whispered.

His dad lifted his head from his arm and stared at Arrow, tears rolling down his face. He looked lost and tortured, like the illustrations of damned souls in the children's Bible Jeri had given him.

"I don't know."

"Stop doing it." Arrow's voice cracked with anger, with tears he failed to fight back. "Just stop and leave her alone."

His dad reached out to him, held the back of his neck, pulled Arrow to him until he curled against his chest. Feeling his father's arms around him, hugging him, siphoned off any power in him, and he cried, his body shaking from it. Arrow pressed his face into his dad's work shirt until he calmed down some.

"Just stop, please, just stop." *Just be normal*, he wanted to shout. *Be normal, be normal.*

"I want to. Sometimes, I do, but..."

His father shook his head as though he were trying to shake out the demons hiding there.

Arrow imagined a younger version of his dad, before his last deployment and returning home, the half-dead glaze to his eyes that only got worse when Arrow's mom became ill.

"She needs me as much as I need her. I help her."

Arrow lifted his head from his dad's shoulder, hoping he misheard his father.

"We went too far this time, is all."

Meredith covered in blood flashed in Arrow's mind.

"Sam knows what she wants. She's strong."

The fervor in his father's eyes, like Jeri's when she spoke about Jesus forgiving all sinners, dying for them—he knew his dad really believed Sam enjoyed what he did and that scared him more than anything.

He let go of his father and crawled backwards to the ladder.

He ran back to the house, but where he wanted to run was to the hospital, to Sam, to tell her it wouldn't end, he knew it now. It wouldn't end until he made it end or died trying.

Chapter 26: Sam, 2009

Sam looked away from her mom's puffy, powdered face, the face she got after crying and trying to hide it with makeup. She wished she hadn't suggested meeting her mama halfway to Blanchard at an IHOP during her lunch break, which had ended five minutes ago. If she weren't a manager at the bank, she'd expect a reprimand from her work.

"I know I look a mess, honey," her mama said. "I haven't been sleeping well."

"Because of Isaac?"

"No." Her mom did that fluttery blinking she always did when she lied.

"The detectives talked to me."

Her mom's face crumpled into her hands. "Oh, Lord. I'd hoped they would leave you alone."

Sam saw an older couple staring at their table.

"Please stop crying, Mama. It's going to be fine."

Sam didn't know why she said that to her mom. It was a reflex answer she gave to coworkers, her boss. She was fine, everything was fine. She hated seeing her mom cry. Really, she didn't like seeing anyone cry. It made her want to sink into the ground until it was safe to come out again.

Her mama dried her eyes on a paper napkin, glancing at the people eating around them as if they were secretly listening in. She looked back at Sam, her composure mostly intact again.

"I saw you and Eric are friends on Facebook now."

Sam sighed. This was exactly what she expected.

"So? What do you have against him?"

Her mom stared at her uneaten country omelet. "I never trusted that boy, not from the moment I met him."

"Why? Because of a bunch of small-town gossip?" Sam drank some of her lukewarm coffee, eyeing the server for the creamer he still hadn't brought her. "Come on, Mama. Eric didn't rape that girl. You know him better than that."

"Certainly not better than you." The hard look her mom gave her made her redden.

"I don't want to talk about it," Sam said.

The server brought her mom's requested ketchup but no creamer.

"You never want to talk about it, yet you want me to be okay with him?" Her mom struggled to open the ketchup cap. "After Isaac? And Eric said nothing when he knew it was happening?"

"Mama, stop it," Sam hissed through her teeth.

She couldn't have this conversation without her insides tightening around something absent yet always there, a seed poised to blossom outward until it ripped her apart. Someday, it probably would and she'd go crazy from it, but not today in front of her mom.

Her mama squirted ketchup, sufficiently drowning her hash browns and half of her eggs. "Fine, but you know Eric had every reason to kill Isaac."

"So did I. He fucking attacked us." The older couple nearby gave Sam the stink eye.

Her mom swallowed her bite of hash browns. "Watch your language, Samantha Grace."

Nothing changed with her mama; she still skimmed right over the small fact that Isaac raped Sam right under her roof.

Sam banged her plate with her fork. "Can I please get some

goddamn creamer like I've asked for the last thirty fucking minutes?" she yelled.

Her mom's fair skin flushed, her mouth a thin line. When the server rushed over with an entire bowl of creamer, her mom smiled, eyes downcast, and said a quiet "thank you."

In that moment, Sam saw why Isaac had chosen to marry her mom. She was the perfect submissive female, hardworking and a firm believer that women shoulder know their place. She wondered at what point Isaac realized her mom wasn't into his sexual proclivities, his need to dominate and cause pain. Maybe he always knew and didn't care. A thought shivered through her, one she couldn't believe she had never thought of before: what if he married her mom to get to her?

"I don't know why you have to be like this," her mom softly said, her eyes tearing up again. "Bringing up the past like I can change any of it."

Her mom lifted her knife to cut through her omelet, her swollen fingers quickly dropping it. She rarely talked about her lupus, but Sam noticed her mom having more trouble performing simple tasks. Her mom's graying blond hair was much shorter than Sam had ever seen it, right below her chin, and she saw how limp and greasy it looked. Sam imagined her mama losing the ability to get around on her own. She'd have to move from Blanchard, get better care for her symptoms. Sam didn't want her mama living with her, knew they'd drive each other nuts, but she couldn't picture her living on her own, and Sam would never put her in a nursing home. She was too young to be around a bunch of elderly people pushing walkers.

She reached for her mom's hand, so strangely warm from the inflammation caused by the disease. She remembered her mom's hands being so cold when she was younger. She used to have her mom press them to her face after she played outside for hours in the summer heat, her skin a furnace by time she'd come indoors.

"Mama, I'm sorry."

160

Her mom smiled a little, but the hurt remained in her pink-rimmed eyes.

"I should've done something to help you," she said, gently squeezing Sam's hand. "All that time you two spent together. Then that time you were in the hospital. I knew it in my gut he hurt you, but I was so stupid. I loved him."

Sam's stomach dropped. She could never talk to her mom about Isaac, about anything that happened, because it would mean telling her everything and everything, she knew, would kill her mama.

"All those rumors about that poor girl in Anadarko, but I didn't want to believe."

A pool of acid formed in the back of Sam's throat. "Do you mean Meredith Lang?"

Her mom's blue eyes widened. "So, you know about Eric's cousin? Well, cousin by marriage. Isaac said she was a disturbed girl who made up stories, and I stupidly believed him. He was so good at making people trust him."

Meredith was Eric's cousin by marriage? Sam slowly shook her head, feeling numb as the pieces she'd struggled over seemed to come together.

"Meredith's mother—is her name Vickie?"

"Yes, honey," her mom said. "I didn't think you knew about what happened."

"I'm not sure I do."

She didn't know what to believe, there were so many rumors floating around after Isaac and Eric moved to Blanchard.

She thought of Caleb, how much he looked like both Isaac and Eric. Only a paternity test would tell for sure. The probability was nauseating, but she knew people would think the same thing about her having sex with Isaac and Eric, father and son.

Eric wanted her to stay away from Meredith either because it was true, he raped her, or because he didn't want Sam to find out he might've had a kid with her. If it was Eric, not Isaac, who raped Meredith, there'd be no reason Sam could think of for Meredith to kill Isaac, and then she'd be back to the only other person she knew about who had a motive besides herself: Eric.

"Mama, did you ever talk to Meredith's mother, to Vickie, about Eric and what really happened in Anadarko?"

"No. At the time, I didn't have any reason not to believe Isaac. And look at what Eric put you through."

"He never did anything I didn't want." *Unlike like your husband*, she wanted to add.

"You say that like it's something to be proud of."

Sam's laugh came out low and humorless. Her sexual history something to be proud of? Her mama would die on the spot if she knew the half of it. Eric might too.

She touched her throat, hoped the makeup she had used was concealing the bruising Eric made.

Heat flushed her face and she looked away from her mom. She wouldn't be ashamed about what she enjoyed, she refused to be. Eric's hands on her neck the other night, the sounds of pleasure he made before she stopped him—maybe he could accept what she needed. She knew he'd probably try, and she believed him when he said he still loved her. She also knew there was something missing to the story he fed her, even those years ago, some detail he left out about Meredith.

"Mama, did you send Eric away to foster care?"

Surprise entered her mom's face.

"You told me he ran away, but he says you put him in foster care. Is that true?"

Her mom gazed at her plate for a long time, her mouth twisted in a frown.

"I didn't have a choice. He kept sneaking off, and I couldn't handle him. You remember how out of control he got."

Memories came to Sam, unwanted. Memories of being in the

hospital after the attack, sitting next to Eric's hospital bed, his left leg bandaged. Her mom had left to go back to the house to get some things for them. Grandma Haylin stayed behind at the hospital until she got a call and left for a long time. Eric woke up startled like he was having a bad dream. He looked around the room, frightened until he saw Sam. "Is he dead?" he had asked and promptly fell back asleep.

She thought about that February night again all those years ago, the night Eric came home without his coat and that odd grin on his face.

"Sammy?"

Sam looked at her mom and then to the server offering her more coffee.

"No, thank you," Sam said.

"You okay, honey?"

"I'm fine, Mama."

Chapter 27: Eric, 2009

Eric left Vickie's apartment, the wallet-sized photo of Caleb clutched in his right hand. When he got inside his truck and blasted his air conditioner, he glanced at her upstairs unit. She stared out at him from a small window that had a long crack stretched across it. After all these years, he knew one thing about Vickie: she still loved his father. He would never understand why.

He turned up his car's stereo, the gyrating guitar and lacerating vocals of The Walkmen blaring, trying to drown out his next thoughts. No matter what Sam said, he knew she had loved his father too. What Eric never knew was if she loved his father more.

He needed a drink. Seemed like since he'd been around Sam again, he'd been drinking every day. He'd end up like his father if he didn't watch it, chasing ghosts away with drink and drugs.

Eric held up the photo of Caleb and looked at himself in his rearview mirror. Same wistful eyes, same straight nose and full mouth, but Caleb wasn't made out of love. He and Sam had made something out of love—his love anyway. Any time he glimpsed a child with chestnut hair and dark eyes or sturdy tan limbs made for climbing trees and digging in dirt, a hand gripped his heart and held on tight, crushed until every breath left his body.

He pulled out of the gravel parking lot of the apartment complex and vowed never to see Vickie again. Her daughter was another story.

By the time Eric made it back to Oklahoma City, the August heat peaked, and the sun teased the horizon. Sam's silver Subaru sat in front of his house, and he cussed under his breath. He wanted to see her, but he didn't have the energy to do anything but have a beer, microwave something to eat, and crash out on his couch.

Sam got out of her car and came over to his truck once he parked.

He had dressed in a button-down blue shirt and nice jeans for his visit with Vickie, something he couldn't explain to himself, but he was glad he didn't look like shit now. Sam stood near the back of his truck, her arms crossed but with a calm face.

"You look nice," she said with no hint of a smile.

"You too."

She did, her blue tank top draping just right over her breasts.

"Let's get a drink. There's a bar down the way, right?"

"Yeah."

Something about her energy worried him. She looked ready to attack, but he started walking and she followed next to him.

The bar was less than a block from his house, and they didn't talk the entire way. He was close enough to her that he could breathe in her scent—the true scent of her, hiding under her spicy perfume. He reached for her hand, but she avoided his touch and pretended to dig in her purse for something.

Inside the bar, people were enjoying happy hour, laughing and talking loudly over the indie music pumping through the overhead speakers. Sam spotted a couple leaving a two-top near the windowed front of the place. She waited at the table while he ordered them two draft beers.

He set the beers down on the tiny round table and sat across from Sam. She took a long pull of the beer and carefully put the glass down like it was a porcelain teacup. He noticed that about her now, her odd deliberate movements as if she were hyperaware of how she appeared to others. She was never like that when she was younger. She didn't care what people thought about her. She was free. The only time he'd seen her close to being free now was when his hand had closed around her throat.

"So?" he prodded when she remained a silent force across from him.

"So, you have a son," she said. "Or should I say second cousin? By marriage, right? I guess that makes it a little less fucked up."

Eric picked up his beer and drained it.

"It's true then?" she said. "That Vickie person you were so afraid to talk about is Meredith's mother? She's your Uncle Jobe's widow?"

Either Meredith said something or Sam found out on her own. He took the picture of Caleb from his wallet and placed it in front of Sam.

"Was this the boy you saw when you talked to Meredith?"

Sam touched the edge of the photo, but she didn't pick it up. "Yes. That's him."

He didn't know why, but Sam's confirmation evaporated some doubt he had felt since his meeting with Detective Eastman at the police station. He hadn't told Sam about any of it because he didn't want to see her reaction.

"So, is he yours?"

Eric reached for his pint glass and remembered he had emptied it. "I don't know."

Sam caressed the top of her glass in careful, measured strokes, her eyes boring into him. "Why did you lie to me about him? You let me believe the rumors, what people said about Meredith's baby, and you knew he was alive all along, didn't you?"

"I didn't lie to you. Until this week, I had no idea about him." He could tell Sam didn't believe him. She lifted her glass and finished her beer. A server came by and asked if they wanted another round. Eric nodded.

He watched Sam look out the window at people walking on the sidewalk. A couple, holding hands, kissed outside of the bar. Eric reached across the table and tried to take Sam's hands, but she pulled them back and onto her lap.

She had that familiar ozone surrounding her, the dense apprehensiveness of it he could almost taste.

"Did you rape Meredith?" she asked.

Eric would've been less stunned if she punched him in the face.

"You're really asking me that?"

"It makes sense, you not wanting me to see her." She paused when the server dropped off their beers. "Did you hope Caleb would disappear like Isaac?"

"Oh, so now you believe I killed my father?"

Sam looked lost on that question, but her scowl returned.

"That night you said you were at the Stewart farm, the night you came home late covered in dirt with no coat, you said you were hunting feral hogs. Were you?"

Eric swallowed over the lump in his throat.

"I was."

Sam looked down at her lap and shook her head. "No, you weren't. I contacted both of Stewart's sons through Facebook the other day. Neither remembers ever shooting hogs with you that night."

He leaned back in the chair, arms crossed. "So, that automatically means I killed him?"

"It means you lied to me."

"I lied because I didn't want you to worry."

Sam shook her head again. "Then what did you really do that night?"

He dug his fingers into his crossed arms, trying to keep the memory of that night buried.

"I just went for a walk. I needed a break from your mom. From everything."

Sam let out a long exhale. "It was so easy for you, wasn't it?"

"What's that supposed to mean?"

"To get over everything that happened, to go mess around with

167

your friends, *go for a walk*, leaving me behind."

The thing he regretted the most back then was not knowing how to help her. At least Sam had Jeri and Grandma Haylin to help her work through what happened.

"I wish it had been easy for me like it was for you," she said.

"Nothing was easy for me, Sam. Nothing."

She looked up at him, eyes steady and drilling.

"Tell me then, what exactly did you lose? An older girl willing to fuck you? Someone to distract you from your sad life while you knew— the whole time you knew what he was like and you let it happen."

Eric pushed his chair back until it slammed into the faux brick wall. He stood up, pulled a twenty from his wallet, and threw it down before leaving the bar.

A moment later, Sam ran up next to him on the sidewalk. She shoved the photo of Caleb in his face. "Don't forget this."

Eric stopped and grabbed the hand Sam was holding up. He snatched the photo from her fingers but held onto her wrist.

"You don't know a goddamn thing about what I've been through these years. You spew shit like it doesn't hurt, like you can take it back, but you can't, Sam."

She attempted to jerk her wrist free, but he held on. "Let me go!"

"What—isn't this what you like? Or was my father the only one who could do it for you?"

He released her and she backed away from him. He saw tears form in her eyes, but her mouth was tight with anger.

The fire in her eyes speared through him. "He understood me in ways you'll never know because you don't want to know."

"Right."

He turned from her and headed back to his house.

Sam yanked on his forearm.

"Yes, Eric, if you wouldn't have been drunk off your ass, I would've let you, okay? But, you were, and it wasn't safe for either of us. Does that make you feel all better?"

He didn't like the taunting in her voice, as if he were a little boy whining about some toy he wanted and not about something real and meaningful.

"You wanted to fuck my father the other night, not me. But it's all about what you want, right? So *you* can feel all better?"

Sam opened her mouth but quickly closed it again, tears falling down her cheeks. Her tears pooled inside his chest until he felt like he was drowning in them.

He pulled her to him, caressing her hair.

"I was just a kid," he said. "If I could go back and do things differently, I would, but I can't and neither can you. You can't keep blaming me for something I can't change."

Sam drew back from him, tears still streaming down her face. "Who should I blame? Myself? I should've dressed differently? I asked for it, right? I asked for all of it and got exactly what I wanted. Is that it?"

"No." Eric held her face, ran his thumb along her jawline. "My father is the one who hurt you, who made you like those sick things. Not me."

She backed away from him. She half-smiled as if she pitied him. "I used to suffocate myself when I masturbated, did you know that? I was probably twelve, thirteen the first time. And I'd do other things to cause pain, long before Isaac. So, I've always been like this. I don't know why."

She had never told him this, and he didn't know what to say.

"But for everything Isaac did..." She paused, looking down and shaking her head like she was trying to shake loose a bad memory, a painful memory Eric knew he could never fully understand. She looked back up at him. "He never made me feel ashamed of it like you do."

He tried to hold her again, but she pushed away from him. She ran back toward his house, Eric right behind her, wanting to run after her but the pain in his left leg stopped him.

Sam dug through her purse for her car keys, glancing back at him like he was a monster coming at her. He didn't want her to leave this way after what she revealed to him. He tried to pry the keys from her hand, but she held on to them.

"I don't know what you want, Sam. You want me to be like him? Is that what you want from me?"

She stared at him and he saw her thoughts turning inward, away from him. He pressed her against her car and kissed her hard to bring her back to him and away from the anguish on her face.

"I can't do this, Eric." She twisted in his arms.

All he wanted was to take her inside his house, push her to the wood floor, and sink himself as far as he could in her. He would hurt her if that was what she wanted. He would be whatever she wanted or needed, he didn't care. He just wanted to make her feel something, anything, other than the torment he saw on her face.

"I can't," she repeated louder.

Sam slid out of his arms and unlocked her car.

She pushed him aside and got into her vehicle. Eric watched her taillights disappear down the street before entering his house.

He didn't know what to think, what to do. He wanted to reverse time, to tell Sam he didn't mean to make her feel ashamed for her desires, but he couldn't be like his father. If he admitted liking it, hurting her, what else would that make him?

He lay on his couch for a good two hours, his blanket pulled up to his waist. He thought about the Edmond job he had delayed, how long it'd take him and how it had pushed his other jobs back two days. He tried to think about everything else, anything but Sam. Then he imagined seeing Caleb for the first time, whether the boy would be happy to see Eric—brother, father?—and a pain in his stomach grew and he remembered he hadn't eaten dinner.

He was microwaving a burrito when his cellphone vibrated on the kitchen counter. He didn't recognize the number, but it was local. Maybe a potential client?

"Arrow Contracting."

"Eric, listen to me."

It was Sam and she sounded panicked.

"I'm at the downtown police station. I need you to do something for me."

Chapter 28: Arrow, 1994

Arrow rushed through his after-school chores, cleaning the chicken coop and running fresh water for the animals. He was eager to spend time with Sam since she was finally home. His dad probably would've noticed his half-assed completion of chores if he weren't doing side work at the Mabel farm. Sam's hospital bills kept rolling in, and even Jeri was working longer hours at the feed shop to pay them down.

The November afternoon was in that in-between state Arrow hated—too much chill in the air to go without a jacket but not cold enough not to sweat through his T-shirt. He ran toward the back of the house to the kitchen, thoughts of drinking a gallon of water making him forget how terrible he smelled. He saw the back door to the kitchen was open, the screen door letting the smell of something burnt mixed with the intoxicating scent of bacon drift to him. As he got closer, murmuring voices joined the smells. He stopped at hearing his name, his heart banging in his chest from the amount of venom in the voice saying it.

"It's the truth, Mama," Jeri said. "You don't know the whole story."

"What—the story Isaac told you? Any fool could see it for what it is."

Arrow moved to the side of the screen door to listen without Jeri or Grandma Haylin seeing him.

"He has no reason to lie. And now this with Sam. She has bruises all up and down her back, Mama, and it wasn't from any fall from a ladder. And, Lord help me, she has other wounds—down *there*— I

172

can't even think about without wanting to kill that boy."

"*That boy* wouldn't do anything to hurt Sammy. I'd stake my life on it."

"But you heard what happened with that Anadarko girl and Eric."

"You always believe every bit of gossip?" Gandma Haylin said. "'Sides, I heard some mighty nasty rumors about Isaac and that girl. Maybe those are true, and here you are letting him spend so much time with Sam."

Arrow's chest pinched until he could barely breathe.

He heard Jeri let out a grunt of frustration. "Don't even mention those lies to me. God'll strike this house."

"I've yet to see God strike anything down, truth or not."

Arrow smiled a little.

"How can you talk like that, Mama?" There was a pause. "When I'm not here, he's not to be left alone with her, you hear me?"

He heard Grandma Haylin answer with a grumble that sounded like "foolish woman."

Arrow thought about entering the house from the front and getting a drink from the bathroom faucet to avoid Jeri, but her words had stoked a fire in him. He entered the kitchen, and Jeri did a little jump at seeing him before turning to the stove where she was frying cabbage with bacon. He looked over to the Formica table where Grandma Haylin sat staring at a loaf of burnt bread as if it were a holiday centerpiece she couldn't quite get right.

He went straight for a glass and poured some water from the tap, drank it down, and smiled at the women.

"Something smells good," he said.

Grandma Haylin shook her head at him. "Since when does bread blackened to nothin' smell good, boy?"

Arrow saw Jeri shoot Grandma Haylin a look he couldn't interpret, but it made him feel queasy, like he was something Jeri wanted to scrape off the bottom of her shoe and Grandma Haylin wasn't helping her.

"You do your chores?"

Jeri had to know he did by the smell and look of him, but he said, "Yes, ma'am."

She pushed a loose strand of her blond hair from her face, her blue eyes worrying a hole through him. "Well…don't be going up to Sam's room and bothering her. She's still recovering."

Sam wasn't in her room. Arrow had seen her walk to the barn while he was scooping out old poop-covered hay from the chicken coop. He delayed taking his shower and left the kitchen to see her.

He entered the barn, zipping his jacket up to his neck. The evening was coming in fast with icy fingers tickling down his back.

He found Sam sitting in one of the goats' stalls, gazing at Antigone, a new dam that'd given birth to her first offspring two days before. Sam watched Antigone lick the kid, which was black and white like his father.

"Whatcha gonna name him?"

Sam looked up at Arrow, her smile the saddest one he'd ever seen. She wasn't wearing much of anything—a baggy short-sleeved T-shirt and jeans.

She shrugged her shoulders. "It's just a goat."

No animal on the farm was just an animal to Sam. Outside of Maddie, she had named all the goats on the farm after Greek gods and goddesses, sometimes making up elaborate backstories for them as if they were human. It was one of the weird things he loved about her.

Arrow tried to remember some of the unsolicited Greek tragedy lessons Sam used to give him.

"What about Polynices? Wasn't that Antigone's son or something?"

Sam rolled her eyes at him.

"Polynices was her brother. She ignored King Creon's orders and buried her brother's remains, so she was sealed up in a cave as punishment."

"Well, that would totally suck." He grinned at her and she smiled

174

some in return.

"I can think of worse things."

She returned to studying the mother and her baby, and Arrow sensed the ozone around her, the strange crackle of something telling him a storm was forming inside her. A breeze blew through the barn and Sam shivered. She did nothing to make herself warm, and this bothered him. He sat on the hay-covered ground and removed his jacket. She didn't say anything when he draped it over her shoulders, and he wrapped his arms around her to warm her further.

A memory of his mom hit him. He had been six or so and was playing in the snow in nothing but his underwear and his mom chased him back into the house, calling him her crazy naked bear cub. She had wrapped him in her favorite thick flannel blanket and cradled him like a baby on the couch, his dad in the kitchen getting something warm for them to drink. Arrow had felt so protected in his mom's arms. Nothing in the world could harm him.

"Sam," Arrow said. "Your Aunt Shelley still lives in Dallas, right?"

"Uh-huh."

"And you're close with her?"

"Sure."

He squeezed her as a way of giving himself courage. "Let's go there—to your aunt's. Let's run away."

Sam snorted out a laugh. "Are you insane? That's nuts."

"It's not. I still have money from when I mowed lawns over the summer. I'm going to start chopping wood soon too. I was going to use the money for your birthday present, but we can get bus tickets."

She turned in his arms and asked, "How much do you have?"

"Almost eighty dollars."

She slumped against his chest.

"That's not enough for both of us."

"You'll get money for your birthday. We can combine it."

As he said it, Arrow saw the plan coming together. They'd wait until after Sam's birthday, hitch a ride to Oklahoma City through Sam's friend Chrissy, who just got a car, and buy bus tickets to Dallas. Sam would be safe from his dad. They'd both be safe.

Sam was quiet for a long time, rubbing her stomach as if it were bugging her. Arrow shuddered from the cold and hugged her closer to him. Sam brushed her lips over his cheek, barely a kiss.

"Okay," she said, and he kissed her lips. They were freezing but he kept kissing her until warmth flowed through every part of him, surrounding them both in a promise.

Chapter 29: Sam, 1994

During her entire last period in school—biology—Sam thought about the baby growing inside her. Mitosis, chromosomes in the nucleus separating and reforming new cells on repeat, creating organ tissues, eyes…fingernails. Almost eleven weeks, and the baby had toes and ears too. Could it hear? The book she had read at the library didn't say, but she imagined it could so she tried not to cuss too much.

She thought of her Aunt Shelley. She could call her from a payphone or maybe Chrissy's private phone line, but she had a feeling her aunt would call her mom and ruin the plan. If she showed up with Arrow, if she explained their reason for running away in person, she couldn't imagine Aunt Shelley turning them away.

Aunt Shelley's first husband had been physically abusive. Sam wasn't supposed to know this, as her aunt pointed out during Sam's last visit to Dallas. "You think I had it bad, your daddy wasn't too nice to your mom either," Shelley had told Sam while they drank huge lattes at a small café, the intimate conversation making Sam feel like an adult.

Her aunt had left her husband and married a much younger man who "couldn't keep his dick in his pants." Now, Aunt Shelley lived alone in a large downtown high-rise apartment filled with expensive, uncomfortable contemporary furniture she paid for with her pharmaceutical sales job. Everything in the apartment was red, black, white, and gray, and Sam couldn't picture Arrow lounging on the blood-red couch.

The final school bell rang, and Sam exited the building with the throng of students, walking past Chrissy, whom she hadn't spoken with much in the last few weeks. Chrissy had cut her blond hair shorter and was wearing Doc Martens with one of those popular baby doll dresses, all short and low-cut, like she was a grunge girl, which she wasn't. The dress showed off Chrissy's ample chest, and Sam felt oddly jealous when she remembered Isaac talking about how developed Chrissy was. Sam thought hers were getting bigger or at least more painful when she tried to touch them.

Chrissy called out to her, but Sam kept walking. She was about to walk in the direction of where she usually met up with Arrow when she saw a white Chevy pickup in the high school's circle drive.

Isaac's truck.

Isaac leaned over and opened the passenger door. Sam looked back at the school to see Chrissy's brown eyes darting back and forth between Isaac's truck and Sam's face. Her best friend seemed to give her a look saying, "Don't."

Then Chrissy called out, "Hi, Mr. Walker. I was going to give Sam a ride home today."

"That's quite all right," he called back. "Maybe tomorrow."

Sam smiled at her friend for her attempt. She went to the passenger side and set her backpack on the floorboard before climbing into the truck.

They drove for a minute before Isaac spoke. "Put your seatbelt on."

She secretly hoped they would get into a wreck and she would fly out of the truck, magically unscathed while Isaac smashed his head on the steering wheel, blood everywhere. The fullness of her belly made her comply and she buckled her seatbelt.

He didn't pull onto the normal street going toward their house and a sweat broke out over Sam's body.

"Where are we going?"

"Just someplace nearby."

"Why?"

He gave her an incredulous look as if she should know why, and her stomach cramped.

"I—the doctor...she said I shouldn't..." Her voice faded into the sound of the truck's tires whooshing over the pavement, kicking up fallen leaves.

Isaac didn't say anything and kept driving for the next ten minutes until they came to the edge of a large pond. He got out and she followed, staying farther behind him. It was a pretty spot, spires of golden grass lining the narrow rock beach, trees still laden with orange and red foliage, the gray water emitting a gentle lapping sound, but Sam couldn't focus on anything but the back of Isaac's denim jacket, at his large hand reaching back for her own. When she took it, his grip was unexpectedly gentle, and a flutter of need flickered through her lower half, surprising her.

They sat at a bench someone had fashioned from stone many years ago from the look of it. Isaac leaned into her and she knew he wanted to kiss her, but she turned her head, hoping he'd think she didn't notice.

"Look at me."

He took her chin in his hand and forced her to face him.

"Look at me," he said, each word punctuated.

She did but it was hard to hold eye contact with him when his voice turned demanding.

"I didn't mean to hurt you. I never wanted that."

She didn't see how he could be serious, but his eyes were so intense, she had to blink a ton to keep looking at him. It made her think of being at the lake when she was younger. "Don't stare at the sun, Sammy," her mama would say, "you'll go blind."

"I'll never hurt you that way again, you understand?"

That way. Not never hurt her period—just not that way. She wasn't sure if she was relieved. Even now she craved his pain, but she knew she wouldn't survive that kind again.

She nodded.

He pressed his lips to hers, soft, like it was their first kiss, and she thought of Arrow's lips, not Isaac's, of Arrow's hands tugging a handful of her hair until she whimpered.

Isaac pulled back from the kiss and yanked on her hair harder. She held in her cry because she knew that was what he liked. He grinned, pleased with her, and she felt their familiar exchange rekindled; he took, she gave, and he gave back just enough to make her want more.

"Did you miss me?"

"Yes."

"Did you miss Arrow?"

She didn't know how to answer him, and fear scratched at her throat.

"Do you love him?"

She closed her eyes, afraid he would see the answer in the blacks of her pupils. Magic 8 Balls giving her away.

"You love me," he said. "What I do for you."

Not a question. She opened her eyes and nodded, wanting to see his approval, hopeful it would put him in a good mood. When he was in a good mood, his punishments didn't last as long. Sometimes, she wanted him to be in a bad mood, and she'd push all his buttons to see how far he'd go. This wasn't one of those times. Her gut told her to be careful.

Isaac motioned to the huge pond.

"You know, used to be good fishing here, but people kept dumping their trash—wrappers, bottles, old tires and such. Bodies too. Fish got too fat and started dying. They can barely swim now."

Isaac's sudden smile didn't reach his eyes.

"They can eat a body to the bone. Probably love nibbling on young flesh the best."

Sam squirmed next to him, and Isaac's hand grasped her thigh, his fingers digging into her jeans and she knew there'd be bruises.

180

"What'd you tell those doctors at the hospital?"

"Nothing," she said.

"You told them about us, didn't you?"

"No. I didn't say anything."

Isaac's fingers dug deeper, pain shooting throughout her left leg. It wasn't the good kind of pain and she wanted him to stop. She ran her hand across his chest and down to his jeans and he tightened his grip on her thigh.

"Such a little whore, aren't you? It's all about fucking to you."

She stopped moving her hand, unsure of what he wanted now. She wasn't used to not knowing.

"Tell me you're a whore."

His fingers felt like they were touching bone.

"Say it."

Tears sprang into her eyes and she mumbled, "I—I'm a whore."

He gathered a chunk of her hair at the nape of her neck and pulled hard again. "Louder."

"I'm a whore," she said, loud enough to echo across the pond.

"Yes, you are, and you make me treat you like one."

He unzipped his jeans and took himself out. She knew what he wanted her to do, but she never enjoyed doing it for him. It wasn't the same as with Arrow. Isaac used it as a punishment, pushing her down on him until she would almost pass out from lack of oxygen.

He shoved her face down onto the salt and sweat of him. He was barely inside her mouth before her stomach rose up and kept coming up until everything in her came out onto his lap.

"Fuck!" Isaac jumped up, vomit covering his jeans.

Sam jumped up too, hands hovering near her mouth, the acid burning the back of her throat. She had to stop herself from laughing as Isaac rubbed a fistful of dead leaves over his groin in an attempt to clean himself, dry heaving as he did it.

"I'm so sorry, I—"

"Get in the goddamn truck!"

She ran to the passenger side and tried to clean herself while she waited for him.

It was dark by the time they made it to the house, Isaac cussing under his breath most of the way back, the truck filled with the sour smell of puke. Isaac shot through the front door and called out, "Taking a quick shower."

Sam slowly trailed him inside, feeling weak and exhausted. She vaguely thought about her calculus homework on her way up to her bedroom, ignoring her mama's voice coming from the kitchen. Arrow waited at the top of the stairs, annoyance on his face.

"Where'd you go after school? I waited forever."

Sam stared through him. She wanted to tell him about his cells multiplying in her, making her throw up anything she tried to keep down. He should just know without her saying it. Didn't anyone notice her gaining weight and throwing up all the time?

"I saw Chrissy drive by," he said. "She told me she saw you after school."

Sam pushed past him toward her room. "Yeah."

"You left with him?"

She flopped onto her bed and Arrow shut her bedroom door behind him.

"Why would you go with him?" he asked.

"I had to."

She reached for her headphones, but Arrow snatched them from her hands.

"Don't you hear your mom? It's time to eat."

"Not hungry."

"What'd he do to you?"

"Nothing."

"You're lying."

"Get out."

182

"No."

"Get the fuck out!"

Sam grabbed the headphones back from him right as her mama busted through the door. She looked at Sam and then at Arrow standing by her bed, inexplicable anger crossing her face.

"What'd I tell you about coming around Sam? Get downstairs right now."

Arrow darted out of the room, hurt in his eyes when he glanced back at Sam.

"Sammy, it's time for dinner," her mama said, her tone softer.

"I'm not hungry."

Her mama sat next to her on the bed. "You've been saying that a lot lately, but I've seen you munching quite a bit here and there. Like a lil raccoon sneaking into the kitchen at night." Her mama touched her stomach, making Sam jerk back from her.

"Are you saying I'm fat?"

"No, honey, I didn't mean it like that."

Her mama stared at her as if she expected her to say something, and Sam felt like crying into her pillow.

"Honey, we have to talk about what happened. If someone hurt you, and—"

"I fell from the ladder. That's it. God, can you please stop talking about it all the time?"

Her mama looked down at her lap.

"But those marks you had on your back, and…and down there. I don't see how falling could've done that."

She couldn't tell her mama about Isaac, all the things she let him do to her. It would destroy her. But maybe she could tell her about the baby. Her mama would cry and yell at her, Sam knew, but maybe she would be a little happy too. She loved knitting tiny blue and pink caps and booties for the preemie babies at the hospital.

"Sammy, you know you can talk to me. About anything."

"Mama, I…"

Before her words could form, Sam remembered the large pond, the dead look in Isaac's eyes when he told her people dumped bodies there. She imagined herself sunk to the bottom, fat fish swarming and biting tiny chunks out of her tongue and eyeballs.

"Sammy?"

She smiled at her mom.

"Actually, I am hungry."

Her mama paused, looking unsure, before she patted Sam's hand.

"Okay, honey. Wash your hands before you come down."

Her mama paused again at the door.

"Do you need any help with your homework after dinner?"

"It's calculus. You wouldn't know how to do it."

"Okay."

Hurt crossed her mama's face before she left the room, but Sam didn't feel the sting of it; she still felt like she was sitting at the bottom of the pond, her voice swallowed by murky water.

Chapter 30: Sam, 2009

The police called it escorting, as if they were gallant men from a fairytale sweeping up to Sam's house to take her to an extravagant ball. They didn't handcuff her before they helped her into the back of the police vehicle, but they weren't exactly gentlemen either.

All she knew was that they were bringing her in for questioning. An officer checked her in at the downtown Oklahoma City police station and took her to a small room containing nothing but three crappy plastic chairs and a small desk. It was freezing in the room, and she wished she had a jacket, but no sane person wore a jacket in this kind of August heat wave. She never wore padded bras, but she began to wish she owned one when the officer kept ogling her blue tank top before he left her, shutting the door behind him.

For several minutes, she sat alone in a chair against the wall, no access to her phone, which an officer took during the check-in. She guessed it was about seven-thirty and realized she had two beers and no food in her stomach.

Detective Eastman entered the room, grinning at Sam like she was a good friend he hadn't seen in a long time. He set what looked like a shoebox on the desk, took one of the chairs across from her, and told her they were recording the conversation. Sam placed her hands on the table but quickly moved them back to her lap. Her instinct was to twist the bottom of her tank top, but she made herself be still, a mannequin who wouldn't react.

185

"Miss Mayfair, it's been a while. I bet you're wondering why you're here."

"I'm sure you'll tell me."

"What I'm interested in is what you have to tell me."

He took off his gray suit jacket and draped it across the chair next to him before leaning forward, elbows resting on the table. It was silly, she knew he was trying to intimidate her by taking up space in the tiny room, but that simple act was enough to make her heart rate pick up.

"As you know, we determined the cause of your stepfather's death to be blunt force trauma to the head. He also had some obvious stab wounds to the back of his torso, which likely caused a collapsed lung and internal bleeding."

Sam's jaw tightened so much her back molars hurt. She avoided looking at the box between them.

"It wasn't a pleasant way to die."

Sam wanted to say *no shit*.

The detective smiled again, that same self-assured grin Isaac always wore, and Sam had to fight to control her breath. In and out, in and out.

"How's your stepbrother handling all this?"

"Not that well." Or maybe too well. She couldn't decide.

"It's a difficult thing, losing a loved one like that." He examined her face for a moment, his eyes lowering to her neck. "How are you handling it? You were close to your stepfather, right?"

Be a mannequin. Don't react. In and out, in and out.

She shrugged.

"Not really. I mean, it's sort of hard to feel close to someone who attacked you. I'm upset but mostly for Eric."

"Not close to him, huh?" He sat up in the chair, his smile faded. "That's interesting. Your mother seems to think you and Isaac were very close. He took you fishing a lot. Things like that."

She wondered how much her mom had told the detectives. Did

they know Isaac raped Sam? It wasn't something they told the police those years ago after the attack because Sam didn't want them to know. The thought of Isaac coming back to fight rape charges, the possibility of seeing him in a courtroom telling everyone how much she enjoyed what he did to her...she couldn't do it.

"The reason why I brought you in, Miss Mayfair, is this."

The detective slid the small box over to him and removed the lid. He pulled out a plastic bag containing a pocketknife, and Sam's stomach coiled tight. He pushed the bagged knife in front of her.

"Do you recognize this pocketknife?"

She didn't want to pick it up, look at the intricate mother of pearl handle, the blade that appeared too clean.

"No."

"We found it on your family's old property, hidden in the barn loft. It tested positive for your stepfather's blood. Has Eric Walker's prints all over it."

The beers from earlier stirred acid that threatened to climb up to her mouth. Why would they have that knife? It was supposed to be gone forever. She felt dizzy.

"Miss Mayfair, do you remember being hospitalized at Norman Regional when you were sixteen?"

The question came from nowhere and the room was suddenly hot. "Yes."

"And you know they performed a rape kit on you?"

"Yes." She didn't want to think about all the prodding and swabbing.

She knew what was coming next, but it was impossible to brace for it.

"Who raped and beat you, Miss Mayfair?"

Sam looked down, keeping her eyes on the edge of her shirt, mind spinning through words to say. She couldn't simply say she fell from a ladder when they had a rape kit. She looked up and the detective's body language said he could wait all night.

"My boyfriend at the time…he got a little rough."

Detective Eastman released a heavy sigh.

"Okay. What about now? How'd you get those marks?" He motioned to her neck.

She grazed her throat with her fingers. She thought the crap ton of concealer and powder had covered the finger-shaped bruises Eric made that brief time when he was drunk.

"You have a boyfriend now who gets a little rough too?"

Sam glared at the detective.

"Yes, but it's consensual. I enjoy it."

Her words didn't faze Detective Eastman as she'd hoped they would. His face remained calm and controlled.

"Did you enjoy it rough with Isaac Walker?"

His smirk reappeared, this time like a dare.

Her hands found the edge of her tank top, but she fought the urge to twist the cotton around her fingers.

"I wouldn't know."

What about Meredith Lang? Would she know?"

Acid shot up against the roof of Sam's mouth, but she swallowed it back.

"Yes, we know you paid her a visit about Isaac." Detective Eastman leaned forward, his clasped hands on the table. "Guess you don't trust us to handle the investigation, but we know all about Miss Lang and everything that allegedly happened with your stepfather. Trust that we're looking at all possibilities." He nudged the bag with the pocketknife closer to her. "So, perhaps you cared more about his murder than you thought. Would that be a fair statement?"

She decided no answer was better than a lie.

"Listen, I'm sure you've been through a lot in your life, Miss Mayfair." A shadow of genuine concern seemed to cross Detective Eastman's face. "I'm sure you want the truth to be known, for that burden to be lifted from your shoulders."

Sam knew this game, give her the illusion of being on her side, protecting her. She knew he was on no one's side but his own.

"I don't know what you mean, sir."

"Let's be honest here. You know there are inconsistencies in what you and Eric Walker reported to police in 1994, and now we have a knife testing positive for Isaac Walker's blood and his son's fingerprints hidden in a barn loft. Is there anything you'd like to add to that story?"

This wasn't good, not good at all.

"My grandmother—Delia Haylin—she gave a statement to police back then, my mother too. My grandmother witnessed him attacking us, and she confirmed that Isaac was fine when he left. That is the truth."

Detective Eastman paused a moment, looked to be in deep thought.

"You and Eric Walker, you were close?"

"We were."

"And now?"

What could she say? It felt like a trap.

"Your mother says he had an unhealthy attraction to you," the detective said, pressing back into the plastic chair and stretching his hands. "Says he sent you many what she considered *inappropriate* letters. So, how would you describe your relationship with him back then?"

Sam sensed the lie rise to her lips, the one she'd told so many times—to police, to her mom...to herself—but she pushed it down. The lie could never deflate the swell in her chest still there when she thought of Eric. She knew he would always have a hold on her, whether she wanted him to or not.

"We were...he was more to me than anyone. I loved him. Not like a stepbrother."

She'd never said it aloud to anyone and it made her lightheaded and terrified to admit it.

The detective was quiet for a long time like he was waiting for her to say more.

"Did you have a sexual relationship with Eric Walker?"

She paused a few beats. "Yes."

"And your stepfather knew about this?"

She nodded.

Detective Eastman let out a long exhale, nodding a little in return, and she knew what he was thinking.

"Eric didn't kill Isaac." Saying it, she hoped in her gut it was true.

"That's for us to determine, Miss Mayfair, but you telling the truth helps us with that. There's something else we're trying to figure out and maybe you can assist me with it."

His blue eyes didn't waver from her face.

"Your hospital records from Norman Regional showed you were pregnant. What happened to the child?"

The air left the room. An invisible vacuum sucked and sucked, and Sam couldn't breathe, cold running down the back of her neck to her spine, tightening every muscle in her. She had to get out of the room, get away from this detective staring her down. Now.

"I want to speak to my lawyer."

Chapter 31: Eric, 2009

Eric scanned the downtown police station parking lot again for Dan Baumann, Sam's lawyer friend she asked him to call for her. The evening was balmy, but he felt chilled when he imagined the questions detectives were asking Sam.

Five more minutes passed, and he saw a black BMW pull into the lot. A tall man got out of the car and made his way directly to the entrance until Eric stopped him.

"Are you Dan?"

"Yes. You're Eric?"

"Yeah."

Dan's dark hair was damp as if he'd just taken a shower, his moss-colored eyes analyzing Eric with cool detachment. "Never thought Sam would end up here," Dan said, "and I've seen her in some interesting places. And positions."

Dan smiled at him, but it wasn't in a friendly way, and Eric decided the guy was an asshole.

They entered the station, and Dan pointed to a small waiting area.

"Wait over there. I've got to speak with the officers holding Sam."

Eric wondered if Detective Eastman was there and how Sam would handle his questions. He searched out a tucked away spot in the waiting area and sat on the most uncomfortable plastic chair imaginable.

Every time he checked his phone, only a minute or two had passed. A couple of officers walked by carrying take-out, the smell of something deep-fried making Eric's stomach grumble. He longed for his beef and cheese burrito abandoned in the microwave as soon as Sam called. He didn't want to read too much into her calling him and not Dan or her mom, but he couldn't help it.

Dan reappeared fifteen minutes later and they both followed an officer back to the tiny room where Sam waited. She stood up as soon as she saw them and embraced Dan hard. She gave Eric a guarded hug. She had goosebumps from the overly air-conditioned room, and Eric tried to rub some warmth into her arms before he realized how intimate the act looked. He doubted Dan knew anything about their relationship and he really didn't care if the man did, but Sam widened her eyes, so Eric stopped.

Sam sat while Dan and Eric remained standing near the closed door.

"You do remember I'm an estate lawyer, right?" Dan said.

"An estate lawyer?" Eric shot Sam a look he hoped conveyed a big *what the fuck.*

Sam ignored him. "Are they releasing me or not?"

Dan gave Eric that artic stare again. "Do you want *him* present?"

Him? Like Eric was some nosey bystander and not the person who called him.

"Yes," she said, "you can tell him anything you'd tell me."

It annoyed Eric how grateful he was for those words.

"They're releasing you, but if this goes any deeper you might need a criminal defense attorney." Dan sat next to her. "I don't think they suspect you in your stepfather's murder," he said, giving Eric a sidelong glance, "but don't talk to anyone without a lawyer present, okay?"Another hour later, officers signed Sam out of custody. She needed a ride back since she didn't have her car at the station. Eric replayed their fight earlier and fully expected her to go with Dan, but she asked Eric to drive her home.

They didn't speak much on the way back, something he was fine with. He didn't know what to say to her, how to take away the shame he made her feel before. Why did he have to use the word sick to describe what she liked in bed? He didn't really think that was sick, but what his father did to her? There was no other word for it.

They pulled up to Sam's house, and he walked her to her front door like they were ending a first date and about to have an awkward kiss. She looked tired and he wasn't sure if the police gave her anything to eat at the station, which made him regret not asking if she wanted to stop by someplace for food.

She dug in her purse for her keys and turned to him, her face troubled.

"Do you want to come inside?"

He did, but something pulled and nagged in him. His lie to her.

"Earlier, you asked me what I really did that night I said I was at the Stewart farm."

Sam unlocked the door as if she hadn't heard him, and Eric held her shoulders, turning her to face him. As soon as he looked into her eyes, he almost changed his mind about telling her. She looked like she was on the verge of breaking.

"I did go for a walk that night, but I went to the barn first." He could almost smell the chimney smoke as he had walked away from the farmhouse, could hear the crunch of the snow under his shoes. He'd gone to Maddie's empty stall, the place where his father had done terrible things to Sam, things Eric hadn't stopped. He stood there for a long time, letting the emptiness in his chest expand and engulf him. "I got some rope, and I went out into the woods." He swallowed over the swell in his throat. "I tied the rope to a tree limb...put the other end around my neck." He could still feel the coarseness of the rope rubbing his skin raw as he climbed higher up in the tree.

Sam took his hand, but his mind was in the woods, crouched on a tree limb with a rope around his neck, the winter air sucking any reservations out of him.

"I was going to do it," he said.

Sam held his hand so tight, her nails dug into his palm.

193

"Then I felt my mom." He smiled as the memory surged through him. The pain, the grief, the guilt—it all washed away, replaced with the rich spice of Opium. "I know it sounds crazy, but I felt her all around me. I could smell her perfume."

He had felt so weightless, he thought he'd float out of the tree and up to the moon.

"I was so damn happy to feel her. I hadn't felt that happy in a long time, and I forgot why I was in the tree." He blinked and tears fell. He wasn't ashamed for Sam to see them. "My coat got stuck on the branches, so I left it there and came straight back to the house."

"Eric."

Sam had tears in her eyes now too. He held her, his hand rubbing the back of her head. He pulled back from her and squeezed her upper arms.

"Before, what I said, I didn't mean it, Sam. It's different with us. I don't want to change you and I don't think you're sick. I just don't know how to be what you need."

She stared at him for a long time. Then she pressed against him, hand low on his back. "Do you want me to show you?"

He nodded.

They entered her house, and she led Eric to her bedroom, her hand never leaving his. She told him everything she wanted him to do to her, and how to cause her pain without harming her. She said this as she slowly undressed. She told him to do whatever else he wanted and not to ask her permission first; she would let him know if it was too much by saying a simple word they would both remember.

"What if you can't speak?" he asked.

"If you're choking me, I'll pinch your wrist like this. Just never press here." She motioned to her windpipe.

He soaked in her every curve as he started to undress too.

She took his hand, stopping him from unbuckling his belt. "Not yet." She paused, her eyes downcast. "Please."

She kept her eyes down, not looking at him directly, and he knew why she wanted him to stay dressed for now. She needed to feel vulnerable. She was giving him permission to overpower her.

He grabbed the back of her head, pulled her hair hard as he kissed her. He thought his body would explode from how good she felt against him.

He leaned back from her, heard her breath as rapid as his own. She was waiting. Patient.

He could do this. He wanted to do this for Sam.

He held her by her throat like she taught him, and slapped her hard across the face, the sting racing up his arm. Nothing about it felt natural to him, but it was what she wanted, so he did it again.

Sam closed her eyes and smiled. Then she opened herself to him like she never had before.

Eric glanced at his cellphone resting on Sam's nightstand. It was almost two in the morning, but his mind wasn't tired. Sam was, though. She had fallen asleep almost as soon as they were done.

He got up to the use the bathroom, and she was awake when he returned and stretched out next to her.

"How do you feel?" she asked.

"Strange."

"Strange bad or strange good?"

"Strange good."

It was the truth. At first, it was difficult for him to relax and do what she wanted, but hearing her pleasure transcended his reservations. Now, though, worry disturbed the strong arousal he had felt in giving her what she needed.

"When you were at the station, what did the detectives ask you?"

Sam sighed.

"Why did you hide your knife in the barn?" she said. "Your prints are all over it. And Isaac's blood."

He knew he should've told her the detectives found the knife, not let her get blindsided. "Did you tell them it's mine?"

"I'm not an idiot. Why the barn? Why not any place else in the world?"

"I know, it was stupid. I should've tossed it in the stream. Something."

"No. We should've told them the truth."

It was too late for that. They had been young and afraid of jail, scared the truth would send them there to rot.

"Eric…they know about us."

"How?"

"They just do," she spat out.

He was screwed. Detectives had a weapon and a motive—to protect the person he loved from his father. No way around it now, but he didn't want Sam to worry.

"All right. It's going to be okay. What they have, it's mostly circumstantial."

"They have your fucking knife," she said. "I'd say that's more than circumstantial. Don't you see that?"

Of course he did. Everything led to him. He fit the narrative of the troubled son with the disreputable past, his father the normal, hard-working provider for his family.

"We'll figure it out, okay?"

He pulled her to him, held her tight. He kissed her and her lips tasted like mint, like the lip balm she used instead of lipstick. This beautiful mouth that hurt him earlier, her words coming back to him, broken glass in his stomach: *He understood me in ways you'll never know.* Was it true or was it just her way to stab him where it'd do the most damage? Did it matter now?

He hugged her tighter to him and tried not to think that it could be the last time he'd ever be with her.

Chapter 32: Arrow, 1994

Arrow counted out four twenties, two tens, three fives, and eleven badly crumpled ones. Would it be enough? He stacked them, twenties on top, rolled the money and stuffed the wad into a white tube sock, buried it under the pile of other socks in his top dresser drawer.

Sam's seventeenth birthday was next week, Thanksgiving the week after that, but they would be gone before then. Arrow's chest tightened when he thought about how upset Jeri would be. She probably wouldn't shed a tear for him, but Sam was her only kid. And Grandma Haylin— he didn't know what she would think. He imagined she would she hate him, or maybe she would guess their reason for running away.

Arrow had caught a small cold from splitting firewood after school during the prior week, his nose running and his hands so numb from the icy weather that pain exploded up into his arms every time the axe pierced through to the chopping block. Every job he did for neighbors brought him closer to being able to buy the bus tickets for Dallas and getting away from his father. Sam told him her friend Chrissy agreed to drive them to Oklahoma City. There was no bus service in Blanchard and Chrissy said she'd make the trip so long as they covered gas. He hoped Chrissy wouldn't change her mind because he couldn't think of anyone else to drive them.

Sam, he noticed, had been retreating to her room more. She was always listening to music and rarely came to Arrow's room to talk much less anything else. Not that he wanted to do anything but hold her since her hospital stay. She seemed to avoid that as well. Now since the weather turned colder and Jeri was still working longer hours, Sam usually got rides home with Chrissy, which meant Arrow had to walk home alone. It wasn't far, so he didn't mind, but he missed walking with Sam, talking and laughing with her over dumb stuff that had nothing to do with home or his father. It made him want to hurt his dad even more, to make him give back the old Sam who smiled easily and didn't mope around the house.

Soon it wouldn't matter. They'd be gone, far from Blanchard, and that was more important than hurting his dad.

Arrow counted the days before Sam's birthday. He could maybe get in four more wood splitting jobs before then without his dad getting suspicious of him working so much. That'd be another twenty or thirty dollars plus whatever Sam would get for her birthday, assuming her family gave her money. Tickets to Dallas ran about sixty dollars with tax each plus money for food and money to Chrissy for driving them. Then they'd probably need money for a taxi to get to Sam's aunt's apartment. He counted the money again in his head. They would have to make it enough.

Sam's dog yelped outside. Arrow went to his window. The moon was high, illuminating the fields below. Two glowing red eyes receded into pinpoints as they pulled farther from the house. His father's truck. Probably going to drink and gamble a little in town. *Good.*

Arrow went to Sam's room, opened her door without knocking first, something he never did. She had her headphones on, eyes closed as she lay on her back, her bedspread covering only her legs. She had her nightshirt pushed up and was rubbing circles over her stomach.

His heart somehow moved up into his head, thud-thudding in his ears.

Sam's eyes fluttered open and she saw him. She quickly pulled her shirt back down over the fullness of her belly, but it was too late. He had seen it and he knew what the bump meant.

Sam sat up, her eyes wide and anxious. She yanked off her headphones.

"I was going to tell you when we got to Dallas. I promise I was."

A horrible thought crossed his mind, making his stomach lurch.

"Is it mine?"

Sam jutted her chin at him. "Of course."

She stood up and walked over to him, hands covering her stomach like she was hiding a present. She took his hand and placed it under her nightshirt, over the warm bump. He didn't feel anything, no movement, but he wasn't sure when that was supposed to happen. Her skin was hot, and he pictured a little ball of fire inside her.

"How many—I dunno—months or whatever?"

She smiled. "About twelve weeks or so."

"What is it?"

"Don't know yet. Not until like twenty weeks."

He sat on her bed, feeling like someone had just handed him a hundred pounds of split wood to carry.

"She has eyes and ears and little fingers and toes. She can hear us."

"Thought you didn't know what it is."

Sam sat next to him.

"I don't, but I don't like saying 'it.' Feels like a girl, though."

Why hadn't she told him? He thought about Meredith, seeing the small bump so strange on her tiny, slender body.

"Are you going to keep it?"

She held his hand. "Is that what you want?"

He didn't know what he wanted. He was sixteen with no job or car. He knew babies cost a lot of money.

"What do you want?" he said.

"I don't know yet."

Arrow knew if his father found out Sam wouldn't have any choice.

"You need to leave now," he said.

"What?"

199

He couldn't believe he was saying this to her, but he knew it was right as he thought of it.

"I want you to go to Dallas now, not after your birthday. Take the money I have and get Chrissy to take you this weekend when my dad's doing work at the Hunt farm."

Sam stared at him in disbelief.

"Without you?"

"You'll need the money, and I can come later." But he knew that wouldn't happen. As soon as his dad found out, he'd likely try to beat the information out of him, and he'd watch Arrow's every move after that. He would never lead his father back to Sam.

Tears formed in Sam's eyes.

He touched her belly, moving his hand in a slow circle like Sam had done. She did such a good job hiding the bump from him, from everyone, but then it wasn't that big yet.

"If you don't go now, he'll find out," he said.

A hardness entered Sam's face and she placed her hand over Arrow's.

"I'll go this weekend."

She squeezed his hand hard.

"But not without you."

Chapter 33: Sam, 2009

Sam sat at her desk staring at her computer screen, trying to make sense of the numbers flashing back as hieroglyphics. Katelyn, one of the lazier tellers, stood at Sam's desk, her fingers tap-tapping on the glossy faux Cherrywood until Sam wanted to rip off each one of the young woman's acrylic nails.

She avoided looking at Katelyn so the teller wouldn't see the puffiness of her eyes. After Eric had left her place that morning, there was nothing distracting her from the detective's questions the night before. *What happened to the baby?* She had cried in her bed until she fell asleep. She couldn't talk about it, least of all with that asshole detective, and she knew asking for a lawyer would be the quickest way to stop the questions.

"You have a customer waiting," Katelyn said as if it would push Sam to hurry and approve the large cashier's check.

"Are they here for a loan?"

Sam was no longer a loan assistant after taking the management position, but she was still qualified to handle them when the bank was too backed up, which hadn't happened in a long time.

"Nah, I don't think so."

"Well, did you ask them what they need?"

"No."

Sam took a slow, deep breath. She hated how inept her younger staff could be sometimes, but she was reluctant to fire anyone. The recession had killed enough jobs.

"She looks like a meth-head," Katelyn said, "and she asked for you—doesn't want to see anyone else."

Sam shot up from her desk and peeked down the short hallway at the lobby's sitting area. She saw the back of Meredith Lang's head, the jagged burgundy bob.

Fucking hell.

Katelyn gawked as Sam sped through approving the cashier's check, the fog in her head lifted and the blood in her body boiling with her rapid thoughts. She didn't know why the hell Meredith was at her work, but she knew it wasn't to open a checking account.

The teller took the cashier's check and a minute later Meredith was at Sam's office door.

"Come in and shut the door," Sam said, no smile.

Meredith shut the door and sat across from her. She kept her large messenger bag on her lap, her hands gripping it as if someone planned to snatch it from her. Sam noticed Meredith's legs bounced constantly, the same habit Eric had when he was nervous about something.

"How do you know where I work?"

Meredith wasn't wearing make-up and her face appeared much younger without the heavy eyeliner and lipstick. She almost looked innocent, childlike.

"What did Eric tell you about me and Isaac?" Meredith said.

"Oh, so now you admit you knew him?" Sam leaned back into her chair, arms crossed. "Why are you here?"

"I'm here because some detectives were all over my ass asking questions about Isaac, and I know one of you brought me into this shit."

"What did they ask you?"

Meredith leaned forward, her small chest pressed against her messenger bag.

"I bet you'd like to know."

202

There was so much twitchy energy coming from Meredith, Sam wasn't sure what the woman was capable of doing. It made her want to call the bank's security officer.

"What did Eric tell you?" Meredith asked again.

"He said he lived with you and your mom, Vickie." Sam used the same gentle tone she used with erratic bank customers. "He told me about what Isaac did to you, but he didn't know about Caleb. Why did people say you lost your baby? What happened in Anadarko?"

Meredith looked down at the nameplate on Sam's desk, a haunted expression on her face as she said nothing.

"Is he Isaac's child?"

Meredith's small mouth remained shut tight.

"If Caleb's Isaac's son, Eric deserves to know."

Meredith glared up at Sam. "Eric didn't tell you what happened then."

A sickening dread ran down Sam's back.

"What do you mean?"

Meredith gave a half-grin. "What happened in Anadarko—there were two stories people liked to tell. One where Eric's the hero who saved me, and one where he raped me and tried to kill his father."

Sam thought about Eric's weight on her the night before, how he easily overpowered her, how he could easily overpower her when they were younger too. He didn't want her to see Meredith, but she still didn't know if it was because he had lied about having sex with her and knew Caleb could be his, or if it was because he raped her.

"Which story is true?" Sam asked.

Meredith smiled but that same heavy, haunted look was in her eyes. "I know which one you hope is true. It's all over your face."

"This isn't a fucking game. The police are looking at Eric as a suspect."

"I know."

"Better him than you?"

203

Anxiety flashed in Meredith's eyes, so quick Sam almost didn't see it.

"If Eric did something to help you, you need to tell the police."

"Why?" Meredith asked. "So he'll look good?"

"Yes." Sam didn't mean to yell the word, and she hoped her boss hadn't heard her from his office next door.

"Wow." Meredith smiled again. "You really love him, don't you? How fucking sad."

"Not as sad as you risking your child's life to protect Isaac." Sam remembered the articles she had read fifteen years ago and all the rumors. "Why did you tell the police you were gang raped at a high school party, yet you didn't name a single person or press charges?"

Meredith stood up, slung her bag over her shoulder.

"Are you really going to lecture *me* about protecting my kid? *You*?"

Meredith opened the office door, paused, and turned back around. She shook her head, disgust in her eyes.

"Fucking baby killer."

Meredith left, and Katelyn floated over to Sam's office, her long fake nails clacking against the doorframe.

"What did she just call you?"

Sam couldn't speak, couldn't feel her body. She could only hear Meredith's words playing on repeat: *baby killer, baby killer, baby...*

Chapter 34: Eric, 2009

Eric had started early at his Edmond job, tearing out the old kitchen backsplash and prepping the space for the new tile, his mind constantly slipping back to thoughts of Sam, of the night before in her bed. He surprised himself with how much he enjoyed hearing her pleasure in the pain he inflicted, but he still had trouble not associating what he did with his father. Sam had told him it was different because she consented, she controlled what she wanted, so he tried to see it from her perspective.

He was about to mix the thinset when the homeowners called to say they wanted different tile from what they'd taken two weeks to pick out. The new tile wouldn't arrive until the next day, so he found the late afternoon free to start on his next job. As he left Edmond, he drove north to Guthrie instead of south, knowing it was a bad decision to put off work, but he couldn't stop himself.

Meredith's apartment complex was a small, rundown place near the highway. Eric checked the address he had pulled up on his phone before exiting his truck. He climbed the narrow stairs, past a dirty toddler playing with her even dirtier baby doll. He saw what looked like a bullet hole in one of the windows, another window with taped up plastic tarp in place of glass. If anything, he thought the place was worse than where Vickie lived.

He found Meredith's apartment number but didn't find a doorbell, so he knocked. His heart climbed into his throat and stayed there. He paused a minute and knocked again. No one answered, so he tried to find a gap in the cheap window blinds to get a glimpse inside.

"You looking for Meredith?"

Eric turned to see a woman, rail thin and wearing a strappy tank top, no bra.

The woman scooped up the dirty toddler with one arm, the little girl reaching for her doll that fell to the concrete. Eric picked it up for her. The girl smiled at him and he smiled back.

"Yeah, I am. This is her apartment, right?"

"She left," the woman said.

Eric's stomach was an immediate painful knot.

"Probably went to work early or something. She's always at work."

"But this is her apartment?"

The toddler squirmed in the woman's arms and she let the child slide back down to the concrete. "Yeah, but not for long. She's moving in with her boyfriend, next month I think."

She looked Eric up and down and smirked.

"You her boyfriend too?"

"No."

He stepped around the toddler and made his way down the stairs toward his truck. He glanced at a teenage boy hovering near the back of the parking lot, his thumbs clack-clacking on the cellphone in his hands.

Eric slowed to a stop.

He blinked hard and the teenager was still there, his unruly dark-blond hair curling around his ears, his eyes—Eric's eyes—shifting up from the cellphone to Eric's stunned face.

It was him. Caleb.

"Hey, man, you gotta light? Mine's out." Caleb dug a pack of cigarettes from his baggy jeans.

"Uh, yeah. Sure."

Eric's hands shook as he reached in his back pocket for the Zippo lighter he only owned because a fellow contractor buddy gave it to him, saying, "You never know when some pretty lady might need one." It had worked too. His last girlfriend smoked American Spirits, same as the pack Caleb withdrew from his jeans. Caleb had to have stolen them from Meredith, or maybe her boyfriend.

Eric handed the lighter to the boy. For the briefest second, his hand touched Caleb's in the exchange and he stopped himself from pulling the kid into an embrace.

Caleb held up the silver lighter. "Thanks."

The boy was tall, almost as tall as Eric. He was too thin, though, and his sagging jeans only accentuated this.

Caleb moved over to the side of the apartment building, trying to get out of the wind. He lit the cigarette and flipped the Zippo over and over in his long-fingered hand.

Caleb sucked hard on the cigarette, and Eric thought of Vickie. Did Caleb ever see his grandmother? The thought settled in Eric's stomach, an ice cube chilling him.

The boy coughed, a wet rattling deep from within his chest, and Eric wanted to yank the cigarette from his mouth.

"Maybe you shouldn't be smoking."

Caleb rolled his eyes, huffing out a laugh. "What the fuck is it to you?"

The boy glared at the ground like he was suddenly mad at the parched grass. He coughed again, harsher this time, and spit out phlegm that thudded near Eric's boots.

"Your mom know you smoke?"

Caleb's glare turned on Eric. He took another long drag and blew it in Eric's direction.

"What do you think?"

"You should quit before you get too old to stop. Harder when you're older." That's what Eric had heard, anyway.

The boy continued to burn his way through the cigarette before throwing it on a dry patch of grass. Caleb watched it smoke where it landed, the grass starting to catch. Eric pressed the cherry out with his boot.

Caleb stood there, avoided looking at Eric, almost like he knew this man who looked so much like him wasn't a coincidence. He didn't want to scare Caleb but something too powerful to ignore stirred in him as he watched the boy fiddle with the lighter.

"Do you know who I am?"

Caleb grinned at him, his brown eyes weighted with a loathing Eric felt, a punch to his ribs.

"Sure, I know you. You're the asshole who gave me a light and then preached at me to quit."

He walked past Eric, handing him the lighter.

"Thanks a lot."

Eric held onto Caleb's hand, the lighter hugged between their palms.

The sarcasm on Caleb's face melted into fear and confusion.

"Hey, man…I'm not into gay shit."

He jerked his hand from Eric's.

"What the hell are you doing? You're supposed to come straight home, boy."

Eric and Caleb both turned to see Meredith rushing toward them from the parking lot. Her eyes barely registered Eric's presence but he knew she recognized him when she stiffened.

"Get upstairs and do your homework. Now."

Caleb made his way up the stairs, feet dragging all the way.

"Hurry your ass up. And I swear—I better not catch you smoking again."

Eric was stuck, unable to pry his feet from the ground and move. He couldn't do it, he couldn't see Caleb and Meredith in the same space together. It was all too real and unreal at the same time.

After Caleb entered the apartment, Meredith's full focus turned on Eric, hands on her slight hips. She looked so different from the fifteen-year-old blond girl he remembered. She was still bird-boned, small all over, but her look—clothing and hair—was now dark. He saw she had her nose pierced but wasn't wearing jewelry, so the hole looked like a blemish.

"What are you doing here, Eric?"

He looked up at the apartment unit Caleb just entered. The boy stared out from the pushed down window blinds.

"I think you know why."

"So now you suddenly care about him?"

"Suddenly? You say that like I knew he existed." Eric didn't want to raise his voice, didn't want Caleb to overhear them, but he couldn't help it. "You lied. This whole time."

Meredith glanced up at the window, at Caleb's sullen face. When she gazed back to Eric, her empty expression chilled him.

"Yeah, I lied. I didn't have a choice. Isaac made sure of that."

"What about Vickie?"

"Well, you know how it was with my mom. Isaac's word was gospel."

That was true, but Vickie was no pushover. She got what she wanted from people, one way or another. She would've known she could hold Caleb—the proof of Meredith's rape—over his father, extort money for drugs, whatever she needed so long as she kept his secrets. His father didn't know what went on in Meredith's bedroom, Eric dealing with his grief as he cuddled close with her, the closeness quickly turning to something more one night. It only takes one time, though. If his father knew and thought Caleb was Eric's kid, Vickie would've had nothing to keep the man she loved matted to her messy life.

"Is Caleb my son?"

Meredith's face was blank.

"I have no idea, and I don't care to know."

"I care to know, and I would've cared before if you told me."

"I did what I needed to do, and that included staying the fuck away from you. I guess you did what you needed too. Can't say I blame you."

Eric swallowed, his throat hurt-dry. It wasn't that hot out, but it felt like a hundred degrees. Something tingled deep at the base of his spine, something telling him Meredith didn't believe what she was implying. She had to know Eric didn't kill his father, and he wondered if she knew who did.

"My father—he came back to Anadarko, didn't he? Your mom took him in, and then what? They fought like they always did, and he left?"

Meredith's eyes widened, briefly, and she shook her head.

"You're unbelievable, Eric. You really think she'd take him back after what happened?"

"Yeah. I do, and for a lot less."

Meredith laughed, high and unnatural. "You're probably right. Isaac could've killed me three times over and she would've taken him back, but he didn't come to Anadarko. I'm sure he went to that Les guy's place."

"What makes you say that? Is that what your mom told you to say?"

"Like I listen to anything she says."

She was lying. Her body was still, her arms too stiff at her sides. She was nervous.

"Listen, I need to know the truth. The police—it doesn't look good for me, but I didn't kill him."

"I can't help you."

Meredith repositioned the large bag slung over her shoulder, and Eric touched her forearm. She jerked away like he had stung her.

"Don't touch me."

"I'm sorry—look, I just need to know. Anything you can remember, anything at all about where he went after he left Blanchard."

Meredith's face was grim as she stared at him. Her eyes darted up to her apartment window and back to Eric.

"I told you everything I know."

Eric knew he wouldn't get anything further from Meredith. Maybe she didn't want the police looking too closely at her. Sam was right; Meredith had every reason to kill his father and he would've deserved it.

"Meredith—I know it means nothing now, but I'm sorry for—for what happened. And I'd like to know Caleb, if you'll let me."

Meredith looked down at the gravel parking lot where they stood. She sighed, her lips curled slightly, not in a smile, not even close.

"You're right. It means nothing now." She turned and started toward the metal stairs. Once she climbed to the second floor, she looked back at Eric. "Don't come back here again."

Meredith entered the apartment and Caleb disappeared from the window.

Eric stood there a few moments, wanting to leave but unable to draw his eyes away from the window. He felt gutted, completely empty.

Finally, he got in his truck and sped off, not sure where the hell he was going and not caring what happened. He pulled onto the highway. Sixty, seventy, eighty miles per hour—he kept going, hoping his head would clear with the recklessness but it didn't.

He didn't deserve to know Caleb, he knew it. He didn't deserve anything good, not after what he let happen to Meredith, not after Sam. He should've killed his father—in Anadarko, he should've, but then Caleb wouldn't be alive, and Eric never would've moved to Blanchard. He never would've met Sam and everything that happened, all the horrible things that happened to her...

He should've jumped from the tree that night in the woods.

Red and blue lights flashed behind him. Eric ignored them until a siren blared. The unmarked vehicle pulled him over on the left shoulder. He looked in his side mirror and saw the officer approaching his truck was a short redhead. Speeding—that's it. He was just getting pulled over for speeding.

"I'm sorry, ma'am," Eric said as soon as he rolled down his window, his ID and insurance ready to hand to the officer. "I was in a hurry for work, and—"

"Eric Walker, I'm going to need you to step out of your vehicle."

He felt his driver's license and insurance card in his hand go slick with sweat.

"Why?"

"Step out of your vehicle, nice and slow. I'm not going to ask you again."

He saw she had her hand hovering near her gun holster. Then he glanced at the police vehicle to see another officer, a male, on stand-by next to the passenger door. Eric shut off his engine, making sure the female cop saw his hands at all times, and exited his truck.

"Turn around. Put your hands behind your back."

Eric did, and she pressed him into his truck as she placed handcuffs on him.

"You're under arrest for the murder of Isaac Walker. You have the right to remain silent. Anything you say can and will be used against you..."

Eric couldn't wrap his mind around what was happening. This had to be a nightmare; it wasn't real. He expected it but it felt like he was watching it happen to someone else.

The metal cuffs cut into his wrists as the officer thrust him toward the back of the Charger. She roughly pushed his head down and he fell into the backseat, smacking his head against the opposite passenger window. He searched the officer's face for any sign of consideration while she quickly buckled his seatbelt, but her face was severe and all business. The male cop climbed into the front passenger seat and reported the "suspect is detained" to the station on a two-way radio, the static buzz in between responses surreal to Eric.

This was happening. This was really fucking happening. They knew where he was and they waited, hunted him down fast and efficient, and he had no defense but the truth wrapped in layers upon layers of his own lies.

Chapter 35: Sam, 1994

Three more days. Sam sat on the couch, watching some new TV sitcom about six stupid New Yorkers, all apparently in love with each other. Her mama giggled next to her and asked, "You think I should get my hair cut like her?"

Sam watched her mama's face light up with more laughter as Grandma Haylin smirked at the TV screen, answered a blunt "no," and excused herself to her bedroom.

Three more days until Saturday, and Sam and Arrow would be gone. The thought sent a sick chill down her back. She'd be away from Isaac, the baby safe, but she wouldn't see her family.

The show cut to commercial, and Sam touched her mama's hand. "Mama?"

Her mama turned toward her and took her hand.

"Yeah, honey?"

The expectation on her mama's face felt like a force pulling her closer. It was as if her mama knew there was something itching to escape, a confession that would absolve Sam if she could only get it out. She just had to open her lips and tell the truth, tell everything.

"Mama, I…"

Her mama wrapped her other hand over Sam's, gave her squeeze.

"What is it, Sammy?"

She thought of when Isaac had exploded at dinner, beating Arrow into a corner. Her mama stood there and did nothing. If she said anything now, she couldn't imagine what Isaac would do to Arrow, to her mama or grandma.

"Mama…you should cut your hair however you want." Sam smiled. "That hairstyle would look really pretty on you."

Her mama wrapped a throw blanket around them both and swayed Sam gently side-to-side with her on the couch. "I might just do it then. Not sure what Isaac would think of it, but then it's my hair, right?"

"Right."

She noticed her mama used Isaac's name around her now, didn't force daddy on her like before.

They watched the rest of the show together and the show after that, waiting for Isaac and Arrow to come back from repairing a busted water pipe at the Woodland farm. It seemed like Isaac had been over at the Woodland farm a lot, helping the elderly couple with various chores when he wasn't working side jobs. He rarely touched her since that time at the pond, and part of her wondered if he somehow knew about her pregnancy and no longer wanted her. She knew she should be happy about it, but she wasn't. Yet another reason why she needed to leave. Arrow was right. She must be brainwashed or something.

It was after nine-thirty when Isaac and Arrow banged their way through the kitchen door, waking her mama who had fallen asleep on Sam's shoulder.

The two entered the living room, and her mama, still groggy, stood up to greet Isaac with a peck on his cheek. They exchanged words she couldn't hear as Arrow, covered in smears of mud, smiled at Sam from behind Isaac's back.

"Go clean up and getcher homework done," Isaac said, and Arrow scurried up the stairs to his room.

"I'm turning in. Been too long of a day." Her mama kissed Isaac on the lips and turned to blow a kiss to Sam. "Don't stay up too late, honey."

Isaac went to the kitchen and came back to the dark living room with a bottle of Miller High Life. Sam remembered a time when her mama refused to keep any alcohol in the house, but it wasn't long after Isaac and Arrow moved in that beer became their third staple along with bread and cheese.

Isaac sat next to Sam, stealing some of the blanket covering her legs. She watched him drink down the entire beer in two long pulls.

"Whatcha watching?" he said.

Sam had switched the station to MTV's *Real World* once her mama fell asleep.

"Just some dumb show."

"So dumb you like watching it?"

"Yeah."

"What does that make you then?"

He winked at her and she smiled a little.

"You get the pipe fixed?"

His grin withered and he appeared tired, more tired than she'd ever seen him, the lines around his eyes highlighted by the TV's glowing screen.

"Yeah, we got it fixed. A shame they don't have any kids to help them."

"They did have a kid—Davey. He died from cancer."

Isaac shook his head. "Not right. People oughta have someone to take care of them when they can't do for themselves."

"Yeah, it's sad."

Sam absently caressed the bump under her shirt until she saw Isaac staring at her. She pulled the blanket up to her neck, making sure every part of her was covered.

"You cold?" he said, almost a whisper.

She nodded.

He scooted closer to her, tucked his hands under the blanket. He reached under her shirt, found her breasts, grasped one and squeezed hard until she whimpered. The pain rushed hot and fluid to her head, between her legs.

"Warmer?"

She nodded again and he gave her a quick kiss.

She needed to do something to stop him, she needed to get up and go to her room. She knew the look in his eyes—he wouldn't stop himself and they were in the open, not her room, not the barn or out in the woods. Someone could see them.

She wore loose pajama pants, which he ordered her to remove. She paused, frozen under the blanket.

"You want the barn?" he said, lips against her ear.

She slowly shook her head. Nothing good happened in the barn. No pleasure with pain there. At least on the couch, she knew he wouldn't do anything to make her want to cry out too loud and wake her mama.

She pulled down her pajama pants and his hand was on her. She didn't know how long it went on—thirty minutes, an hour—but she couldn't take it anymore. She struggled to get out of his grasp; she felt like she'd split open again at any second.

She was going to scream, she had to scream, and her mama would see, and she'd know. Everyone would know what Sam let him do.

Isaac kissed her, so hard his teeth clinked her own, his hand more forceful on her until her release ruptured from her in waves she thought would splinter her body. She buried her face in his shoulder to muffle her cries.

She heard a floorboard creak and her heart stopped. She searched for the sound's source. Arrow stood just outside of the living room. She wasn't sure how long he had been there, watching them, but his face was a death mask, drained of any emotion, good or bad. Isaac didn't seem to notice her distraction and moved her hand on him under the blanket until he groaned with that suppressed animal sound telling her he was through. Slowly, Arrow turned and went back upstairs.

Done with her, Isaac left for the downstairs bathroom and then, Sam guessed, to his bedroom to sleep next to her mama. He didn't come back to the living room. Just left her alone, like always.

She went to her bedroom first, changed into new pajama bottoms since Isaac had soiled the other pair. Arrow's bedroom light was off, but she doubted he was asleep, so she entered his room.

He was lying on his side, away from her.

"This whole time," he said, his lowered voice cracking with anger, "I really thought you hated it."

She didn't know what to say to Arrow. She did hate it, but then a part of her sometimes liked it. She liked that she didn't have to think with Isaac because he forced pain into her, made her want it as much as the pleasure. She hated herself for liking it with him, but she hated Isaac more for taking what he knew she liked and turning it against her.

"I do hate it," she said, pushing back tears.

"That's not what it looked like."

She sat on Arrow's bed and tried to touch his arm, but he shot up from the bed so fast it made her flinch out of fear he'd hit her.

"I hope you do leave," he said, "but it won't be with my money and it won't be with me."

He had worked so hard, she knew it—so hard earning money for them to leave, for her to be safe.

"What about our baby?"

"Have it, get rid of it—I don't care. Probably his anyway."

Get rid of it? The words repeated in her head, boiling hotter and hotter.

"Fuck you!"

She didn't care if anyone heard her scream at him. She ran to her room, placed the latch on her hook lock. She sat on the edge of her bed, rocking the rage out of her body.

She had a little money but not enough to get to her Aunt Shelley in Dallas. She'd get there, though, and Arrow could die by Isaac's hands for all she cared.

Chapter 36: Arrow, 1994

All throughout the night, Arrow fought with his nightmares, ones filled with blood and knives, hateful laughter and red hair…a gun fired but missing its target. He awoke to the Thursday morning in a daze until he remembered the night before. That wasn't a nightmare. It had been real, witnessing Sam and his father together, seeing how much she enjoyed it with him.

Maybe Meredith enjoyed it too—until she didn't anymore, until his father took too much from her and left her with nothing. Just abandoned her in Anadarko with her mother, the one person Meredith probably hated more than Arrow for not helping her. He couldn't imagine his dad leaving Sam alone, though, even with the baby growing inside her. People could get rid of babies. He had told Sam he didn't care if she got rid of it, but he didn't mean it.

He finished dressing for school and slipped on his tennis shoes. He didn't hear Sam getting ready next door, though. No loud music playing like usual as she put on a little makeup, no drumming down the hallway to get to the bathroom before him.

He went to her bedroom, opened her door. She wasn't there.

He followed the scent of frying bacon to the kitchen. His father sat at the table, reading the local paper and waiting for Jeri to serve him breakfast.

Jeri eyed Arrow and said, "Go tell Sammy to hurry up and get down here."

A sinking dread settled in his stomach. He went back upstairs, passing Sam's room and going directly to his room, to his sock drawer. He didn't have to dig for the tube sock at the back of the drawer. It lay on top, a flat, curvy snake, empty of the lump of rolled money he'd saved.

He knew right then Sam was gone.

He made his way back to the kitchen as slow as possible.

His father looked up from the paper in his hands, saw Arrow's expression.

"Where's Sam?"

Arrow directed his answer to Jeri, not his dad. "She's not here."

"What do you mean she's not here?" Jeri said, turning off the burner on the gas stove.

"She's not upstairs."

Grandma Haylin, up unusually early, sat at the table, chewing on a piece of crispy bacon and looking apprehensive.

"I think she said something last night about having to get to school early to finish a project," Grandma Haylin said.

Arrow could've come up with a better lie in his sleep. His father wasn't buying it either, but Jeri's face softened.

"That girl." Jeri sat at the table, grabbed a couple of slices of bacon for herself. "You could learn a thing or two from her, Arrow. That's why she's on honor roll."

Arrow had lost any appetite the minute he saw his sock drawer, but he knew his father would be more suspicious about Sam if he didn't eat breakfast. So, he sat and gobbled down two eggs, buttered toast, and three slices of bacon with his tall glass of milk.

He ran back up to his room to get his backpack. Grandma Haylin caught him before he ran down the stairs.

"Where's Sammy?" she hissed, clutching his arm. "I know you know, and I just need to know if she's run away or not."

"I don't know, ma'am."

Grandma Haylin puckered her lips, thinking. "Will she be safe, where she went?"

He wanted to look away from her pleading gaze, but he couldn't. He could only assume Sam took the money and was on her way to Oklahoma City and then to Dallas.

"Yeah. She'll be safe."

She held onto his arm. "You didn't hurt her, did you? It's not you she's running away from?"

"No, ma'am."

Grandma Haylin glanced down, her face looking as if she had finally determined something.

"It was him, wasn't it?" she asked.

Arrow paused a beat. His breakfast felt like it was about to come up, but he needed Grandma Haylin to know the truth.

"Yeah. It was him."

"I knew it." She shook her head.

She moved her hand up to his shoulder and squeezed hard.

"Get yourself to school before you're late."

Arrow knew she wouldn't say anything to his father, but he also knew it wouldn't matter. His dad knew Sam was gone and that Arrow probably knew where she went.

He had to run most of the way to school and he was still five minutes late. At the end of the day when the bell rang, signaling the end of his last period, he didn't look forward to walking home and seeing his father.

Chrissy, Sam's friend, was waiting for him outside of the school. She used to be weird around him, but she had warmed up to him some. Now, though, she didn't look at all happy to see him.

She shoved a note into his hand as she said, "Hope you're happy." Then she ran to her car parked in the circle drive.

He opened the note and read Sam's messy scrawl: *You won't have to worry about me or "it" anymore.*

Chapter 37: Eric, 2009

The police cruiser pulled into the Oklahoma County Jail, and Eric thought for sure he would throw up. He had heard plenty from the news about the corruptness and inhumane treatment in the county jail and now he'd get to witness it firsthand.

The two officers took him inside. It took a couple of hours before they officially booked him, every fingerprint taken along with his mug shot. He kept his eyes down as they walked him from place to place, not wanting to make eye contact with anyone.

They moved him to a holding cell and left him there for a long time. Hours—he wasn't sure. They didn't give him any food or drink and his mouth was dry, his stomach twisted in painful cramps from hunger. The holding cell contained a dozen other men. It was hot, it stank of urine and body odor that threatened Eric's stomach to rise up, and there was one metal toilet out in the open just in case that happened. There was no place to sit but for the crappy benches lining the walls. He sat, unable to get his bad leg comfortable. He saw a pay phone along one wall, but a man was using it, alternating between sobbing and yelling into the receiver.

He didn't know how, but he had fallen asleep slumped on the bench until someone nudged him awake. It was a male officer. Eric stood up, his left leg numb and throbbing with pain, and the officer cuffed his wrists in front of him.

The cop walked him through several hallways to a small room in another part of the building. Detective Eastman was waiting for Eric in the room. His face was grave, his usual smile replaced with a tense jaw brushed with gray stubble.

Eric sat at the cheap table across from the detective.

"Would you like some coffee?" The detective motioned to his own. "Too damn early for me to be up."

Eric was thirsty enough to drink his own piss.

"Yeah. Thanks."

Detective Eastman raised his coffee, nodded his head to a surveillance camera secured to the wall behind Eric.

"Black, right?"

Eric nodded, surprised the detective remembered. A moment later, an officer entered the room and set a small Styrofoam cup in front of Eric before stepping back out. He had to be careful with his hands cuffed, but he took a cautious sip, his gratitude for the coffee bordering on obscene.

"We'll get you something to eat soon enough," Detective Eastman said.

Eric set the cup down and held the detective's stare.

"I shouldn't be here. This is a mistake. I didn't kill my father."

"Yeah, we've been through all that." The detective crossed his arms and gave Eric a tiny shrug. "The thing is Vickie Lang contacted us— said you paid her a little visit in Anadarko, threatened to hurt her if she kept talking to us about you."

There was only one reason why Vickie would tell lies about him. She knew what happened to his father, she knew who killed him. He didn't know if she was protecting herself or Meredith, though. Hell, maybe she was protecting someone Eric didn't know. Some drug dealer of Vickie's who didn't like Isaac coming around. It could be anyone, but he figured it was a man from the description of his father's head wound. That would take force, and Vickie and Meredith were both small women.

"We know you went to see her, Mr. Walker." The detective paused, assessing Eric slumped in the chair, tired and starving. "Whatever threat you made didn't faze her, I'm afraid."

Eric never had to clench his mouth shut so much as he did right then. He knew whatever he said was being recorded, would be picked over until it fit whatever narrative the police had invented.

Detective Eastman took a slow sip of coffee and leaned forward.

"You know, I've been struggling trying to piece everything together. This hasn't been an easy case for many reasons. Frankly, your father was one sick piece of shit, and if I weren't in this job and on this case, I wouldn't blink twice at someone killing him."

The detective leaned back in the chair and Eric noticed the man's white button-up shirt wasn't pressed and starched like usual. There was a deep crease just below Detective Eastman's neck and Eric couldn't look away from it.

"But, I am on this case and I have a responsibility to see it through, to look at all the pieces, even the ones that don't seem to make sense at first. You see, I knew your father's murder had something to do with your stepsister and Meredith Lang, but I just couldn't get that last piece to fit and give me the full picture. But, it all came down to an unborn baby."

Color drained from Eric's face. He felt it as his body went cold, every inch of it.

"Yeah, we know about Samantha Mayfair's pregnancy. I can only guess the child was yours, though it's hard to say isn't it? Your father, it seems, took a liking to many girls, girls like Miss Mayfair and Miss Lang."

Eric sucked in his bottom lip, his teeth pressed hard enough to draw blood.

"Looks like your father found out about the pregnancy and your sexual relationship with Miss Mayfair. He attacks you two—that I believe. But then you stab him multiple times, maybe hit him on the head with something heavy—a hammer? He dies and Miss Mayfair helps cover for you by helping you bury the body and driving your father's Chevy into a pond. Is that how it went?"

It was like Eric was back at the Blanchard farm, stuck in the middle of some wild bramble lining the woods, thorns pricking him and no easy way out. The truth was right there, edging its way to his lips, but he couldn't say it.

"No. That's not what happened."

Detective Eastman glanced up at the surveillance camera and gave a short, strong nod. A minute or two later an officer brought in a familiar box, perfect for holding shoes but Eric knew what it really held.

Detective Eastman took the plastic-wrapped pocketknife out and set it right next to Eric's cuffed hands resting on the table. His pinkie finger brushed the plastic and he pulled his hands back.

He looked down at the knife, the opalescent handle shimmering under the florescent lights. His head felt like a thousand-pound weight when he lifted it again.

"Jeri Walker informed us that this knife belongs to you. Your father gave it to you on your sixteenth birthday. She remembered that very clearly. Guess her memory is better than Miss Mayfair's. Or yours." Detective Eastman loudly exhaled. "So, Mr. Walker, would you like to explain why you lied about owning this knife, how your father's blood got on it, and how it made its way to a barn loft on the property where you used to live?"

For a long time, Eric couldn't exhale, his lungs expanded, full to bursting with words, words that could easily damn him, but they were the truth, or at least enough of the truth to be believable.

"I—I was scared."

"Scared of what?"

"That police wouldn't believe me."

"Believe what?"

"What I did."

"And what did you do?"

"I hid the knife. I was just a kid. I didn't know what to do, so I hid it."

He should've thrown it in the river, but he had kept it, the only real gift his father had ever given him.

"So, you stabbed your father?"

Eric swallowed.

"He was on Sam, he was going to kill her, so I had to—I had to do it."

"Why do you think he was going to kill her, Mr. Walker?"

Eric sat, face numb, the scene of that day playing out in front of him, a projector beaming images on a waving white bedsheet—his father pinning Sam, Eric's knife burning hot in his back pocket—all flashing and gone within seconds.

"Mr. Walker, we have record of Miss Mayfair's pregnancy but no record of the birth. What happened to the child?"

Eric didn't know what happened, not exactly, but he knew enough to tell Detective Eastman. Only Sam knew the entire horrible answer.

Eric cradled his head, pressed his palms into his closed eyes to stop the tears from finding their way out of him.

"Mr. Walker?"

He couldn't do this. Not this, not now, not ever. It would seal everything for him, for Sam, nail in coffin.

"Mr. Walker, I need you to answer the question."

Eric lifted his head, stared at the detective straight on.

"I want to make a call."

Chapter 38: Sam, 1994

Sam watched Aunt Shelley finish the last of her large glass of red wine. She gazed down at her own untouched wine, which her aunt had procured for her because she was friends with the server at the small bistro-style restaurant. The two women had laughed and chatted as if Sam were invisible. When the server finally stepped away and silence settled over the two-top, Sam knew her aunt was digging for something to say to her. Sam bit the

Sam had arrived at her aunt's apartment late that Thursday night three days before, tired and hungry, her face stained from dried tears and eyeliner. Sam said little on the drive to Oklahoma City while Chrissy yapped the entire way about how it was a huge mistake to run away, how Sam needed to talk to her mama about her pregnancy and Isaac and figure things out.

Her mama. Her mama was as blind to everything going on as Betty Woodland had become after her stroke. Isaac could say anything, and her mama would believe him.

On the bus ride to Dallas, Sam had found a seat in the back, away from anyone else. A middle-aged brunette woman with kind eyes kept glancing over at her, her mouth parted as if she wanted to say something. Even after Sam tried to muffle her crying with her backpack, the woman remained silent, but her eyes seemed to ask, "Are you okay?"

No, she wasn't okay.

Aunt Shelley took ten minutes to answer the security guard in the apartment building, the guard holding the phone and eyeing Sam like she was a homeless kid trying to break into the place. Her aunt didn't come down to get her but gave permission for Sam to come up to her thirteenth-floor unit. Sam said nothing when Aunt Shelley opened the door to let her inside. Her aunt had taken one long, sleepy look at her and hugged her, her frosted hair teased into platinum cotton candy tickling Sam's cheek.

Aunt Shelley, sitting across from Sam, tapped her empty wine glass and ordered another pinot noir while flashing a quivering smile.

"It's really not a big deal, sweetie," she said, patting Sam's hand. "I had two in college. Super-fast—you don't feel a thing."

Sam wasn't dumb. She knew an abortion would hurt. She tried not to think about what her baby would feel.

"We'll go there after our lunch, okay? It'll be fine."

"Okay."

Sam lifted the glass of wine. She and Chrissy drank a little peach schnapps at Ricky Stover's house once, but they didn't have enough to get drunk or even buzzed much. She drained the glass, the wine burning down her throat, and her aunt laughed.

"You want another? Jenny's cool."

Sam found the server, Jenny, flirting with the bartender on the other side of the restaurant. Jenny caught her eye and swooped back over with more wine for her aunt.

"Sammy?"

"No, thanks."

All the wine in the world wouldn't numb her enough to make her forget what she was going to do.

Aunt Shelley nodded and nursed her wine.

That was one thing Sam loved about her aunt; she didn't ask too many questions. She didn't ask who the father was or how Sam had sex under her mama's roof without getting caught. She didn't mention calling Sam's mama either, although Sam knew her mama was close with Aunt Shelley, her younger sister and only sibling. Aunt Shelley also didn't ask what Sam planned to do after the abortion. Maybe she assumed Sam would go back to Oklahoma, which was the last place she wanted to go. She imagined staying in Dallas, living with her aunt and getting a job to save money for her own place. She didn't want to think about what Arrow was doing back in Blanchard or how upset her mama probably was by now.

They drove over to the Planned Parenthood after their lunch. The place was a small, red brick single-story building that looked nothing like a medical facility. At first, Sam thought they went to the wrong place until she saw the waiting room. It was filled with women, mostly young, some white, some black. Aunt Shelley filled out forms next to her, mumbling under her breath, and they waited two hours before someone called and ushered them to an exam room.

An older nurse took Sam's vitals, asking questions she wasn't sure how to answer until she was asked to verify her date of birth. Aunt Shelley made a sudden coughing sound as Sam answered. The nurse looked at the form on the clipboard and back to Sam, a frown etched on her face.

"Someone will be in to see you shortly," the nurse said.

As soon as the woman left the exam room, Aunt Shelley gawked at Sam.

"Why did you tell her your birth date?"

Her heart raced. "Because she asked."

Her aunt groaned. "Didn't you hear me in the waiting room? I told you what date of birth to say—the one I wrote down."

Before Sam could ask why, a woman entered the room. She introduced herself not as a doctor but as a PA, which Sam wasn't sure what that meant.

The PA looked at Aunt Shelley and asked to speak to Sam alone. Sam knew from her aunt's thin-lipped scowl, so much like her mama's, that she had done something wrong. She wanted to hop down from the exam table and run out of the room with her aunt.

"Samantha," the PA said once they were alone, "how old are you?"

She thought about lying but she didn't hear what date her aunt had told her. She recalled her aunt saying something in the waiting room, but she had been too absorbed with watching the nervous faces of the other young women, including one girl whose belly looked ready to burst open.

"I'll be seventeen next week."

The PA nodded her head with the answer and circled something on the chart she held.

"Samantha, I know you came here for abortion services, but there's a problem with that."

She guessed as much when the nurse hadn't told her to get undressed and into an exam gown.

"First, you would need parental consent for an abortion to even be considered at your age. The other problem is that we don't perform those services here. We only refer patients to other places. Do you understand what I'm saying?"

She nodded, realizing tears were streaming down her face. The PA was telling her she was stuck.

She stopped listening as the woman rambled on about referring her to a good prenatal doctor and, if she wanted, adoption services.

Aunt Shelley drove them back to her apartment, her BMW pushing over sixty on the city streets every time she blasted Sam with a barrage of comments.

"You should've listened to me. Now what are you going to do? You'll have to drop out of school. How will you go to college? How will you get a good job?"

Sam took a hot shower in her aunt's huge bathroom, the black and white tiles as cold and sterile as the rest of the place. She ran her hand over her growing stomach.

Eos.

That was the name she had for the baby. The Greek goddess of the dawn, of new beginnings. But the baby wasn't a new beginning. She was the end of everything, but Sam now knew for sure she wouldn't be able to go through with an abortion even if she were allowed the choice. It'd be like killing a part of herself, a part of Arrow. She held the tears in, forced them down into the space she usually saved for Isaac, the space that felt pain but allowed it to wash over her and away.

She got out of the shower, wrapped a towel around her body and hair. She walked into the red, black, and white living room, her aunt sitting on the blood-red couch talking on the phone. She saw Sam and stopped talking.

"I have to go. I'll call you back."

"Who was that?"

Aunt Shelley smiled, nervousness flitting across her face. "No one, sweetie."

Sam's heart fell to her toes.

She knew. Her aunt had called her mama, and now everyone would know, everyone would find out about the baby and make her come back home, back to Isaac. She couldn't hold the tears in again. She had cried too much over the last few days, so they were always right there, ready to surface.

Aunt Shelley didn't move from the couch, the phone sitting on her lap.

"Sweetie…I'm sorry. You really should've listened to me."

Chapter 39: Sam, 2009

For the longest time, Sam couldn't move her body as she sat in her office. She pressed her eyes with her palms, the words Meredith said to her still repeating: *Fucking baby killer.*

Tears didn't come. Instead, pain settled deep and heavy in her chest, steadily simmering and growing into fury.

Her workday finally ended. The sun's light was waning by time she pulled up to her house. Her grass was getting too high, she noticed as she walked up to her front porch. A child's singsong voice whizzed by her. She turned her head and saw a neighbor's kid riding by on his bike.

Then she lost it. She stood outside the front of her house sobbing, the rage and pain so great she thought she might die from it.

When the neighbor kid rode by again, slower, Sam forced herself back to a somewhat calmer state. She walked her long driveway to the back of the house, opened her garage door and went straight for the lawnmower.

Thirty minutes later, she was drenched in drying sweat, the grass bagged in plastic and sitting next to the curb, but the rage was still humming in her body.

She went inside, fed Zeus, and took a quick shower, trying to talk herself out of doing what she knew she'd do the moment Meredith left her work. She told herself she should call Eric, let him know what Meredith said to her. He'd talk her out of going to Meredith's place, which was exactly why she didn't call him.

Keys in hand, she grabbed her purse and cellphone and was about to sweep out the door when Zeus ran up to her, whimpering. She paused, looking down at his sad dog eyes, and scooped him up.

She drove straight to Guthrie. It wasn't until she pulled into the gravel parking lot of the apartment complex that a rush of anxiety made her question her decision. The front windows to Meredith's apartment unit glowed a soft yellow. Someone was home, for sure.

Sam reached for her cellphone, ready to shoot Eric a quick text letting him know where she was just in case things turned bad. She cussed when she saw her phone was dead. She lowered her car windows an inch, allowing a balmy breeze to flow in, and left Zeus in the car.

She walked up the stairs to the unit, pushed down her nerves. She knocked on the door hard enough to redden her knuckles, trying to resurrect the fury she felt an hour before.

The door cracked open a few inches, revealing a tall teenage boy, the wavy mop of honey-blond hair Sam wanted to reach out and touch, it was so much like Eric's at that age.

"Caleb?"

He opened the door wider, leaning against the doorframe, casual but his stance told Sam he was wary.

"Yeah. What do you want?"

Any anger she had summoned evaporated. "Is your mother home?"

"She's out."

"With her boyfriend?"

"Maybe."

"Could I come inside and wait for her?"

Caleb scanned her again, his sullen expression eerily like Eric's.

"You're the lady my mom yelled at that one day."

Sam heard Zeus's whine spiked with an occasional yip coming from the parking lot. She knew she should leave, but there was too much she needed to ask Meredith.

"Yeah, I'm helping your mom with a bank loan. It's very important

232

that I speak with her as soon as she gets back." She quickly added, "The number she listed on her application isn't working so I can't call her."

The boy smirked at her, completely altering his demeanor to one reminding her too much of Isaac—charming, dangerous. It was like Caleb was suddenly interested in her.

"You're not a very good liar."

He opened the door fully and left the entryway, which Sam took to mean "come inside." She shut the door and followed Caleb into a tiny living room with ancient green carpet. The furniture, a sagging beige couch and recliner, looked to be from Goodwill but the apartment was clean and a lot tidier than Sam expected from the place's exterior.

Caleb sat in the center of the couch, a video game controller next to him. She saw he had a game paused, the onslaught of attacking zombies frozen on the TV screen. The fact he didn't immediately start playing again made her feel stupidly flattered.

She sat on the recliner, and Caleb seemed disappointed she didn't sit next to him.

"So, what do you really want with my mom?" Caleb said after an awkward minute.

"That's for your mom and me to discuss."

He sank back into the couch, his expression so dramatic and sour Sam had to stop herself from smiling. She didn't miss being a teenager, everything seeming so life or death. Her breath caught in her throat a second. Sometimes it really was life or death at that age.

"Does my mom owe you money? Is that why you're here?"

"Does she owe a lot of people money?"

Caleb appeared to roll the question around.

"Sometimes." He looked away from her, staring at the game controller.

Sam felt sorry for the kid. Eric had told her about Vickie's addiction issues, and it sounded like she had passed on the same issues to Meredith.

"No, your mom doesn't owe me money."

Caleb started to say something and paused. "Sometimes she has to borrow so she can go to the clinic for her medicine. She gets sick without it."

Sounded like Meredith was going to a methadone clinic. At least she was trying to stay sober.

"She works a lot, though. She always pays people back."

Sam noticed his vintage-looking Misfits band T-shirt, which swallowed him. He seemed so thin, but she thought that of a lot of teens; she had a strong urge to feed him.

"Can't your father help your mom out with money?" Sam hated to ask it, but she wanted to see what the boy knew. Maybe Meredith had told him his father's name.

The look Caleb shot Sam said the answer was obvious. "I don't have a father."

"I'm sure you do." Where her own father was now, dead or alive, she didn't know, and she told herself she didn't care.

Caleb reached for the video game controller, and Sam knew she was losing him. His thumb hovered over a button, ready to shoot zombies again.

"What if I know who your father is?" she said, watching his face change from apathy to intense alertness.

He set the controller down, not taking his eyes off her.

"Are you fucking with me?"

She already regretted the words making his eyes drill into her. "No. I'm not."

What the hell was she doing? She didn't know for sure who this kid's dad was—Isaac or Eric—and here she was stirring hope in him that could just as quickly be dashed to nothing.

"Caleb, I—I don't know for sure."

The boy cradled his head in his hands. "You're totally fucking with me, aren't you?"

"I promise, I'm not. My friend—" Friend? She didn't know what to call him, but friend was far from accurate. "Eric Walker is his name, and I think he might be related to you."

Caleb looked up at her. "Is that why you came here? Was it really to see me? To tell me this?"

She was already forgetting her true reason for coming, to interrogate Meredith. The mixed pain and hope in Caleb's face struck her like a slap.

She stood up, slung her purse over her shoulder. "Yes. It's why I came, but don't tell your mom."

"Who are you?"

She was surprised he hadn't asked her before. She heard him ask her again while she made a dash to the front door. She opened the door and slammed into solid muscle.

"What the fuck?" A tall man with a shaved head and two full sleeves of tattoos sidled past Sam into the apartment and got a good look at her. "Who the fuck are you and why the fuck are you here?"

"I—" Sam's eyes darted to the doorway and there stood Meredith, holding an ice cream sundae in one hand, her cellphone in the other.

Caleb, mouth agape, crept up near his mother, whose face was slack with shock.

Meredith quickly composed herself and flashed a smile as huge and fake as her waitress smile. She turned to the man, keeping the smile.

"It's—it's okay, babe. I know her." She motioned for Sam to follow her outside. Caleb trailed them, but Meredith pushed the sundae into his hands and nudged him back toward the apartment, saying, "Extra nuts—like you wanted." She added a playful but strained, "Get inside, boy, before it melts all over," after he failed to move.

Meredith shut the front door and followed Sam to the parking lot, her smile dropped along the way.

"You better have a damn good reason to be here."

235

The anger and pain from earlier in the evening came back to Sam. "What did Isaac tell you about me, about what happened in Blanchard?"

Meredith's face was stone.

"'Baby killer.'" Sam whispered, fighting the cries wanting to escape again, surfacing in her voice. "Did Isaac tell you that? Did he?"

Meredith's hard expression fell. "No."

"Why did you say it?"

Her eyes were wide and searching Sam's face and then the ground.

"I overheard them—Isaac and my mom—talking...about you."

Sam pushed the tears down, swallowed them, but her heart continued to hammer in her ears. "Your mom? What did they say about me?"

"How you weren't pregnant anymore," Meredith said and paused. "And Isaac told me before why you went to Dallas, so I—I thought..."

Sam felt like she was choking on her own breath.

"He told you about me?"

Meredith looked as sick as Sam felt.

Sam wanted to collapse right there on the gravel. Vickie knew what happened in Blanchard, what Isaac did, but Meredith didn't. If she had, she wouldn't have said those hateful words to Sam. There was something else there, fuzzy, out of focus, but so close she almost caught a glimpse of it. Vickie knew, but what else did she know? She for sure saw Isaac sometime before the attack and his escape. Maybe she knew how he ended up dead and buried near the Blanchard farm.

"So, you didn't do it—when you went to Dallas?" Meredith asked.

Sam glared at her.

"No. I didn't. Not that it matters."

Meredith looked down at the ground again.

"But you don't care what really happened, do you?"

Meredith crossed her arms and glanced up at Caleb, who was watching them from the window.

"You didn't want to be dragged into this mess, right?" Sam said.

"Don't want police knocking on your door and looking too closely at your past, especially with you being clean now."

Meredith smirked, but she couldn't hide the alarm in her eyes.

"Are you fucking threatening me?"

"Do I have to?"

"I didn't have anything to do with Isaac's murder."

"I know." Sam wiped away her tears.

"Then what do you want from me?"

"The truth. What happened in Anadarko, with your mom and Isaac, with Eric?"

Meredith stood completely still, her expression blank. Then she slowly nodded to herself as if she were having a conversation in her head.

"Fine," she finally said after a long pause. "But you may not want to know it once you hear it."

Chapter 40: Arrow, 1994

Arrow tried to ignore the yelling downstairs, but it was impossible. He didn't know Grandma Haylin could get so loud, her voice effectively drowning out Jeri. They were fighting over Jeri sending his dad to get Sam from Dallas. The fighting started the night before when Sam's aunt called and continued well after his dad left early the following morning.

It was past dinnertime, his dad gone much longer than even Jeri could explain. Yet, she tried. Maybe they had a flat tire. Maybe they saw how late it was and stopped for a bite to eat. Maybe they couldn't find a phone to call from.

Arrow had skipped school that morning. He ate breakfast and left the house as usual, but he went to Sam's favorite spot in the woods, the place where she loved to sketch. By lunchtime, the November cold had sunk into his bones, making him shiver all the way back to the house where he snuck inside, stopping by the kitchen for a sandwich before hiding in his room. It wasn't long before Jeri and Grandma Haylin started back up with the shouting.

The noise downstairs ceased, too sudden, he thought, to be natural, which made him leave his room to see what was going on. Maybe Sam was back. He went to the kitchen and saw Jeri slumped on the linoleum floor, crying, Grandma Haylin on the floor with her, rocking her like she was a child.

"Is she okay?" Arrow said.

Jeri jolted up from the floor and went straight for Arrow. She slapped him hard across the face, knocking him back into the refrigerator.

"You did it to her!" Jeri screamed, shaking him as he tried to get out of her arms. "I know you did, I know you did it!"

"Enough, Jeri Anne!"

Grandma Haylin pulled Jeri back, freeing Arrow from his stepmom's grip.

"He didn't do anything, you stupid, blind fool," Grandma Haylin roared, and Jeri ran from the kitchen. A moment later, a bedroom door slammed shut.

Arrow held his cheek, felt the raised skin from where Jeri slapped him. Grandma Haylin took him by the shoulders, looked up into his shocked face. She shook her head.

"I told you I didn't wanna raise no great-grandbabies."

Her disappointment went through him, and he wanted to tell her they had used the condoms she gave him but it had been too late. It didn't matter now. It wouldn't change her or Jeri's feelings about him. It wouldn't change the fact that his father probably already had a plan to get rid of the pregnancy and Arrow would have no way to stop it. He didn't want to think about why his dad and Sam were delayed in getting back.

Grandma Haylin touched his sore cheek, her labor-worn fingers softer than they appeared.

"You better sleep with one eye open and that pocketknife of yours under your pillow, boy. She's not going to protect you and, frankly, she might be the one you should be afraid of right now."

She left him in the kitchen. He stood there next to the refrigerator for a long time, his will to move gone. He looked down at his left forearm, at the bruises his father made when he tried to squeeze out the truth of where Sam went, but Arrow took the pain, swore he didn't know. His father then said if anything happened to Sam, it was Arrow's fault.

He was right. It would be his fault, just like Meredith.

239

Arrow opened the refrigerator door and, without pause, took one of his father's beers. He twisted the top off and chugged it. He had never tasted beer before, never had friends brazen enough to steal any and he had been afraid to steal from his father until now. It wasn't as bad as he expected. He took another from the fridge and drank it down as fast as the first. He decided to stop after the fourth. He buried the empty bottles in the trashcan outside and climbed the stairs to his room, his stomach empty but for the alcohol sloshing around.

Arrow fell onto his bed and closed his eyes. His head swam from the beers, a gentle lapping that would rise into sharp, spinning terror until he opened his eyes again. Soon, he could keep his eyes shut without the lurching fear. His breath became an even stream, flowing in and out of him, drifting him into sleep.

"Eric," a voice whispered right into his ear.

He opened his eyes, but no one was there. Lightning flashed outside and a crack of thunder followed. He looked around his room again and sat up. This wasn't his room. It was Meredith's bedroom, the room in the crappy Anadarko rental house. He could make out her Color Me Badd poster taped to the wall.

A hollow scream tumbled into the room. Arrow got out of the bed and opened the bedroom door. Down the longest hallway he'd ever seen, he saw a dim light. He didn't want to walk to it, but his legs moved him against his will. The light grew closer, the screaming louder, and then he saw her: Meredith on the square dining table in the kitchen. Something was holding her arms down, but he didn't see anything or anyone around her. She was naked from the waist down, her legs spread obscenely wide, the pregnant swell of her stomach as pale as the light shining down on her. Thick blood streaked her thighs—from what, he wasn't sure, but he was terrified for her. Meredith gazed at him, quiet and calm now.

You have to kill her, she spoke to his mind, her lips motionless.

240

He looked around the kitchen. "Who?"

She turned her eyes down between her legs. *Her.*

There was a dark, spectral mass—a dense evil—prying something from inside Meredith and more blood poured from her, her face sweaty and white with pain. Then he saw another shadowy mass, much taller and larger, holding Meredith's arms down.

Get the gun, Eric.

The gun. His father's gun in the closet. He ran down the hallway seeming to go on forever and he found the master bedroom. He opened the closet and a mountain of handguns toppled onto him. Arrow picked one up and quickly realized it was plastic. He picked up another and another—all of them plastic toy guns. His heart pounded in his ears as Meredith's shrieks started again. He had to get to her. His eyes caught a glint of metal that disappeared into the pile. He dug for it, scraping his hands raw until he secured something cold, heavy, and solid—the real gun. He ran back down the hallway, heavy rain pelting the roof, wind rattling the windows and more thunder, louder, louder, crashing and rumbling from all around him.

He made it to the kitchen, panting, and aimed the gun for the dark creatures, but they were gone. Meredith was gone too. There was a pool of dark blood on the dining table, some of it smeared into a frown. Vickie was there, her body turned away from him as she rinsed a bloodied sponge out in the sink, her red hair burning in the light.

She came over to him, holding the sponge.

"You look just like your daddy." She grinned. "You're just like him, aren't you?"

"No, I'm not," he forced through gritted teeth.

"You sure love to watch us." She laughed. "Yes, you certainly do, don't you?"

"I don't."

"What would your mother think of you? Her perverted son."

"I'm not perverted."

"Look what you did." Vickie pointed to the bloody table. "You killed it."

"You did it, you did it! I saw you!"

"You're too late." Vickie moved closer to him. "It's done and it's all your fault. Everything's your fault."

Arrow aimed for Vickie's chest and pulled the trigger—BAM! BAM! She cackled at the bloody holes. She fingered them, her long nails disappearing into the ripped flesh, and laughed more when blood trickled out of her.

"Just die!" he screamed. "I hate you! I hate you!"

"Arrow."

"I hate you!"

"Arrow!"

"I hate you!"

"Arrow, wake up!"

He gasped, eyes wide.

"It's okay. You were having a dream."

Sam.

His lips paralyzed, Arrow reached for her to see if she was real. She was, and he clutched onto her, feeling as if he were about to be swept away again by his panic.

"Jesus Christ, you're okay." Sam untangled herself from his arms and stood up from his bed. "You almost woke up the whole house. It was just a stupid dream."

No, it was a nightmare, only it was real. His failure, the police arriving at Vickie's place after the missed shots fired…Meredith taken to the hospital and Arrow taken into custody. And the baby dead.

Sam crept over to his doorway, her figure a blur of shadow bleeding into the dark.

Panic rose in him again as he remembered the horrible words he had said to her before she ran away, that she should get rid of it.

"You didn't do it, did you? I want you to keep her."

He wanted to touch her stomach, to feel the bump and know their baby was safe.

Sam turned around, her shadow figure still.

"No. I didn't do it." He heard her inhale, hold it for a moment, and release. "When we were driving back from Dallas, your dad…he asked me if…I—I told him the baby's his."

Arrow sat up in the bed.

"Why?"

"Because he—because I had to."

Arrow lay back down on his pillow and closed his eyes tight.

"Arrow?"

He swallowed over the lump rising, cutting off his ability to speak again.

"Eric?"

He pictured a scene from one of his favorite horror films, the part when the young, pretty girl circles through the dark woods and goes back into the house she had escaped from two scenes prior, the monster not far behind her. Only, this time, she doesn't come back out.

Chapter 41: Sam, 1994

Sam refused to look at her mama. Instead, she played with the tie string of her blue exam gown, waiting for the ultrasound technician to enter the room. She heard her mama pick up another magazine and turn the pages rough enough to rip them.

Déjà vu. She imagined that's what her mama was feeling, but it wasn't her this time, waiting in an exam room with Grandma Haylin perched ready to berate her for her poor decisions. This exam had been her mama's idea anyway, taking her to what Grandma Haylin called the "lady parts doctor."

Sam was the one who had a right to be angry. She still couldn't believe her mama sent Isaac to pick her up. She knew Aunt Shelley noticed her fear upon seeing Isaac at the door, yet she let her go with him. Sam knew it was her own fault for not telling her aunt about him. She had come close to saying his name when she first arrived at her aunt's place. Her aunt even asked her if she had been raped, but she didn't know how to answer. She always imagined rape as something brutal with the victim clearly not wanting sex and screaming no the entire time. Sam had never said no to Isaac. She didn't even fight him.

On the long drive back to Blanchard, Sam asked Isaac to stop twice so she could throw up. She knew it wasn't from being pregnant. It was nerves. She knew something bad would happen with him.

He had pulled off the highway into a tiny Texas town. He drove up to an old motel and told her to stay inside the truck. Just when she got up enough courage to run somewhere, anywhere to seek help, he was back with a room key.

The room smelled of mildew. Dust suspended in bands of afternoon light slipped through the broken window blinds and splashed across the peeling nicotine-stained wallpaper—brown and orange flowers against what might've been a cream backdrop once upon a time. He told her to undress, which she did. She wasn't sure what he would do, but every muscle in her tensed.

She had never seen him fully naked before then, and definitely not in the middle of the day. It was unnerving how quick her body responded to the sight.

He took her to the firm bed and lay next to her, his leg hairs tickling her. Then he stroked her, tenderly, from her head to her feet, but he touched no part giving her any relief. He didn't hurt her; no biting, no drawing blood from scratching, no pinching or hitting with a belt. Nothing. No words.

It was the worst punishment he could inflict.

He had kept her in that state of need for almost four hours, his restraint amazing her, and then he stopped, got dressed without a word.

She didn't ask permission. She ran to the bathroom and locked it. She removed one of her stud earrings, paused, and shoved the fake gold post under her middle fingernail. A dark dot of blood appeared under her nail as she leaned against the bathroom vanity and touched between her legs, pleasure mixing with the pain radiating up her hand.

They ate in silence at a nearby crappy diner before driving back home.

The florescent highway lights made Isaac's face appear jaundiced while he drove.

"It's mine," he had stated after he glanced at her.

"Yes." She knew Arrow would be dead with any other answer.

"We'll have to take you outta school soon. And get you to a doctor—find a family for it."

Adoption? She was sure Isaac would beat the baby out of her or find some other way to get rid of it. He could've done anything to her, and no one would know. He could've killed her, told her family she ran away during a pit stop, but he didn't.

Isaac had reached for her hand, held it the last forty minutes to Blanchard.

"I won't let anything happen to you," he told her.

"Samantha Mayfair?"

Sam let go of her exam gown, the fabric twisted into a stiff blue point.

The ultrasound technician introduced herself as she tugged on a pair of gloves, the latex snap-snapping on her wrists. She pushed up Sam's gown and squeezed a cold gel onto her stomach. Her mama stayed seated near the exam bed at first, but she arose as soon as the technician let Sam hear the heartbeat. One hundred and sixty beats per minute. Her mama clasped her hand, held it to her chest so that Sam heard the thrumming from the baby's heart monitor and felt her mama's quickened heartbeat at the same time.

"Oh," the technician blurted in delight. "Today's your birthday?"

"Yeah."

"Well, happy birthday, Samantha. You've got a healthy baby."

Chapter 42: Eric, 2009

Second-degree murder. Minimum ten years in the state penitentiary. It's what the Blanchard police hoped to charge Eric with, but the prosecutor was apparently sitting on it. That's what the state appointed defense attorney had told Eric during their brief meeting.

Eric sat on the hard lower bunk bed in his jail cell, staring at the stainless steel toilet/sink combination against the wall, his gut rumbling, threatening to release the only meal he'd been offered since his arrest: a bologna sandwich, no cheese or condiments, and a bruised apple. His cellmate, a black man who didn't look older than nineteen, slid down from the upper bunk. It was impossible for both to be up and moving around at the same time. The man went to the toilet and stared at it, the look on his face a strange mixture of defeat and defiance. Eric looked away when the man pulled down his pants and squatted.

Eric made three calls early that morning. One was to Sam's lawyer friend, Dan, who reminded him he wasn't a criminal defense lawyer and referred him to an attorney Eric knew he couldn't afford, which meant he was stuck with the state's attorney. He made his second call to Sam, whose phone went directly to voicemail. The third call he made sucked everything left in him to dial it.

He had been positive Jeri wouldn't accept the collect call, but she did, and he spent the first minute thanking her. She had to guess he had no one else to go to other than Sam, but that wasn't why he called her. He asked Jeri to see him, told her he had some important things to tell her. When she told him to tell her over the phone, he said he wanted to do it in person. Reluctantly, she agreed to drive to Oklahoma City, but she made sure to tell him how difficult it was for her to drive longer distances.

Jeri arrived at the jail that morning. A detention officer escorted Eric to the visitation room to wait, sat him down facing a thick Plexiglas wall and told him he had fifteen minutes, all of it monitored.

Eric hadn't seen Jeri in almost fifteen years. Even now, he couldn't help but think of Jeri as his stepmom. After his father ran off, Jeri still treated Eric like he was her responsibility, making him get up for school every morning and harping on him to do his daily chores and homework. Over time, though, he noticed a shift in her when she looked at him. It was like she couldn't stand to see him. Soon after he was released from the hospital, he snuck into the master bedroom when Jeri was at work. He opened the top dresser drawer where his father had kept photos of Eric with his mom and keepsakes Eric had made him when he was little. His heart felt like it dropped out of his body when he saw the drawer completely cleaned out. He looked everywhere and saw she had removed every last trace of his father from the house.

Eventually, Jeri stopped caring if he did chores or went to school. She also didn't seem to care when he stopped coming home and started hanging out with the Stewart boys, who were known to drink and get into mischief.

There was no comfort at the farmhouse, not with Jeri, Grandma Haylin, or with Sam, who had fallen under a depression she wrapped tight around her like a cocoon. He was almost relieved when Jeri placed him into foster care less than three months after his father left. Vickie, his only traceable family member, had been serving time for drug possession. Foster care with strangers wasn't as bad as he thought it'd be, though. The family he lived with the longest—eight months—was strict and religious, but they had been kind before he turned eighteen and aged out of the system.

He thought of the letters he had written to Sam, one per week for the first year he was in foster care—all opened and read by Jeri, he was sure, before she got rid of them. Jeri knew his deepest thoughts from those letters, his confessions of loving her daughter, but she didn't know everything. Eric never wrote about what happened with Sam. He never wrote about his father at all, as if Sam would forget if Eric didn't mention him.

Motion caught Eric's attention; he looked up to see an officer directing Jeri to the stool attached to the wall on the opposite side of the Plexiglas. Besides her ivory complexion, Sam looked nothing like the short, graying blonde across from Eric. Jeri wore an ankle-length, green summer dress with a long-sleeved white cardigan she wrapped tightly across her chest after she sat. She looked shaken, like she'd passed a ghost right before visiting him. Eric pointed to the phone on the wall next to him and Jeri picked up the one on her side.

"Thank you for coming," Eric said, unsure of how to start.

Jeri pursed her lips.

"Have you spoken with Sam?" He still hadn't heard from her, and he couldn't see her ignoring the message he left for her saying he was under custody.

"She hasn't answered her phone," she said. "I've tried all morning."

A trickle of fear went through him. "You try her work?"

"Of course. Several times."

"I've tried to call her too."

Jeri widened her eyes at him.

"Why did you want me to come here, Eric? To help you?"

Eric looked down at his hands, at his thumb kneading the other, his knee bouncing.

"No."

He knew she couldn't help him. No one could help him.

Jeri looked at the phone in her hand as if a bug had crawled out of it.

"Then why?"

Eric pulled himself up, holding Jeri's gaze.

"You know I didn't do this. I should have killed him a thousand times to protect Sam, but I didn't."

Jeri stared at him, her arms relaxing a little from holding her sweater closed. He saw the painful-looking swollen knots that were her fingers now from her lupus, and he wanted to reach through the Plexiglas to button her sweater for her.

"Is that what you wanted to tell me? That you didn't kill him?"

He shook his head.

"Then what?"

Eric's mouth was too dry. His eyes weren't, and he held them open until he was sure he wouldn't lose it in front of Jeri.

"I wanted to say I'm sorry for not telling you what he was doing to Sam, for not stopping him."

Jeri just sat there, lips tight.

"And I'm sorry I wasn't the one who killed him."

Jeri's mouth went slack for a moment before she tightened up again.

"Sam wasn't the only one," Jeri said, her eyes avoiding him.

Meredith wasn't the first, and Eric knew Sam wouldn't have been the last. They had been his father's favorites, though, maybe because they were smart and strong-willed. His father used to say it was a lot more fun breaking in a wild horse than one that gave in at the first tug.

"No, she wasn't the only one."

"And you could've stopped it." Jeri looked him in the eyes, her resentment shooting into him, reigniting his own.

"You could've stopped him too." He watched the pain shadow across her face. "I saw him abuse her while you were asleep in the next room."

Jeri put the phone down, her face pale. After a minute, she gathered herself and held up the phone again.

"I was a kid, Jeri. Yes, I should've said something, but you had to know something was happening. After the hospital, after she went to Dallas."

Jeri slowly shook her head. Then she buckled in her seat, the phone in her lap. Her crying echoed through Eric's receiver. He wanted to hold her, to tell her there was nothing they could do now.

Jeri pulled herself together and took up the phone again.

"My sister…Shelley told me something was off when he got Sam. She said…" Jeri paused, collecting herself. "She said Sam didn't want to leave with him."

Her voice broke off on the last words, and Eric's heart was an iron weight in his chest. He never knew what happened when his father picked Sam up in Dallas, but he knew whatever happened wasn't good. He thought about when she was in the hospital, the rip his father made in her flesh, and he was glad he didn't have much food in his stomach.

The hospital had failed Sam, and Jeri failed her too. So many people failed her, not just Eric.

He thought of everything he had told police those years ago, about Meredith and his father, and a realization hit him: people had failed Eric too.

The officer hovering at the end of the visitation room walked over to them, warned Eric they only had a few minutes left. Jeri wiped tears from her face with her cardigan's sleeve.

"The baby—it was yours?"

Eric nodded, unable to say it aloud.

"I'm glad," she said with a sad smile.

He wasn't sure what else to say to her. There was too much he wanted to say, but he knew everything was being recorded.

"I know you didn't kill him, Eric."

Hearing her say it lifted some of the weight from his chest, but not all of it.

"Why did you send me to foster care?" he asked.

She twisted her cardigan sleeve, the same habit he noticed in Sam.

"You look too much like him."

Disappointment fell over him at being right. She had changed the course of his life all because she didn't want to look at him.

"Why did you throw away his things?"

He used to wonder why his father never came back for his clothing. He had left everything at the farmhouse, even his favorite boots.

Jeri appeared lost in her thoughts for a moment.

"I didn't want Sam to see them."

"He never tried to come back for them?"

It was quick, but Eric caught fear flash in Jeri's eyes.

"No. He couldn't have come back anyway." She released a long exhale. "We got a protective order against him before you were released from the hospital."

He never knew this. He wondered if Sam did.

"Eric, I let the detectives know about something, something I think you should know."

His chest tightened. He knew she was going to talk about his pocketknife, how she pretty much put a target on his back.

"Your father was sending your Aunt Vickie money. I never knew why, and he didn't know that I knew. It wasn't a lot, not enough for me to notice at first until he was giving her more, but I thought the detectives should know."

His father gave Vickie money? More like Vickie extorting money to keep his secrets. He thought of all the side work his father did in Blanchard, even after Sam's hospital bills were paid off. More and more, he could see Vickie doing something to his father, although killing him would mean killing her cash cow. Besides, she had loved him, was obsessed with him. All her talk to the detectives, feeding them lies about Eric and what happened in Anadarko, he wasn't sure if it was to lead them away from herself because of what she and his father did to Meredith or because she killed him. He tried, but he couldn't get the pieces to fit the narrative of her murdering him.

"I'll do what I can," Jeri said. "I don't have much money, but you need a better lawyer."

"I don't want your money."

"Just take it."

He didn't understand why she would want to help him. She didn't owe him anything.

"Thank you."

She gave him a little nod and hung up the phone.

Chapter 43: Arrow, 1994

Arrow let Lisa Doss lace her fingers with his as they exited the high school, their backpacks low and heavy against their backs. He didn't want to hold her hand or watch her glossy pink lips as she talked to him in bursts of giggles at his locker each day, but he needed her attention like it was oxygen allowing him to breathe and move when all he wanted to do sometimes was go to sleep and never wake up.

"Is that your stepsister?" Lisa asked him as they walked along the road toward downtown.

The wind blew through him, his coat barely keeping him warm. Sam walked in their direction, some distance off. She wore a long, chunky purple sweater over black leggings with her black combat boots laced up to her mid-calf and her backpack slung over her right shoulder. He didn't see how she was warm enough with the December weather getting colder by the day. He pictured the baby in her shivering, and irritation at Sam rubbed raw in him.

"Yeah, that's her."

"She's pretty."

Sam was out of breath when she caught up to them. "Hey. I waited for you by your locker."

"Sorry," he said. "We're going to the drug store for drinks."

Sam glanced at his grip on Lisa's hand, her jaw tight. "You promised to help me clean the stalls."

Arrow looked at Lisa, who squeezed his hand as if to say, "It's fine."

Lisa smiled at him. "I'll see you later."

He didn't know why Sam suddenly wanted to be around him. He hadn't promised to help her with her chores.

The two weeks since she had been back from Dallas, he felt like he had a splinter in his chest and it was slowly festering. She was hanging out with his father more after school, and that's what confused him the most. She told him she was only talking to his dad so he'd side with her when her mom brought up the issue of school. Sam's stomach had grown more noticeable but not enough for her to leave school yet. Every time Jeri mentioned it, Sam would fight her on it until his father stepped in, ending any discussion. Sam would stay in school through the rest of the fall semester. Period. The only battle Jeri won was not allowing Sam to come with them to church. Sam seemed fine with this. Maybe she was happy because it gave her all Sunday morning free with his dad while Arrow sat on a pew, imagining, in turns, Sam naked and flushed with pleasure with his father and then her thighs dripping with thick, neon-red blood, like a horror film come to life.

Sam nudged Arrow's arm as Lisa walked away from them. "Do you like that girl? You know she's Pastor Doss's daughter." She smirked. "She'd probably fuck a picture of Jesus before she'd do anything with you."

Arrow ignored her and hurried into the nearby woods, the shortcut to the house. He heard Sam behind him, rustling the brown needles and dead leaves from the surrounding pine and elm. She made a sudden pained grunt and he turned to see her holding her abdomen. He ran to her.

"What is it—the baby?"

She inhaled sharply, her face pale. "Yeah. I think so." She took a few shallow breaths as he held her arm. "It's better now."

"Are you sure?"

She furrowed her brows, fear still in her eyes. "Yeah."

He took her backpack and led her over to a tree stump so she could rest.

After a few moments, color returned to her face. "Your dad's been giving me this stuff to chew to help with the nausea." She laughed a little. "I think it's making it worse—tastes like shit."

Arrow gaped at her, unable to speak.

"What?" she said.

He wanted to slap her, but he satisfied himself with kicking the stump she sat on. She jumped up, surprised.

"What's your problem?"

"You!" he screamed. "You're my problem. You fuck my dad and now you're letting him poison you so you'll lose the baby."

A sharp laugh escaped Sam as she pulled a plastic sandwich bag from her backpack. She threw it at him, and he caught it. He didn't know what it was—greenish seeds of some sort.

"It's fennel seed, you asshole. You chew it and swallow the juices. You really think I'd take something without knowing what it is first?"

Arrow held onto the bag of fennel as he sat on the tree stump, his anger subsiding. It didn't make any sense to him, his father helping Sam. After what happened in Anadarko, he couldn't see his father protecting Sam or the baby. Why her and not Meredith? His heart sank with his guess; his father never loved Meredith. He used her, but he never loved her.

"He loves you," he mumbled.

"What?"

He looked up at her as he stretched the plastic baggie with his finger. She gazed down at him, her hardened face faltering, softening the longer she watched him.

He stood up and handed her the bag of seeds. "Nothing."

"Eric." She took his icy hand, her own so cold it somehow neutralized into odd warmth. "Nothing's happened with him since…

since before Dallas. I promise."

Resentment rose in him again. "But you want something to happen. That's why you're always around him, flirting with him."

Fire lit in Sam's eyes. "So, I can't talk without it being flirting?"

Had he been wrong? Hadn't he seen her smiling with his dad as if nothing had happened? He knew he had. Yet, he wanted to believe her.

"You're the one who's been avoiding me," she said. "Do you like that Lisa girl now?"

"No."

"You were holding her hand. Do you want to kiss her?"

How many times had Sam kissed his dad? The thought made him want to throw Sam down on the leaf-strewn ground and tear off all her clothes.

He roughly pulled her to him and kissed her. He tried to block the thought of her kissing his father on the couch those weeks ago, her cries of pleasure, her hand moving on him under the blanket, but he couldn't, and he found himself grabbing her hair and pulling hard, wanting to hurt her for hurting him. He thought he saw a flicker of a grin from Sam, and something deep in him held in place by the thinnest thread snapped.

Using his full weight, he pushed Sam to the ground. She gave him no struggle as he lifted her long sweater up and over her face, locking her arms above her head in the heavy knit fabric. She looked curious, maybe a little excited, until he bit her as hard as he could on the side of her neck. He didn't know why he did it, but it felt good, right even.

Her mouth parted in panic. Her fear drugged him, made him feel powerful and outside of his body as he loosened his jeans and tugged down her leggings, felt her air-chilled thighs as he kept her arms pinned with his other hand.

She didn't say "no" or he didn't want to hear her if she did, but he saw her face, the terrible calm acceptance on it. Her face—it was Meredith's face with his father, and it said, "Go ahead. I can't stop you."

He released Sam's arms and scooted away from her, the fog in his brain lifted, leaving a chunk of lead in his stomach in its absence. He slowly stood and pulled up his jeans, his hands shaking as he did it. Sam remained on the ground, unable or unwilling to move, he wasn't sure which. He tugged her sweater back down and helped her to stand. She drew her leggings up and brushed the dead leaves and pine needles from her backside, not making eye contact with him.

"Why did you stop?" she finally asked.

Because for a moment he was his father, and he could never take it back. Sam even asking the question made his stomach hurt further. Right then, he felt like he didn't know her at all. He wasn't sure if he knew himself.

Hands still shaking, he grazed Sam's neck near the place where he had bitten her. Blood had dried some, but he saw the skin around the bite was turning purplish-red. He needed to clean it for her before it became infected.

"You okay?"

She nodded, but her face was flushed crimson and she kept nodding. He watched as sobs consumed her body with terrifying swiftness. He had never seen her cry like this.

He held her tight, stroking her hair. His fingers snagged on a frail leaf and he slid it from her chestnut strands.

He didn't know what to say to her to make it better. There was nothing, and he wanted more than anything to be normal like Lisa Doss and for Sam to be a normal girl, but he knew it would never be that way for them.

He hugged Sam tighter and felt her bump press into his lower stomach and a surge of apprehension speared through him. He placed his hand on the front of her belly and let the vibrations of her crying transfer into him, thinking maybe if he held her close enough he could extract some of her pain. Then he remembered he had tried the same thing with his mom when she was in the hospital for the last time, her gaunt body in a fetal position, and she had told him, smiling, "I'm ready to go home."

So that's where he took Sam.

Chapter 44: Sam, 1994

Sam stared and squinted at her reflection in the bathroom mirror until her vision blurred and the bite Arrow had made on her neck turned into a fuzzy dark spot that could've been a bug bite or a birthmark instead. He had cleaned it for her once they made it home, his hands trembling as he soaked a cotton ball in iodine and dabbed it to her broken skin.

Her face was still puffy from crying, something she couldn't hide from Isaac or her mama. Arrow had apologized several times on the way home until she wanted to punch him. He didn't understand at all. She didn't cry because of what he almost did. She cried because he stopped, just like Isaac had stopped coming to her since she got back from Dallas. When Arrow bit her, it was like he was accepting what she liked, what she needed. She felt overcome by him but loved at the same time. Something she never experienced with Isaac.

But, she had been wrong. Arrow wasn't accepting her; she saw it on his face. Now, she didn't feel anything but shame. Maybe Arrow and Isaac were tired of her since she was pregnant, or maybe it didn't matter that she was pregnant. Maybe everyone would leave her, like her daddy did, and she'd be alone for the rest of her life.

In between commercial breaks for *The Tonight Show* that evening, Sam told Isaac she didn't want to put her baby up for adoption. She wanted to keep her baby, to raise her on her own. She didn't tell her mama this because she was tired of fighting with her. She was scared of what Isaac would say or do as he turned quiet and thoughtful on the couch. Her mama was already asleep in the master bedroom, but Sam imagined her listening in. Isaac gently kissed Sam's cheek, not her mouth.

"We'll talk about it later," he said.

Those might be her least favorite words ever, and he used them often now. Over the last two weeks, it made her sick to think how she had practically begged him to give her pain, but he held back from doing anything outside of the occasional chaste kiss or a placid squeeze of her thigh. She didn't know if he was still punishing her for running away to Dallas, and when she came out and asked him, he ignored her question, told her she needed to focus on school. But she couldn't focus on school, on anything, with Arrow keeping his distance from her and having no outlet for the pleasure and pain she craved through Isaac.

Three days later, Isaac told Sam he'd pick her up after school, and trepidation and excitement pulsed through her. Something in his eyes had seemed as anxious and pent-up as she felt.

She walked over to his pickup as soon as she saw him pull up to the high school. Chrissy shot her a worried look as Sam sped past her, but she tried to ease her friend with a smile.

"Where're we going?" she asked Isaac after they drove a ways.

His eyes briefly left the road to look at her and she saw uncertainty in them.

"Thought we'd just drive for a while."

Sam wiggled out of her coat, the truck's heat blasting her face and making her sweat. She prayed she didn't sweat enough to make the Band-Aid on her neck fall off.

"I brought you a drink." He motioned to the middle console.

Red Gatorade—one of her favorite drinks. She reached for it, but Isaac snatched it up first and took a tiny sip.

"I don't know how you like this stuff," he said.

He held the bottle a long moment before handing it to her. She gulped down two-thirds of it before pausing to catch her breath. She finished it off and set the empty bottle back into the cup holder.

They drove around for a while until Isaac turned onto a dirt road. Sam didn't recognize the area, but they were about twenty minutes away from their farm. She tried to turn her head to ask Isaac where they were heading but she found it took too much effort to move her body, like she had slipped into a mold of Jell-O. She attempted to raise her hands from her lap and was barely able to move them a few inches. What the hell was happening to her?

What was supposed to be Isaac's name came out of her mouth in a strangled moan.

He reached over and squeezed her thigh. "If you feel tired, go on and close your eyes."

She did feel tired, so tired she couldn't move her mouth to form words, but sleep was the furthest from her mind. She was scared. For a second, she thought she was having a brain hemorrhage like Grandma Haylin had the year before, but then it hit her.

The drink. He put something in it.

Fear raced through her at the realization. She forced another weak moan from her lips, and Isaac stopped the truck.

"We're here. Let's get you inside to rest."

She closed her eyes, powerless to keep them open. She heard the passenger door open and felt the cold air whip in. With her coat off, the wind cut through to her bones.

"Come on, girlie," Isaac said. He unbuckled her seatbelt and took ahold of her under her neck and knees, lifting her like she was a child.

"Goddamn, thought you'd never get here," a woman's voice said nearby.

Sam's eyes fluttered open long enough to see a blur of fiery red ahead of Isaac.

"She drink it?"

"Yeah," Isaac said.

"Well, get her ass inside."

So many questions fought to form in her mind, but all Sam could focus on now was her own shallow breathing, in and out, and that spicy, earthy scent of Isaac pressed to her face.

"Put her down there," she heard the woman say.

A pause.

"It's clean enough." There was another long pause. "What—you changing your mind again?"

"Maybe," Isaac said.

"Maybe I'll change mine too."

She felt Isaac's grip on her tighten. "If this goes bad, you know what I'll do to you."

The woman's sharp laughter cut into Sam.

"Don't worry, baby. Your precious girl will be fine."

Isaac carefully laid Sam down on what felt like a pallet of old, lumpy blankets. The sudden smell of cigarette smoke choked what little air she was able to inhale with her shallow breaths. It was like her brain was shutting down, and her body shuddered hard when she thought of her baby's brain turning off too.

Another moan seeped out of her, a sad, croaking sound she didn't recognize as her own voice.

"How long is that shit supposed to take?" Isaac said.

"Not long. Look at her. She's about out."

Within a few moments, Sam was.

Chapter 45: Sam, 2009

The first thing Sam wanted to do after Meredith told her story was drive to Anadarko, find whatever shithole Vickie lived in, and beat her face in with whatever she could find.

She glanced up at Meredith's apartment unit and saw Caleb watching them from the front window. Caleb, who wouldn't be alive if not for Eric trying to shoot at Vickie as she attempted a forced abortion on her own daughter. Jesus Christ, it was too messed up. Almost as messed up as what happened to Sam.

She walked over to the stairs and sat, her mind fumbling in the dark, grasping for yet wanting to reject the memory of that horrific day with Isaac. Her recollections from that day were wispy at best, but she had replayed them enough over the last fifteen years until they were dense enough to bite.

She remembered the December day Isaac had picked her up from school. Afterward, she woke up on a pile of dirty blankets in what looked to be an abandoned shack of a house. She was alone, her clothes on but her leggings haphazardly pulled up and her boots missing. And the pain. There had been so much pain, worse than any cramping from a period.

Her baby.

When she woke again, it was morning and Isaac held her to his chest murmuring to her. She thought she heard him say something like, "Thank God we found you." Her mom was there too, standing near Isaac, her face drawn and pale.

Eight days—how long it had taken for the fetus to fully pass out of her body. Her mom refused to take her to the hospital, afraid the police would arrest Sam for murder even after she repeatedly told her mama she didn't cause the abortion. She didn't believe Sam's story about Isaac picking her up from school and then her passing out. Maybe her mom believed her deep down, but she didn't want to accept what Isaac was capable of.

At the time, Sam thought her subconscious had created the woman's voice, that her mind didn't want to admit what Isaac had done to her, his betrayal. Isaac hadn't done it alone, though. He needed someone who knew what they were doing. Her next thought made her face go numb.

She looked at Meredith. "Did Isaac help your mother…with you?"

The evening was warm, but Meredith shivered. She hugged her body tight as if her insides would spill out if she relaxed too much, which was exactly how Sam felt right then.

"Yeah. He held me."

Meredith had told her about Vickie tricking her into trying a chalky-tasting drink, which Meredith spit out after one sip. Meredith had felt everything until Eric fired a couple of rounds at Vickie and Isaac, missing but prompting the neighbors to call the police.

Meredith wasn't like her. She didn't crave pain. And Eric wasn't like Isaac.

Sam was sure of the answer now, but she felt compelled to ask it anyway. She needed to hear Meredith say it.

"Did Eric ever rape you?"

Meredith continued to hug herself. She looked up at Sam, her eyes glistening from tears.

"No."

Sam felt her muscles relax. For a moment, she wanted to hug Meredith, to tell her she wasn't alone, but a thought stopped her.

"Why did you lie to the police about what happened? You let Eric go to juvenile hall when he protected you."

Meredith hugged herself tighter.

"I didn't have anyone else." She looked Sam in the eyes. "And Isaac and my mother were good liars."

Sam looked up at the apartment window. Caleb was still staring down at them.

"Who's Caleb's father?"

Meredith relaxed her arms. "I don't want to know if it's Isaac."

Sam's eyes flicked to the boy at the window again.

"Don't you think Caleb deserves to know?"

Meredith stopped hugging herself. "Eric and I only had sex one time."

Sam crossed her arms. She understood Meredith's desire not to know, especially since there was a strong chance of Isaac being the father, but she also knew tying Caleb to Isaac could help convince the detectives that Eric wasn't lying about what happened in Anadarko.

"The police are looking at Eric," Sam said. "But if they knew what your mother did, what Isaac did, if they heard it directly from you…"

"Then I could be a suspect."

Sam sighed. Meredith was probably right.

"Did Isaac send your mother money for you and Caleb?"

"Didn't matter if he did. I never saw a dime of it."

Meredith's mouth dropped open a little, as if she knew she said too much.

"Maybe he stopped sending your mother money and she wanted something bad to happen to him."

Meredith laughed, short and harsh. "You don't know my mother at all. She would've done anything for Isaac. Anything. She loved him." She let out another stunted laugh. "More than she loved me."

Meredith started up the stairs. Sam had more questions, but Meredith was clearly done with the conversation.

266

"Tell the detectives what really happened to you," Sam said. "Please."

Meredith paused at the top of the steps and looked back at Sam.

"You just want to pin Isaac's murder on someone else, anyone else but Eric, don't you?"

"He didn't do it."

"You're so sure, huh?"

"Yes." It was the first time doubt didn't try to creep in.

Meredith looked over in the direction of Zeus yipping in Sam's car.

"Well, if you're going to point a finger at my mother, you should get a bigger dog."

Chapter 46: Arrow, 1994

Arrow saw the blood as he was taking a piss in the middle of the night.

His father and Jeri had found Sam out in the woods in some old shack, brought her back to the house wrapped in a baby-blue afghan. Arrow caught a glimpse of her dead eyes and chalk complexion and understood something was very wrong with her. All he knew was she was gone the night before. He overhead his father tell Jeri he had called Sam's friend Chrissy first thing in the morning and that Chrissy had admitted to dropping Sam off near the place where they found her. Arrow immediately recognized it for the lie it was, and he imagined a hundred different horrific acts that could've happened in the shack with his father.

Then, while peeing late at night, he saw it—a glistening, crimson slug slithering down the inside of the toilet bowl, not quite making it to the water. His hand hovered on the toilet handle, his heart on the pink tile floor. He couldn't flush it.

Someone opened the bathroom door as he stared at the toilet. It was Sam, wearing his Tool T-shirt and pajama shorts. She walked past him, not speaking or bothering to close the door. He shut it softly, locking it, and turned to see her sitting on the toilet, her shorts and underwear around her ankles.

She grimaced, holding her breath, and he knew there'd be more blood-slugs in the toilet. He saw mucus-red on a pad stuck to her

268

underwear too.

"I'm going to kill him," he said, loud enough for Sam to hear.

She turned her head to him. There was nothing behind her eyes.

"When your mom goes to your Aunt Shelley's, I'm going to do it."

Jeri was supposed to visit her sister in Dallas the week before Christmas. At least, he hoped she was still going. It didn't matter, but he didn't want his stepmom around. He didn't really want Grandma Haylin around either, but she'd be busy baking for the church fundraiser.

Sam looked at the bathtub. He saw her gaze stuck on his razor, her face blank. After a minute, she wiped herself, going for more toilet paper several times. Each pass, he saw less and less blood. She didn't pause before flushing and his stomach lurched.

She tried to move past him to get to the door, but he stopped her. He held her, and she was a wood block in his arms. He held her tighter and her hands grazed his back before dropping to her sides again.

"I'll kill him," he chanted in her ear. "I'll kill him."

She shook her head against his shoulder.

"You can't." Her voice was as flat as freshly turned farmland. "He'll kill you first."

"I'll never let him hurt you again," he said. "I promise."

He pulled back from her to see her face. It was still vacant.

He walked her to her bedroom and lay next to her on her bed, not caring if anyone walked in and saw them together. It didn't matter now. His father had already taken everything, but he wouldn't hurt Sam again. He'd never hurt her again. Arrow would sleep next to her every night to make sure of it.

Sam didn't cry, didn't move.

He covered them both with her thick comforter, pressed closer to her back as he held her.

He started to drift into sleep when Sam touched his hand.

"We have to do it together," she whispered.

Chapter 47: Sam, 2009

The sun was too bright and high once Sam woke up, her clothes from the day before clinging to her sweaty skin. She forgot to set her alarm and the clock blinked back ten-twenty. At first, she rushed to get ready for work, letting Zeus out in the backyard before taking a quick shower. She got dressed and any desire to go to work drained from her. She was already severely late, which she had never been before, and she couldn't imagine managing a bunch of nineteen-year-olds without wanting to kill each and every one of them. She would save any murderous thoughts for Vickie, whom she found information on within a few clicks and searches on her laptop.

She grabbed her cellphone from her charger and saw several missed calls. No calls from Eric, which she found weird. She dialed his number and it went to voicemail.

She was about to call in sick to her work when her phone rang.

It was her mom. She thought about ignoring the call, but something tugged on her to answer.

"Hey, Mama, let me call you—"

"Eric's in jail. Thought you might like to know."

Shit. Sam inhaled slowly and closed her eyes. She should've checked her messages first thing, but she had been so focused on Vickie and everything Meredith told her the night before.

"I just saw him." Her mom's voice came out in a tremble. "Eric, he—he didn't look good."

Sam swallowed over the desert in her throat.

The tremor in her mom's voice increased as she said, "I'm so sorry, Sammy."

Why would her mom be sorry? Sam assumed she'd would be happy about Eric being in jail.

"The detectives asked me about the pocketknife they found," her mom said.

Sam gripped her phone hard.

"Did you want them to arrest him, Mama?"

"Of course not."

"You wanted him out of my life, right? Is that why you pointed them to him?"

"No, honey, I wasn't thinking that at all, but I knew they'd find out about the knife."

"What if I did it, Mama?"

"You didn't."

"But you don't know," Sam said. "You don't anything about me and what I'm capable of."

"Of course, I know you, honey. Why are saying this?"

"I liked it. I liked what Isaac did to me." Sam knew it wasn't the full truth, but she didn't care. She wanted her words to cut.

"What?"

"He knew I liked pain, so he gave me what I wanted."

"Sammy, stop saying this."

It didn't matter what Sam said now because nothing could change, and she would always be this way, searching out the kind of pain Isaac gave her and never finding it, not with herself, not even with Eric. The thoughts brimmed until they gushed from her, a flooded dam during a storm and she didn't care what debris hit her mom.

"You knew, didn't you, Mama? You knew before the attack. You knew what he did, and you did nothing."

"Sammy, please. Let me come to you. We can talk about this, okay?"

271

Sam took a deep breath. She could manage the anger again; she could hold it in.

"It's fine, Mama. I'm fine now. That's what you want to hear, right?"

"Sammy—"

She hung up, her mom's voice haunting the kitchen.

She sat at her dining table, thinking over everything, Eric in jail and how she could possibly exonerate him. The idea of telling the detectives the truth about the attack crossed her mind, but she knew it was a bad idea. They already had enough ammunition against Eric.

After what Meredith told her, Sam knew in her gut Vickie had killed Isaac. Before, revenge was Sam's only thought, and she had imagined going to Vickie's place, her handgun pointed at the woman until she confessed everything. Sam couldn't be stupid about this. She needed help.

She picked up her cellphone, did a quick search, and called the crappy diner where Meredith worked.

"I need to talk with you," Sam said when Meredith got on the line. "Can we meet?"

Sam met Meredith outside of the diner, which appeared dead even with it being lunchtime. They sat on a nearby bench, the summer heat bearing down on them.

"I only have fifteen minutes for my break," Meredith said.

"Eric's in jail."

Meredith's mouth dropped open a little.

"I know you don't want to talk to the police," Sam said, "but they need to know what your mom and Isaac did to you."

Meredith shook her head. "I can't. Caleb doesn't know about any of this. Going to the police—if he finds out about Isaac, it'll mess him up. He's been through enough already."

Sam expected her to say that. She wiped away the sweat about to

272

drip into her eyes.

"So, you're okay with letting Eric take the fall for something your mother did?"

Meredith's mouth tightened.

"You really think you have it all figured out, huh?" Meredith smirked. "Isaac said you were smart, but maybe he was wrong. Either way, I'm sure he had fun breaking you."

Sam opened her mouth to say he didn't break her, but she stopped herself. She had let Isaac break her because the rush of pain meant more than Eric's love. Because it was tangible. Pain was something she knew how to fight, knew how to accept.

She looked at Meredith, at her spindly arms and legs like a girl's, like what Isaac did to her stunted her growth and kept her in perpetual adolescence.

"He broke you too."

"Fuck you."

Tears formed in Meredith's eyes, and Sam felt the tug to hold her.

"Meredith, listen—"

"No, you listen." Meredith brushed away the tears from her face. "You don't know what Isaac took from me. I'm glad he's dead, and I don't fucking care who did it." She looked down at her lap, her hands pressed together. "I've had to fight to be where I am now, and I'm not going to let this shit destroy that."

Sam took a deep breath, trying to get the words to exit her lips. She didn't want to talk about it, but she needed Meredith to know. She looked up and kept eye contact with Meredith.

"I do know what Isaac took from you." Sam paused, pushing down the pain wanting to explode from her chest. "What your mother and Isaac tried to do to you—they succeeded with me." She took another breath, willing the words out. "I'll never be able to have kids."

Meredith slumped on the bench as if all the toughness in her drained out. She appeared to weigh everything, her face screwed up in thought.

"Shit," Meredith said.

"Please tell the detectives what really happened to you, how Eric helped you and Caleb."

"How will that help Eric?"

"If you tell them," Sam said, "your mother will pay for what she did. Even if it doesn't help Eric, people will know the truth. Don't you want that so you can move on?"

Meredith stared at the ground for several brutally silent moments.

Sam reached out and took her hand. "You can do this."

Meredith looked up at her. She was crying.

"You can. We both can."

Sam squeezed her hand, nodding, and Meredith slowly returned the nod.

Chapter 48: Eric, 2009

Eric was half-asleep, which was as deep of a sleep as he could get with the young man constantly moving above him in the upper bunk. It was the afternoon, but it wouldn't have mattered if it was night because the light in the jail cell was never turned off. The detention officers didn't seem to care when inmates slept or whether they ate what passed as food at the jail. They only cared if there was trouble, and Eric didn't intend to make any, so he stayed quiet and tried to blend into the gray paint of the cell.

He was supposed to have an arraignment hearing within forty-eight hours. That was if a prosecutor filed charges against him. His attorney had told him this, but it had been over twenty-four hours and he still knew nothing about when he'd face a judge or if bail would be set. Even if bail was set, Eric didn't have much to his name with most his contractor earnings going to pay for his house and utilities. He imagined his clients trying to reach him, wondering why the hell he didn't show up to work on their houses. Most of his thoughts, though, were about Sam and why she hadn't tried to call or visit him. By now, she had to know about his arrest.

He guessed it was late afternoon when a different detention officer, this one older with tired eyes, came to his cell. He figured the officer was there for his cellmate, who was sweating profusely and shaking on the top bunk.

"Sir, I think he needs to see a doctor," Eric said to the officer. "He's been throwing up a lot."

The officer barely glanced at Eric's cellmate. "Him? Oh, he'll be fine by tomorrow. You have a visitor."

Eric followed the officer back to the visitation room. Sam was already there on the other side of the Plexiglas, waiting for him. She swallowed hard once she saw him, like she was holding back a wave of tears.

She smiled, but Eric saw she looked pale and exhausted. She was being strong for him. One thing he loved about her, how he could see her and know she was solid and real no matter what crazy shit was happening around him. His mom would've used the phrase "calming presence." That's what Sam was for him.

They both picked up the receivers on either side of the glass. He heard Sam sharply inhale before she said, "We're a goddamn mess, aren't we?"

Then she told him about seeing Meredith. She started to say something else, but she paused.

"She doesn't want to get a paternity test," Sam said. "I think she knows Caleb's your father's kid, but I might be able to talk her into doing one to be sure."

Eric shook his head. "What does it matter now? I'm here."

"It matters because you didn't kill your father." She gave him a slight smile. "Vickie did."

Eric stared at her for a long time, hoping his wide eyes told her to watch what she said to him.

He chose his words carefully, knowing the police were monitoring everything. "Why do you think that?"

"Your father was giving Vickie money, probably to keep her quiet about Caleb. Meredith pretty much admitted it." Sam tucked her hair behind her ear. "I think he wanted to get rid of Caleb since he was proof of what he did, and Vickie helped him and then extorted money from him when Caleb survived. She probably wanted to keep him close to

276

her somehow. Meredith said Vickie would've done anything for him."

Vickie would've sucked anything she could out of his father. He still couldn't figure out what her motive to kill him would be.

"Your mom knew about the money," Eric said. "She told me when she came this morning."

Surprise raced across Sam's face, and he realized Jeri had never mentioned it to her. He couldn't think of any reason why she would withhold the information from her own daughter.

"I think Isaac stopped sending Vickie money," Sam said.

"But why would he stop?"

"I don't know. Maybe he got tired of being her puppet."

He could see that. His father would hate not having control over a situation.

"Eric." Sam's eyes hardened into cold, black marbles. "Vickie...she killed her—the baby. She did it just like she tried with Meredith, and Isaac instigated it all."

Hearing her say it, Eric knew in his gut it was true and the words reached a hand deep in him, yanked his heart out of his chest for a second.

He cobbled together the only words that would form. "Vickie knew about you. I went to Anadarko and spoke with her and she knew about you."

And he didn't put it together. How had he not thought of it, Vickie helping his father get rid of a child that could compete with her ability to blackmail? Maybe she threatened his father, said she'd tell the police about what he did to Meredith if he didn't get rid of Sam's pregnancy.

Sam leaned forward in the plastic seat. "What they did to me—I can't get pregnant." She looked down at her lap, her mouth tight as she inhaled deeply. She looked back up at him, her eyes shining with tears. "She can't get away with it."

He couldn't believe he had never thought of the possibility, and here Sam was telling him she couldn't have children and he knew why she hadn't told him before, because she knew he wanted a family. He wanted to kill Vickie. He wanted to break through the Plexiglas and hold Sam, tell her it didn't matter, it didn't change his feelings for her, and she was wrong to think it.

"I'm not going to watch you go down for what she did," Sam said.

He saw pure revenge on her face.

"Sam, don't—"

She flashed her eyes at him.

"Please," he said. "Don't do anything stupid."

"I won't." She paused, a heaviness in her eyes. "I think I'm going to tell the detectives about it."

"Sam."

"I think Meredith will too."

Eric shook his head. If Sam told the detectives what happened to the baby, they might suspect her of the murder, and it definitely wouldn't help him.

An officer interrupted them, informed them the visitation time was up. Sam stood, slinging her purse over her right shoulder.

"Just wait," Eric said. "Think about it first."

"I will."

Sam looked at the phone in her hand, acted like she was going to hang it up. She stopped and pressed it back to her ear. She opened her mouth slightly, saying nothing. He listened to her gentle, even breathing as they watched each other. The tenderness in her eyes as she looked at him, he wanted to reach through the glass and snatch it before she hid it away again.

"Be careful in there, Eric."

"I will."

She smiled at him.

"I love you, Sam."

She looked down, her smile faded, and the hope of hearing her say those three words back to him dissolved. In that moment, Eric wanted to be his cellmate, awash in a world of withdrawal that at least distracted from reality.

"I—I'll get you out of here."

Chapter 49: Sam, 2009

Every time Sam thought about telling the detectives about what Isaac and Vickie did to her, a sweat broke out over her entire body, and she couldn't catch her breath. She had weaned herself off her anxiety medication several years before, but she felt she needed some now.

She went to her purse laying on her kitchen table, opened it, and eyed her handgun. She thought about Meredith's comment about Sam needing a bigger dog if she was going to blame Vickie for Isaac's murder. Since then, she had kept her gun with her.

She took several deep breaths, released them slowly as she imagined squeezing a lemon, how her old therapist taught her, but she didn't feel any calmer.

She looked over at Zeus, who sat by the front door, anxiously awaiting to be walked.

Sam took him around the block. They passed some neighbor kids running through sprinklers, their giggles so carefree as the sun kissed the approaching evening.

As she walked back toward her house, she noticed an old Buick Regal she didn't recognize parked farther down the street.

When Sam pulled out her keys to open her front door, she sensed movement behind her. She turned around and saw a woman wearing cutoff jean shorts and a green T-shirt standing on her patio.

The woman had dyed fiery red hair that didn't quite reach her roots and a nasty smile on her face.

280

Vickie.

Sam froze, her heart pounding outside of her body.

Zeus loudly barked, and she wished right then he was a biter.

That's when she saw the gun in Vickie's hand.

"Put the dog in the back," she told Sam.

The only way to the backyard was through the house. Sam glanced around. The only neighbors out were the kids playing down the street.

"Do it now." Vickie raised the gun higher.

Sam opened her front door and led Zeus down the hallway to the back of the house, Vickie following her. Zeus immediately started barking and scratching at the back door after Sam forced him into the yard. She pressed her body against her washer and dryer, the already cramped utility space full of Vickie and her gun.

"Go to the living room." Vickie's voice was low and full of threat.

Sam's heart shot up into her throat as she walked to the front part of her house. Her phone, her gun—both in the kitchen—seemed miles away.

Vickie pointed to the couch. "Sit."

Sam stepped backwards toward the couch, almost tripping over one of Zeus's dog toys.

"What's going on?" Sam said, her voice thin and broken. "Who are you?"

"You know who I am." Vickie narrowed her eyes. "You were going to talk to the police about me."

Sam stared at her, eyes wide and trying to appear ignorant to Vickie's insinuation.

"I don't kn—"

"Cut the bullshit," Vickie said. "My daughter called me, told me what you said to her. Said I'd never see my grandson again." She snorted. "Like she ever let me see him."

Sam bit the inside of her bottom lip to keep from screaming. She had no idea why Meredith would tell her mother.

281

"Why did Isaac give you money?" Sam asked. "Because of Caleb? He rapes your daughter and you used the result to get money from him, didn't you?"

Vickie shook her head, smiling. "Isaac always said you were a smart girl. Not smart enough not to get yourself knocked up, though, huh?"

Rage flushed Sam's face, her jaw tight, teeth grinding.

"In a way, we helped you." Vickie sneered. "You weren't tied down with a kid. Got to go to college and get your little degree. You should thank me."

"Fuck you."

Sam wanted to spit on the woman's grinning face.

"What do you want from me?" Sam said. "You want me to give you money like Isaac did?"

Vickie's cackle went straight through Sam's chest. She knew that laugh, had heard it that day in the shack.

"You killed him, didn't you?" Sam felt dazed, like this was a dream and she'd wake up any moment. "Why? Because the money stopped or because he didn't love you?"

Vickie flinched as if Sam had hit her. She licked her lips, her eyes shifting like someone would pop out and surprise her.

"Why did you kill him?"

"He did love me," Vickie said.

"So much that he left you."

Sam clenched her jaw to prevent herself from saying more that could get her shot.

"He said he would come back, to be patient." Vickie took a step closer and Sam pressed her back into the couch. "I knew you would ruin him. I told him so. I told him not to go back."

Vickie's voice trembled on her last words, her eyes welling up, and Sam knew she was so close, so close to hearing the truth. At the same time, she was terrified to hear it.

"Did he go back to Blanchard after he attacked Eric and me?" Sam said, her voice sounding detached and far away.

Vickie ignored her question, stared hard at her and blinked, eyes shining from her tears.

She aimed the gun at Sam's heart. "What did you and Eric do to him?"

Chapter 50: Arrow, 1994

Arrow swore he heard Bing Crosby's "White Christmas" floating through the leafless trees in the dense woods. He knew it was impossible. The farmhouse was almost a half-mile away from where he stood, waiting. He pretended he was back at the house, sitting at the kitchen table, watching Grandma Haylin roll out dough for her famous gingerbread cookies, the Christmas music from the small portable radio chiming throughout the house.

He wanted to be by the fire doing nothing, just sitting and squinting at the Christmas tree lights and wait for the snow to come. It felt like it was coming. He tightened his hold on his pocketknife, ran his frozen thumb over the handle.

Sam was taking too long. He started to wonder if his father guessed what they were planning and did something to her. There was no way. They had been careful, never talking until they absolutely knew they wouldn't be overheard.

Jeri had left early that morning to visit her sister in Dallas, and Grandma Haylin was busy at the house. This was the best time, the only time to make sure his father paid for what he did to Sam.

Sam was supposed to bring his father here, past the large fallen elm, its insides hollowed out. Arrow's plan was to wait, to watch, and find the perfect moment to strike.

He heard the distant crunch of leaves and twigs and hid behind a thick pine tree nearby. Sam entered the small clearing near the dead elm and looked around, eyes searching. He waited and waited, breath held, but he didn't see his father anywhere.

"Arrow?" Sam said, barely loud enough for him hear.

Something was wrong. She scanned her surroundings again, but Arrow didn't want to move. He didn't want to know why his father wasn't with her.

"Where are you?"

He closed the knife, shoved it into his back pocket and moved away from the pine tree. Sam caught sight of him. She slowly walked toward him, her eyes pink and mouth trembling.

"I—I couldn't."

Anger coiled up from inside his chest, struck fast and deep before he could stop it.

"What do you mean you couldn't?"

"I just…I'm sorry, I couldn't do it."

"Why? Because you love him, is that it? You fucking love him after what he did?"

"No, that's not it! I tried. I went to the barn and I talked to him, suggested we go out here, and he wanted to after he finished with chores, he wanted to but I just—I left because I'm not—I can't…." She took a full breath, her exhale a tiny white cloud. "I can't kill someone. *We* can't kill someone. That's not us."

"But it's who we have to be, or he'll keep going and going until you're dead and then I'll want to be dead too and it won't matter if he's alive. It won't fucking matter, so we have to. Don't you see?"

Sam shook her head, tears rolling down her cheeks.

"No." She took his hand. "I don't want you to be like him, and you'll be like him if you do this. We both will. You know that."

He looked away from her, an ache deep in his throat.

"Eric, please. We'll leave. We'll…I don't know, do something."

"Like what—tell your mom? Tell your grandma, the police?" He was serious but heard his questions come out in a mocking tone.

Sam let go of his hand and backed away from him.

"You'd still love me for helping you kill your father? You can really, honestly say you would?"

He swallowed but the ache was still there in his throat.

She was right. He wouldn't look at her the same way. He wouldn't look at himself the same. But it was too much to imagine his father going on in life, moving on to the next person to hurt after Sam. He could leave with Sam, really leave this time and figure things out along the way. They were old enough to work. They could manage it somehow.

But he was only sixteen, Sam seventeen. They didn't know how to pay bills, and he only knew how to drive around the farm, Sam around town on rare occasion. They didn't have a car, a place to live, furniture. They didn't have anything.

He felt trapped, the breath escaping his lungs into the cold air. He sucked in more air, in and out, faster and faster, face tingling and numb, and Sam held his arms.

"Hey," she said, gentle as to a child, "we'll figure it out, okay? Okay? I'm here and I'm not going anywhere. Not without you."

He tried to nod but he couldn't. Sam hugged him tight, her gloved hands moving to his face. She tried to hold eye contact with him, but he didn't want her to see the tears that formed so he turned his head. She kissed his cheek, right where the tears streamed down, and then she kissed his mouth. Her lips pressed into his until he kissed her back, mouth open, warm breath exchanged slow at first and then urgent. Her hands moved from his cheeks to his hair, his back, fingers pressing him closer, hands to his waist, tugging, his hands on her hips, pressing, pressing but not enough, not nearly enough.

He didn't have gloves on, his hands ice seeking warmth under her coat, her sweater, and she gasped when he found skin, bra pushed up. This was crazy, he knew, them out in the open, snow about to fall, and

286

he didn't care. He only cared about Sam and how she felt in his arms right then, the relief that she was here with him and she didn't want him to be anyone else and they could still be together, and no one could stop them. No one.

"Get your fuckin' hands off her."

Sam froze in his arms, her face bone white. They both turned to see his father at the edge of the clearing, maybe ten or fifteen feet from them, he wasn't sure.

"You," his father drew out, his eyes boring into Sam. "I knew it. And you—"

Arrow's instinct was to shrink under his father's glare, but he didn't. He took ahold of Sam's hand.

His father lunged toward them, grabbed Sam by the hair and jerked her into his arms, her back against his chest, a knife at her throat. She cried out and Arrow reached to grab her back until his father swiped the knife at him.

"Let's show him what kind of whore you are. Let him see what he wants to protect so much."

Sam shook her head, her sobs increasing as Arrow's father pushed her against a tree. He kept his eyes on Arrow, darting back and forth from Sam. When his father grabbed Sam's throat and squeezed hard, Arrow rushed a few steps forward before his father pressed the knife to Sam's cheek. Arrow stopped dead.

"Don't be stupid, son."

His father lessened his hold on Sam's throat, and she gasped for air. "She's so innocent, huh?"

"Let go of her!"

Hand still on Sam's throat, his father unbuttoned her jeans and yanked them down. Sam's sobs were uncontrollable now and Arrow's heart thundered in his ears.

His father turned Sam around, pressed her face against the bark of the tree. Her backside was petal white except for the deep purple bruises, some so dark they looked black.

"Look at this. She asked for this. She wanted it. She begged me for it and I gave it to her. You want to save her, son? From what? What she wants?"

Sam continued to cry, the side of her face shoved against the tree as she said, "I didn't, I didn't."

A million thoughts swarmed Arrow's head, none connecting, none making sense except for the one screaming that his father had a knife to Sam and he had to protect her.

"She's a good liar, don't let her fool you."

"Let her go!"

His father laughed, mirthless. "You'll never be able to give her what she needs."

He flipped Sam around, hand tightened on her neck.

"Stop! She can't breathe!"

His father ignored him, turned his back for just a moment as he hissed something in Sam's ear.

Arrow felt like he was out of his body, like his rage would tear him apart. Everything was slow and fast at once as he pulled his knife from his back pocket, opened it, and charged.

The grunt his father made, the carnal sound of it, was almost like pleasure. He let go of his own knife and reached his hands back, touched the knife stuck there in his shoulder blade, and turned to face Arrow.

All color slipped from his father's face as he continued to claw behind him like there was an itch he couldn't reach.

"Oh, shit!" Sam's voice rasped out at seeing the lodged knife.

Without hesitation, she wrapped both hands around the hilt and yanked until the knife came free. She didn't aim any better than Arrow had and stabbed his father's upper back. It was a shallow wound, and his father swung around fast, slamming Sam hard into the tree behind her, her jeans still halfway down her legs. She held onto Arrow's knife, clearly stunned and hurting, but his father easily took it from her, his breath coming out in ragged, white puffs in the frigid air.

Arrow knew if he didn't make a move now, Sam would be dead. He rammed into his father, who fell backwards over a fallen tree limb, knife still in his hand. Arrow grabbed his dad's wrist, grunting as he pressed his thumb deep into the veins and corded tendons there as hard as he could, but he couldn't get the knife loose. They rolled on the ground, his father now on top of him, the knife inches from Arrow's throat. He looked at his father's face, the raw determination terrifying. Arrow's arm was getting tired, the knife drawing closer. Using the last of his strength, he jabbed his knees into his father's groin, used the second to crawl away. Something bit into his left calf, sending a sick, woozy warmth straight to his head.

He turned and looked up, saw his father standing over him, the knife at his side dripping blood. Arrow looked down at his left leg, saw the long, open gash along the back of his calf, and it didn't feel like it was a part of him. After the sharp bite of the knife, he felt nothing, no pain. He couldn't move his leg. His father saw this, but he didn't move. He stared at Arrow's leg like he was examining a lame horse and trying to figure out what to do with it.

There was a sound of cracking wood and his father's eyes widened briefly before he slumped to the ground.

Everything was fading, getting dark around the edges, but Arrow saw Sam, a large tree branch in her hands. She threw the branch and crouched next to him.

"Jesus," Sam said. "I think he cut something big."

He wanted to sleep, so he closed his eyes.

Sam slapped his face.

"You have to stay awake."

He closed his eyes again.

Sam tied something around his leg and then her warm breath was right next to his face.

"Eric, I'm going back to the house to get help. I'll be right back, okay?"

He said okay, but he didn't hear himself say it.

"I'll be right back. You're going to be okay." But her voice trembled, and he didn't believe her.

Chapter 51: Sam, 2009

"What did you and Eric do to Isaac?" Vickie repeated.

Dread rose in Sam, her pulse loud in her ears. She looked over at the dining table across the room, her loaded and ready gun right there in her purse.

"You took him from me." Vickie raised her gun higher, aimed at Sam's head. "And you want to pin his murder on me." The gun was cocked, ready to fire.

There was no time to think. Sam jumped up from the couch and slammed herself into Vickie, her much taller frame knocking the woman back hard onto the wood floor. The gun flew from Vickie's hand, slid somewhere by the couch. Sam tore to the kitchen table, got the gun from her purse.

BAM!

Sam turned around fast, blindly shooting back.

Vickie dropped her gun and clutched at her left shoulder. Sam rushed to it, kicked it across the room.

She pointed her gun at Vickie. "Sit the fuck down."

Adrenaline surged through Sam, making her dizzy, as she quickly examined herself. At first, she thought Vickie had missed, but then she saw a dark-red pool form on her lower abdomen. A bizarre thought flickered in her head that her vintage Siouxsie and the Banshees T-shirt was ruined.

Sam stumbled over to the other end of the couch and fell onto the cushions, holding her stomach. She heard Zeus frantically barking in the backyard as she looked across the room to the kitchen table where her cellphone stared back. She tried to get up. White stabbing pain stopped her, knocked her breath out.

Vickie moaned next to her, her left shoulder bleeding all over the couch. Sam looked down at her stomach again. The blood was pouring out faster.

If she was going to die, she decided she would die with Vickie's confession, with knowing the truth. She held the gun up as steady as she could.

"How did you kill Isaac?" Sam said. Vickie, holding her left shoulder, didn't seem to hear, so Sam spoke louder. "How did you do it?"

Vickie temporarily stopped moaning and looked at Sam, some dawning realization etched on her face when she saw Sam had her gun cocked. Vickie shook her head, and Sam reached over with her gun, pressed the barrel into the woman's left shoulder, deep into the bullet hole. Vickie screeched, horrible and crow-like.

"How?"

Vickie shook her head more as she moaned out, "I—I didn't kill him!"

Sam pressed the gun harder. "How?"

"I didn't. He called me from a gas station…said he needed a place to stay." Vickie kept pausing, and Sam knew she must be in as much pain as she was. "But he had to go back to the house first…for his things…said everyone went to the hospital…so he had to go that night."

Sam fingered the trigger and her head turned fuzzy.

"He never came," Vickie said.

"Never came?" Sam let out an incredulous laugh, stopping when pain pierced through to her back.

Vickie sucked in pained breaths in between crying. "I swear it. I even called your house…that night…when he didn't show up."

Vickie moaned more.

"I don't believe you." Sam felt herself slipping, her body cold and clammy, breaths fast and shallow.

Vickie stared at the gun, avoiding Sam's eyes. When she finally made eye contact with Sam, her eyes were sudden cold steel, the tears magically gone.

"Jeri answered...and she...she said he went to Les Compton's place."

Her mama?

That night at the hospital after the attack, her mom going back to the house for fresh clothes. Grandma Haylin getting a call in Eric's hospital room, Sam watching as her grandma's face turned ashen.

She remembered what Detective Eastman said about Isaac's wounds, the back of his skull smashed in. It didn't take much force to crack a skull with something like a hammer. She pictured her mom going back to the house, Isaac sneaking in to get his things...his favorite pair of boots. Maybe her mom knew he would come back, or maybe he caught her off guard and she confronted him. Whatever happened happens. She imagined her mom calling Grandma Haylin, getting her to help dispose of Isaac's body and truck.

Vickie stared at Sam holding up the gun, her other hand holding her abdomen.

This was not how she saw herself dying, bleeding out on her green couch. Red on green, like Christmas lights flashing, her eyes fierce-blinking, trying to keep herself awake.

Somehow, she smelled cloves, cinnamon, nutmeg. Her grandma's famous gingerbread cookies, how she used to help roll the dough, not too much flour. Ground mustard, the secret ingredient. Not even her mama knew, but she did. She wanted to hug her grandma and touch her silky gunmetal hair. She wanted to make gingerbread cookies with her again, let the spices warm her tongue, but she could only taste copper bubbling up in her mouth.

She tried to swallow, but the muscles in her throat wouldn't work. She choked and coughed hard. A thousand bright red dots misted her jeans.

A soft rupture of laughter next to her on the couch, then words that coiled cold and deep in her bleeding gut.

"You're going to pass out soon…when you do, I'm going to take that gun…and finish you."

Sam tightened her grip on the weapon, her only lifeline.

"Try it."

She glanced down and saw the large, wet circle of blood on her T-shirt was now up to her chest. She tried to get up from the couch again, but her brain ignored her, made her arm go slack at her side, her hand loose around the gun. She shut her eyes, wanted to shut off the pain leeching her life.

This was it. This was really it.

It wasn't that bad, but she wanted her dog next to her, licking her hand. She wanted her mama holding her.

She wanted Eric holding her.

She thought of his face, the sadness and hope always etched in his eyes. She wanted to hear his voice and to tell him the things she should've told him a million times. She wanted anyone else but Vickie next to her, waiting.

"I'll fucking kill you," Sam whispered, unable to open her eyes again.

She felt the coolness of the gun glide past her fingertips, heard the metal clink-clink as it entered new hands.

Maybe it was enough. Maybe it was enough that she tried to make things right. Maybe it was enough, and Eric would know how much she loved him.

Chapter 52: Eric, 2009

Eric wasn't surprised when an officer came to his cell and took him into a small interrogation room that evening after Sam visited the jail.

Detective Eastman entered the interrogation room and sat across from him. He studied Eric's unshaved face, the beginnings of a beard, and the jeans and button-up he'd worn for the last two days. The detective's expression was unreadable, which only served to make Eric more uncomfortable sitting across from him, hands cuffed and resting on his lap, the meager dinner he ate working its way up into his throat.

"So," Detective Eastman began, "I guess Miss Mayfair's been busy doing my job for me."

Nerves hit Eric hard, and he had hold his breath to keep from throwing up.

"We know she's been in contact with Miss Lang." Detective Eastman's regular Cheshire Cat grin was back. "And surprise, surprise, Miss Lang contacts us today with some revelations."

Eric's head was spinning with apprehension. He hoped Sam was right, that Meredith was going to tell the detectives the truth.

"Miss Lang told us an interesting story about the night she ended up in the hospital, the night she almost lost her son."

Eric held his breath again. He didn't like the look in the detective's eyes.

"She certainly presented you as the hero. Maybe you were. But then we know what happened with Miss Mayfair's pregnancy, don't we?"

295

Eric said nothing. He couldn't move. He felt the rope around his throat. Sam hadn't meant to, but she put it there.

"Your father and Vickie Lang forcing an abortion on her? I've seen and heard a lot in my twenty-seven years doing this work, but that—that's some evil shit, right there. Might even say a good reason to kill someone. Avenge the person you love and the child you lost." The detective leaned forward, hands clasped on the table.

Eric looked down at his cuffed hands in his lap, his thumbs digging, digging.

"We know he didn't go to Mr. Compton's place. And we know you told the truth about him being alive after the attack. Several people in town saw his truck when he got gas that evening."

Sweat broke out over Eric's body, making his shirt cling to his back.

"Mr. Walker, let's put this to rest right now. I know you want the weight off your shoulders, I know it's eating at you. No one will blame you for killing him. I certainly don't." Detective Eastman kept his eyes on Eric, watching his every reaction. "Tell me what happened in Blanchard. Tell me what you did when your father came back."

That December day, the air kissed with winter, with the promise of snow at any second. The look on his father's face when he knew, when he knew everything was ending.

"I—" Eric swallowed, looked down again at those thumbs digging. "I wanted to protect Sam."

"And what did you do to protect her?" the detective said, his voice soft and soothing.

"I slept with her in her bed…to watch for him."

"Your father?"

"Yes."

"And then your father and aunt hurt her, and she lost the baby. Is that right?"

"Yes."

"And that made you angry?"

296

Angry was too small of a word to describe his feelings after seeing bloody leftovers of what had been his child in the toilet. No words existed for it.

"That made you angry?" the detective repeated.

"Yes."

"And what did you do after that?"

Eric looked up at Detective Eastman. He just had to say the words: *I was going to kill him. I planned it all. It was me, only me, not Sam, just me.* And it would stop, this would all stop, the guilt and lies. It would stop, and the truth might send him to prison, but Sam would be okay.

"What did you do to your father, Eric?"

Detective Eastman sounded like a parent tending to a child's injury and trying to find out how it happened, his voice gentle yet prodding.

"I just...I wanted him to stop hurting her."

"And how did you make him stop?"

Do it. Say it. He looked down at his hands, his thumbnail bloody, digging, digging.

Blaring static issued from the detective's waist.

Detective Eastman grumbled into his phone, "What?" A horribly long moment passed before he said, "I'm heading there now."

The look Detective Eastman gave him—it was like he was watching a train slam into a person and that person was Eric.

Eric's entire face went numb.

"What happened?" Whatever the detective heard on his phone, Eric knew it was about Sam, he just knew.

A young officer entered the interrogation room, went straight to Eric and lifted him from his seat.

"What happened?" he yelled again, but Detective Eastman was already gone.

Chapter 53: Sam, 1994

Sam tightened her sweater around Arrow's leg the best that she could, but she already saw blood soak through it. She had to get back to the house fast, had to get to Grandma Haylin, to a phone, call for help.

She stood up and looked down at Arrow again. His eyes were closed, his breathing fast. She turned to run, and Isaac was standing right in front of her, his knife in hand, face pale and eyes piercing her.

"We—we have to get help," she said, voice wavering. "He's going to bleed to death if we don't."

Isaac glanced down at Arrow and back to Sam. He rubbed the back of his head where Sam had hit him with a tree limb.

"You tried to kill me. Both of you." His voice was flat yet pained.

She made to run toward the house and Isaac grabbed her arm, swung her around, and she fell to the mattress of dead leaves. He pinned her to the ground, the knife at her throat.

"If he dies, it's because of you," he said.

"If he dies, you'll go to prison. They'll put you to death. I'll make sure of it."

The slap across her face came swift and hard, and Sam tasted metal.

Isaac raised his knife and Sam didn't think, she grabbed. The blade cut through her glove into her right palm and she screamed, unwilling to open her fist.

"Let go before you cut off your goddamn hand!"

She held on, sure he'd cut her throat open if she released it.

298

Isaac slapped her with his other hand and she let go of the knife. He pinned both of her hands above her head, his sweat dripping onto her face. She turned her head, searching until she saw Arrow not twenty feet from her. She couldn't tell if his chest was still moving.

Isaac gasped for his next breath above her. "I would've—I would've done anything for you." He scrunched up his face in pain, took a deep breath and shook his head. "And you turn my boy against me?"

His tears looked real, but Sam knew they weren't.

"*You* turned him against you," she said. "You killed your own grandchild."

Isaac's face contorted with pain, with the truth—she hoped he felt the wound deep. She hoped nothing could ever reach it to heal it and it'd fester slowly, killing him like he'd killed her baby.

He moaned a deep animal sound as he squeezed her, her arms still pinned, and she thought he would keep squeezing until he popped her open. She felt his wet eyelashes brush her face. He kissed her cheek. He kissed her all over her face and hair as if everything would go back to the way it was if he kissed her enough.

"Why?" he breathed against her neck, his body heavy on her to the point where she could barely catch an inhalation. "Why? Why?"

He took her injured hand and pressed her bleeding palm to his cheek. The salt on his skin set her hand on fire.

"I never wanted this. I didn't want to hurt you."

He kissed her lips and she hated herself for the ripple of need that passed through her. She hated herself for having to fight the compulsion to kiss him back.

Isaac pulled back from her, implored her with his eyes.

"I love you."

Sam didn't hear his words. All she could hear was what he had hissed into her ear when he had her shoved up against the pine tree, exposing her fresh bruises to Arrow: *No one will ever know you like I do. No one else will love you.*

299

But Arrow did know her and her dreams and she knew his, and he would die if she didn't do something quick.

With every bit of force in her, she rammed her knee into Isaac's groin. He buckled on top of her, and she rolled out from under him, got to her feet, took a step before Isaac grabbed her ankle and yanked, tripping her back to the ground.

He straddled her again, knife to her throat now, her bleeding hand throbbing, and she screamed as loud as she could.

A thunderous sound came from behind them, and the ground next to Isaac and Sam exploded with dirt and leaves. They both froze.

"Get your goddamn hands off my granddaughter!"

Isaac slowly rose, eyes on Grandma Haylin. She held her hunting rifle high and ready a few feet from him.

"Drop it."

Isaac ignored Grandma Haylin, held onto his knife, until she fired another shot that kicked up leaves by his feet.

"You get your ass to your truck and you pray you get gone before the police get here. I ever see you again, you'll learn how good my aim is."

Isaac looked down at Sam, glanced at her bleeding hand and then looked over to Arrow's ashen face, his eyes still closed but chest moving a little. When Isaac looked at Sam again, she saw a weight in his eyes heavy enough to drag him back down next to her, but he turned and went into a full run toward the farmhouse.

As soon as he was out of sight, she ran to Arrow's side, crouched down and made herself look at his left leg, at his jeans saturated with blood, her sweater wet with it.

Grandma Haylin kneeled as best as she could next to Sam.

"Eric. Eric, honey, wake up," she said, nudging him.

He stirred enough to open his eyes a little. Grandma Haylin went to work inspecting his leg wound. She took off Sam's sweater and removed Arrow's belt from his jeans. She tightened the belt around his

300

upper left thigh and the bleeding seemed to slow down some.

Sam stood up and looked around for Isaac. She couldn't help but feel as if he would come running back to attack them.

"Sammy, I need you," Grandma Haylin said. "You have to be my strong girl now."

Sam looked down at Arrow and he didn't look good.

"Okay," she mumbled.

She listened, numb and obedient, to everything her grandma told her to do. A low earthquake rumbled through Sam's body as she helped Grandma Haylin lift Arrow up, both on either side of him. He couldn't hold himself up, but he was semi-aware.

"Sammy, Isaac was hurt. Stabbed," her grandma said. "Did you do that?"

She swallowed and sucked in more cold air.

"We both did."

She saw worry in her grandma's eyes.

"You have the knife?"

Sam scanned the ground and saw the iridescent handle of Arrow's knife.

"There."

They held onto Arrow as they shuffled over to the knife. Sam picked it up and kept it in her gloved hand, wanting to be ready in case they came across Isaac in the woods.

It seemed like hours getting back to the house, Arrow falling in and out of consciousness and making it harder to hold him up. Along the way, Grandma Haylin asked a dozen questions, many Sam didn't want to answer but she did. When they made it to the house, she didn't see Isaac's white Chevy parked in the driveway, and relief flooded her body.

"Call 911," Grandma Haylin said after they had carefully lowered Arrow onto the kitchen floor.

Sam didn't know what to do with the pocketknife. She made the call and placed the knife on the highest shelf in the pantry where her mama couldn't reach.

She turned to see Arrow watching her, his eyes wide and confused. He looked like a little boy, not a tall sixteen-year-old. Grandma Haylin had elevated his leg with a pillow and covered him with a blanket.

Grandma Haylin motioned to the pantry. "You were protecting yourselves. The police will understand that, they'll know."

Sam looked at Arrow and she knew that wasn't true. Whatever she told the police, whatever Arrow told, it couldn't be the entire truth. It couldn't. Their lives would be destroyed.

"Eric will be okay, Biscuit. We need to get your hand bandaged."

Grandma Haylin wrapped Sam's hand, telling her the hospital would need to stitch her up.

"What in the world is going on?"

Sam turned to see her mama standing at the kitchen doorway, a few snowflakes salting her hair and shoulders. Her mama looked down at Arrow on the linoleum floor, her face going pale.

Before her mama could speak, Grandma Haylin went to her and held her shoulders. "Jeri Anne, Isaac did this."

Her mama looked at Arrow again and then to Sam, her eyes wide with shock.

"No. No, he didn't."

"Yes, he did. I saw him with my own eyes." Grandma Haylin pointed to Sam. "And he…he was the one who hurt Sammy, just like I told you."

Her mama's mouth tightened, her eyes narrowed and gazing at Grandma Haylin like she couldn't focus. "No. He—he couldn't."

"He did, Mama." Sam couldn't look at her mama's face, the disbelief in her eyes. It made her want to scream. "I—I was scared to tell you."

Her mama stared at her for a long moment and then at Grandma Haylin's hunting rifle leaning against the wall by the back door.

"Where is he?" her mama growled out. Sam had never heard her mama's voice sound like that, like she was about to chew through flesh.

"I ran him off. He won't come back," Grandma Haylin said, low and authoritative. "He's not that stupid."

Arrow moaned a little, his voice weak and breaking with pain. "Is he really gone?"

Grandma Haylin and her mama looked at each other, some unspoken fear passing between them.

"Yes," her mama said to him, and she sounded more confident than Sam felt.

Chapter 54: Eric, 2009

Eric gently held Sam's hand, afraid to do anything else. Her hand was freezing, her skin a gray hue, a death color he never wanted to see again.

He knew he was lucky to be here, to see her and touch her, even covered in tubes with various monitors constantly beeping, but how he got here was what destroyed him inside. If he had just told the detectives the truth from the start, Sam wouldn't be on life support.

The Anadarko police had been monitoring Vickie on the drug circuit. She apparently frequented larger towns to replenish her meth supply to sell, but Oklahoma City was unusually far for her, which interested the homicide detectives working his father's murder case. When Vickie went straight to Sam's house, the police waited in a nearby neighborhood. They heard reports of shots fired and entered Sam's home just in time to prevent Vickie from putting a bullet in Sam's head.

All this Eric learned through bits and pieces of information, some from his lawyer, some from Jeri, and some from the police. As it stood, the detectives had no choice but to release Eric since prosecutors didn't charge him. Detective Eastman went to Eric's jail cell before his release, standing there watching him for a long time, saying nothing. When the detective finally spoke, he hardly blinked.

"The truth is a funny thing, isn't it? Sometimes, it's too crazy to be real. We start changing things around in our heads to make a new truth, a believable truth." Then Detective Eastman said something Eric would puzzle over for many years afterward: "I suggest you appreciate the truth you believe in now, Mr. Walker, before it changes on you."

Jeri skittered across the hospital room mouse-like while carrying two cups of coffee. She handed one to Eric and he thanked her.

"How long do you think she can stay like this?" she said and took a sip from her cup.

"I don't know. Until she's ready."

Sam had been in an induced coma for three days since her abdominal surgery, which had complications, but doctors were supposed to wean her off the sedatives that day. He saw her for the first time the day before, and he hadn't left her side since, even when Jeri prodded him to sleep and eat. She rarely left the room herself.

Jeri placed a hand on his shoulder and smiled. "She's going to get through this."

He fell asleep sometime in the late afternoon. He woke up to Sam weakly pressing his hand. His mind switched back on, his heart racing. Sam's eyes were open, but she couldn't speak because of the ventilator. In his excitement, he hit the red call button several times on the side of the hospital bed, and a nurse came to the room looking annoyed until she saw Sam's open eyes.

A different nurse came in, checked Sam's vitals, and removed the ventilator. Then a doctor came into the room, checked Sam's vitals again and asked her a few yes/no questions before leaving the room.

Sam croaked something Eric couldn't hear. He leaned in closer to her.

"You shouldn't talk yet. Just rest."

He squeezed her hand and she spoke again.

"You're out?" she whispered.

"Yeah, I'm out."

She smiled a little.

"Good."

"Not good. You could've died."

"Worth it."

"I think you'll change your mind once the painkillers wear off."

"Look forward to it."

He grinned, shaking his head.

"Goddamn masochist."

"Worse things to be."

He nodded. There were many worse things to be.

Sam tried to lift her hand, the one with the IV line taped to it. Eric saw the IV line pull taut since it tangled on the bed's railing, and he lowered Sam's hand.

"Lips," she said, barely audible.

Her lips were chapped to hell and gone. Eric found the tube of hospital lubricant on the moveable tray. He rubbed a generous amount on her lips, which looked ready to crack and bleed.

"Thank you."

"Welcome."

He twisted around to put the tube back on the tray.

"I love you."

He turned back and stared at Sam, thinking he'd imagined her speak.

"I love you," she said again, slower and softer, her raw voice running out and her eyes glinting with tears.

His heart was too big for his chest. He was sure it'd keep expanding and he'd fall over, dead, a grin on his face.

"Kiss me, stupid man."

He did, and he didn't care that her lips were coarse and flaky with dead skin. It was the best damn kiss he'd ever had in his life.

Chapter 55: Sam, 2009

Sam was ready, but she knew Eric wasn't. Every nervous tic he had—the constant leg bounce, the fists clenching and stretching out, him popping every knuckle again and again—was driving her nuts. She knew he needed something to do to keep his mind busy, so she broke her garbage disposal.

"How in the hell did screws get in here?"

"I have no idea," Sam said from her dining table.

Zeus sat next to the kitchen sink as if he were inspecting Eric's work and keeping him in line.

Sam leaned forward, breathed through the sudden pain in her abdomen. It'd been about four weeks since she was released from the hospital, and she had to remind herself to take it easy. Her medical leave would run out soon and she'd have to return to work, but for now she enjoyed watching Eric, wearing nothing but old, holey jeans, fixing her disposal.

"You ready?" she asked when he was done.

He took his time washing and drying his hands at the sink. "I think it's impossible to be ready."

He walked over to her and she slowly stood up from her chair. She wrapped her arms around him, savored the warmth of his naked chest when she pressed her ear over the thrum of his heart. She looked into his eyes and she didn't see a younger version of Isaac; she didn't see the shadow of a scared little boy either. She saw a different person, a stronger person. It made her feel stronger too.

"I just hope he doesn't hate me." He smiled, and it wasn't his usual shy grin.

"I think all teenagers hate everyone, brothers included."

"Well, we better get dressed and go before Meredith and Caleb beat us there."

Eric drove them to a small Guatemalan restaurant Sam had suggested. She held his hand the entire way. It was early enough on Saturday morning, she didn't think the popular restaurant would be too busy yet. She was wrong. There was a thirty-minute wait. Meredith and Caleb weren't there yet, so she and Eric sat on a bench.

Two weeks before, Meredith surprised them by allowing a paternity test. She had said whatever the outcome was—father, half-brother—she would be open to letting Eric into Caleb's life as long as Caleb was okay with it.

Sam looked out to the street, saw Meredith's red Ford Focus pull into the parking lot. Anxiety gurgled up in her from nowhere. Eric took her hand.

"What's wrong?"

"Nothing, I'm fine," she lied.

"You don't look fine."

"I feel a little dizzy is all. I'm going to get some air—I'll be right back."

She ran into Meredith and Caleb as she left the restaurant. They both paused to watch her pass.

"Just have to get something from my car," she told them.

She walked through the September heat to her car parked further down on the residential street. She locked her car doors when she got inside, welcoming the suffocating air. It distracted from everything she was feeling. Eventually, not even the heat worked, and her mind went back to that day, the day Eric almost died, the day she might've died if not for her grandma.

Then every other thought, like dominoes, collapsed one after the other—her baby, dead, Isaac's face when he knew he was betrayed, the pain on Eric's face when he knew his father ran off and left him to die, the way Eric's eyes lit up when Sam told him she loved him at the hospital. She thought of her mom's secret and Vickie's confession about calling the farmhouse, and how Sam knew her gut was right. Her mama killed Isaac.

She would never tell the police. She would never tell anyone. She would've done the same thing in her mom's place.

Everything hit her at once.

Eric inside the restaurant, sitting across from a brother he hadn't known existed, and everything that would mean.

She lost it, her sweat mingling with her tears.

She'd now have this boy in her life, this stranger, and she was scared. She was scared Eric wouldn't have enough in him for her too because she barely had enough for him. And he'd be around Meredith again, and she knew it was stupid to think about because he didn't have feelings for Meredith and Sam knew she had a boyfriend, it was stupid, but she couldn't stop the thoughts from sparking in her head.

She had pictured helping Eric restore his historic house, maybe moving in with him and making it a home once everything settled. Maybe get another dog. When she imagined a child, her stomach twisted, and she swore the doctors missed removing the bullet from her.

Eric told her he'd stay by her side, no matter what, and she hoped she could do the same for him. She knew he loved her, was trying to accept what she needed from him, and she loved him for it, loved him for being equally damaged.

She looked at her car's clock. Almost fifteen minutes had passed. She picked up her cellphone. Eric had texted: *We're in the back right.* And a few minutes later: *You okay?*

She would make herself okay. Something she was used to. She was good at it.

She flipped down her visor, checked her face in the mirror, making sure her makeup wasn't smeared and she looked somewhat normal. She did.

She walked back to the restaurant as slowly as she could. Before she entered, she looked through the glass entrance and saw Eric sitting across from Meredith and Caleb. Eric had a mug of coffee waiting for Sam, one creamer next to it, how she took it. How Isaac took his.

She studied his face and Meredith's. They both seemed weightless. Not at complete ease with each other, for sure, but there was something on their faces that spoke of deep relief. They could do this; they could be okay around each other. And Caleb appeared more engaged than she had seen him before, smiling at something Eric said to him. He looked nervous, but he also looked happy.

A little happiness. It was exactly what she wanted, for Eric, for herself. No matter what. And she felt weightless as she stepped inside the restaurant and walked toward the back table, toward everything that could be.

Acknowledgments

First, I want to thank you, the reader, for taking a chance on a new author. I knew going in this book wouldn't be for everyone, but I also knew this story deserved to be told. Whether or not you relate to Sam's sexuality, my goal was to shed some light from the perspective of someone who understands her lifestyle and to hopefully remove some of the stigma of enjoying pain. However, any sexual activity, including BDSM, should always be consensual and with safety in mind.

Thank you to my wonderful agent, Sandy Lu, for taking a chance and seeing my vision for this story. I'm so glad you requested my manuscript during Pitch Wars! Speaking of Pitch Wars, I'm endlessly thankful for Layne Fargo and Halley Sutton for selecting me to mentor. This book would not have been what it is now without their sharp editorial eyes and support. And thank you to the entire Pitch Wars team for helping so many writers reach their book dreams and to my 2019 Pitch Wars class for being such a creative, positive force.

Big thanks to everyone at Polis Books, especially Jason Pinter, who's editing sharpened the story even more. His team is outstanding, and I absolutely love the cover and jacket design by Mimi Bark.

Before this book found it's way out into the world, my MFA mentors, authors Lou Berney and Allison Amend, offered invaluable feedback and encouragement. I'm forever grateful for them both and for all of my Red Earth MFA family. You are all truly my heart. Special thank you to past Red Earth MFA director Dr. Jeanetta Calhoun Mish, for teaching me so much about life, including how to two-step.

There are so many writers and editors I admire who've offered support, advice, and fantastic blurbs on this journey, and I thank you all. A special shoutout to S.A. Cosby, Kellye Garrett, Alex Dolan, Jamie Mason, Cynthia Pelayo, Jess Lourey, J.D. Allen, Gretchen Stelter, Sara Spock-Carlson, Melanie Hooyenga, PJ Vernon, Kelly J. Ford, Megan Collins, and Jennifer Pashley. Another special thank you to my good friend Mer Whinery, one of the best writers more people need to know about.

My heartfelt gratitude to my family and friends who've been there every step of the way, in particular to my younger sister, Kelli, who lifts me up more than she knows, and to my good friend Dr. Jim Sturgis, who gave me helpful psychological insights into my characters. Although both of my parents have passed, I know they would be proud. I miss you, Mom and Dad.

To my two beautiful babies, being a mother is and will always be the core of who I am, and I'm thankful every day I get to watch you grow into curious, creative, and empathetic people. I love you, my Biscuit and BooBoo.

Finally, thank you to my husband and most brutal first editor. This book much less my life wouldn't be the same without your love and support. You believed in me long before I did, and you've never wavered. Through pleasure and pain, you are my Bambi and I'm forever your Cougar.

About the Author

Heather Levy is a born and bred Oklahoman and graduate of Oklahoma City University's Red Earth MFA program for creative writing. Her work has appeared in numerous journals, including *NAILED Magazine*, *Crab Fat Magazine*, *Prick of the Spindle*, and *Dragon Poet Review*. She authored a nonfiction series on human sexuality, including "Welcome to the Dungeon: BDSM in the Bible Belt," for Literati Press. WALKING THROUGH NEEDLES is her debut novel. She lives in Oklahoma. Follow her at @HeatherLLevy.